OPERATION SUPERGLUE

A PRICKLY PEN INVESTIGATION

Books by Stacy Lee

Prickly Pen Investigations Series
Operation Superglue

Coming Soon!
Operation Cactus Blossom
Operation Desert Blues

For more information
visit: www.SpeakingVolumes.us

OPERATION SUPERGLUE

A PRICKLY PEN INVESTIGATION

Stacy Lee

SPEAKING VOLUMES, LLC
NAPLES, FLORIDA
2024

Operation Superglue

Copyright © 2024 by Stacy Lee

All rights reserved. No part of this book may be reproduced or transmitted in any form or by any means without written permission.

ISBN 979-8-89022-157-5

To Coach Rob Hulse,
whose guidance and mentorship make me better every day.

Acknowledgments

I am truly blessed to be living my dream as a full-time author, and I am overcome with gratitude for the many incredible individuals I have been blessed with along the way. A gigantic thank you to my agent, Nancy Rosenfeld of AAA Books Unlimited, Kurt and Erica of Speaking Volumes, and Lynn and her team at Red Adept Editing. I couldn't do this without you! A special thank you to Allen Redwing of Story Genius. Thank you, Kevin Olough and Megan Stewart for allowing me to pick your brain about high school in 2024. Thank you, Joan E. Childs for your assistance with networking and for your encouragement.

I could never do this without the love and support of my family! To my husband, Paul Barbagallo, thank you for believing in me, encouraging me, and being my rock. Thank you to my children, Paul and Lucy. Paul, you are crushing your second year of high school. I can't believe we are receiving college mail already. We love watching you on the football field, the ski slopes, and the racing track. Lucy, you are a star! We love watching you perform on stage, whether it is singing, dancing, or acting. Congratulations on your acceptance to Central. They are lucky to have you. Always remember, you are both stronger and smarter than you think.

A very special thank-you to my family, friends, and faithful support system. My parents, Karen and Dan DeBruyckere; sister, Kate Giglio, and her husband, Joe; my father-in-law Paul Barbagallo; my sister-in-law, Cheri Grassi, and her husband, Mike; my aunt, Pat Fishwick; and my brother, Dan DeBruyckere Jr. Thank you, Kara Holloway and Marisa Berlin for your encouragement and friendship. Thank you, Leigh Anne Hulse and Jessica Delano for always being there. Thank you to my youngest reader, Ella Berlin. You are truly fabulous, and I can't wait to see what the future holds for you! Thank you, Jaclyn Hannan for your constant guidance and support. I wouldn't be where I am today without you! Thank you, Rob Hulse, for everything you have done for my family, for kicking my butt into shape, and for not allowing me to settle for anything less than what I'm truly meant to be.

Thank you to my friend and private investigator, Ryan Lewis, for your collaboration on the story line of *Operation Superglue*, and for the tremendous blessing you have been to my family. If there were more people like you, the world would be a better place. Thank you, Attorney Josh Mozell, for your assistance during my time in Phoenix, and everything you have done and continue to do for the homeless and mentally ill population of Arizona.

Of course, I need to thank you, the reader! May you continue to love without hesitation and dream the biggest dreams. Remember, nothing is impossible. You are stronger than you think and there is always a way if you follow your heart. Never give up, even in the stickiest of situations. There is always a way.

Prologue

Earworms. No, not earthworms. *Earworms.* I had not heard of them, either, until two weeks prior to this unfortunate experience when studying the human brain in psychology class. We've all had earworms. It's a cognitive itch that causes the brain to itch back, otherwise known as *I have a freaking annoying song stuck in my head.* Since these cognitive annoyances tend to happen more often when we are anxious or stressed out, it makes sense that "Who Let the Dogs Out" by Baha Men is powerfully belting at me from the deepest part of my soul. My fists clench tighter by my sides, thick beads of sweat trickle down my lower back, and the air inside the car's trunk seems to dissipate by the second.

    I'm supposed to stay calm. Car trunks are not airtight, so the chance of running out of oxygen is unlikely. That's a lot easier to believe when you are not stuffed in one. *Think, Lina.* Jon went over hundreds of worst-case kidnapping scenarios prior to his departure, knowing that anything could happen. He explained, in rather boring detail, all of the ways to escape from the trunk of a car. I hadn't realized that automobiles produced post-2002 have an emergency lever inside, but if there is one, I can't find it. I could try to get into the car's dark interior through the back seat, but that isn't budging, either. I could kick out the taillight, but what would that solve? I chose this. I am here on purpose. Escaping is only an option if I want to quit. I should probably mention that I'm not a quitter.

    I tightly close my eyes and attempt, with my entire being, to slow down my breathing and calm my beating heart, which now is pounding in rhythm to my itching brain to the song's lyrics. I vividly remember the snatching of my purse and the sudden removal of my Apple watch from my wrist. They took everything before shoving me so effortlessly into the car trunk. What am I supposed to do now? How had I agreed to something like this? How can I remain calm enough to make this work? Then I remember the small, cheap flip phone that was hidden in my bra prior to the start of our operation.

I dig my sweaty fingers into my cleavage and flip open the cell phone, wondering why they hadn't tied my wrists together. I then select the only number preprogrammed, my ex-husband's. The car swerves from the left to the right and back again as the phone plummets with a thud somewhere near my leg. I vaguely make out the sound of Jon's voice from someplace in the distance as I frantically pat around me then finally breathe a heavy sigh of relief when my hand firmly clasps the device.

"Jon?" I whisper, grasping the phone to my ear while nervously speaking into the darkness.

"Lina." His tone is serious and gravelly, grounding me in a way I don't expect.

"Hi," I whisper.

"Hi."

"Well, this sucks."

"You're doing great."

"I am?"

"You are. How's your head?"

"My head?" I allow the confusion to settle over me but only briefly. I'm instantly aware of a pounding sensation in my left temple. I touch a quivering finger to the injured area, where I'm met with a wetness that could be blood or tears or maybe both. "I don't know," I confess.

"They got you pretty good. You probably have a concussion."

"Okay," I utter because, really, there is nothing else to say.

"Lina—"

"I'm fine, really," I whimper, biting down on my lower lip and shaking away the new memory.

"If you want to end this right now, just say the word."

I consider it for a moment, the idea of this nightmare coming to an end sounding more than enticing. But then I think of the girls... all of them. The way their families have worried and mourned and how completely agonizing it must be for them to not know their children's whereabouts. I think about Max and Lucy and how devastating it would be if something happened to them. The knot in the pit of my stomach tightens.

"Nah, I'm chillin'," I say with conviction. "It smells like our son's dirty football gear—"

"I'm serious. I'm trailing you now, but who knows where these scumbags are taking you."

"I guess we'll find out."

"Do you still have the necklace?"

I nod, securing my fingers around the faux-gold heart-shaped locket that Jon gently secured around my collarbone just hours earlier.

"Lina?"

"Yes." I'm nodding.

"It's a GPS tracker."

"I know." The car takes a tight turn, forcing me from my back to my side. From the cell phone's light, I make out a miniature pool of blood on the upholstery, and I let out a tiny yelp. "Oh, God."

"What? What is it?"

"It's nothing," I lie. "I'm just getting carsick."

"You're a terrible liar." The car picks up speed then turns once more. "Damn it," Jon grunts. "I think I know where they're taking you. Listen to me, Lina. If you really... If you really want to do this, you need to understand that I might… I might not be able to help you. At least, not right away."

"But the necklace—"

"The necklace is not going to save you. If you want out, you need to tell me now." The car swerves again, and this time, I barrel roll twice before landing on my stomach.

"I'm doing this, Jon. We didn't come this far to give up now. We can do this."

"Just do what they say, and don't fight them," he says, his voice growing softer and much weaker.

"I'll be okay."

"I'm sorry for getting you into this."

"Don't be. Operation Superglue for life." I chuckle, but Jon doesn't find this funny, and his silence speaks volumes. "Jon?"

"I'm here."

"I can do this."

"I know."

"It can't be worse than birthing seven-pound twin babies."

"Actually, it probably can."

"Have *you* ever birthed seven-pound twin babies *naturally*?"

"Are we here again? Now?"

"Yes," I laugh. "We are."

"I'll stop underestimating you. Point taken."

"Just do me a favor and tell the kids I love them. I should probably save the phone's battery." My words catch in the back of my throat at the possibility of never seeing them again.

"Just… Just please be careful."

"I will. And Jon? I—"

My words are cut short since the car has come to an unexpected and abrupt stop. My body slides backward, and my head slams hard against the wall. I shake away the sharp pain that has formed at the base of my neck, do my best to power off the cell, and shove it in the back of my shorts just as the trunk swings open. I squint my eyes into focus and gasp in horror at the unexpected sight before me. Very quickly, I realize that maybe, just maybe, there are times in life far worse than childbirth, and *this*... this is one of those times.

Chapter One

Now

I am trying not to kill my teenage daughter, Lucy, when the doorbell rings.

"I'll get it!" she shrieks, surely eager to flee from what must be the most embarrassing moment of her life. Lucy leaps from a seated position on her bed, bolting toward her bedroom door as a sea of blond highlights zooms by me. But I am quick. I barricade myself between her and the door then narrow my gaze and point to the side of the bed, where Oliver, her new and soon-to-be-dead boyfriend, is perched awkwardly. "Sit," I say like I'm talking to a dog as the doorbell rings a second time.

"Max!" I call, not taking my eyes off either of them. Oliver shifts uncomfortably, and if his face were any redder, I could fry an egg on his forehead. "Max!" I call again. "Please get the door!"

"He has his AirPods in," Lucy says, shifting closer to Oliver.

I shake my head and roll my eyes. "Too close," I scold as the doorbell rings again. "We aren't done here." I narrow my stare from Lucy to Oliver and back to Lucy. "Luciana Francesca Cote, you are *so* grounded. Don't move." I shake my head and scurry down the stairs, eager to remove the image of my daughter straddling her shirtless boyfriend in just a bra and Lululemon parachute shorts. "I'm coming!" I holler as the doorbell rings once more. I reach for the cool brass doorknob and fling open my front door, with the dry September late-afternoon Arizona heat smacking me in the face. "Can I help you?"

A middle-aged man stands at my door, wearing a black polo shirt and a matching hat that reads Super Scorpion Pest Removal. He smiles a toothy smile and wipes away golf-ball-sized beads of sweat from his forehead. "Good afternoon, Miss. Is the head of the household home?"

I inhale deeply, determined not to take out my aggression from earlier events on the soliciting pest control man. "I am the head of the household. Can I help you?"

Pest Control Man looks me up and down and sticks his nose in the air like I have attempted to pass for the Easter Bunny. "We are surveying the area and offering you and your neighbors a discount on pest control services."

"Thank you, but we aren't interested," I say, one hand on the doorknob while starting to close the door.

"Maybe if you get your mom or dad?"

I shake my head and laugh. "Like I said, I am the head of the household."

"Well, okay, then," he says skeptically. "It's just that you don't even look old enough to drive."

"I'll take that as a compliment," I say, closing the door further and once again noting that looking younger than I am is both a blessing and a curse.

"Is your husband home? I'm sure once he hears these prices, he'll be interested."

That's it. Pest Control Guy is now the enemy. "I'm divorced," I hiss. "Goodbye."

I slam the door and jog up the stairs, peeking into my son's room, where he is happily playing his Xbox with his AirPods secure in his ears. I look away from the piles of dirty laundry scattered about his bedroom and prepare to machine gun Lucy and Oliver with the most embarrassing birth control lecture ever to exist. The two delinquent teens leap on separate edges of the bed as I enter Lucy's room.

"Mrs. Cote," says Oliver before I can get a word in edgewise.

"It's Rivera," I snap with an unforgiving roll of my eyes.

"Mrs. Rivera—" he starts.

"It's Ms.," I correct. "Mrs. Rivera is my mother."

"Ms. Rivera," he sighs. "I'm sorry. I meant no disrespect."

Lucy inhales deeply and braces for impact, as she has known me long enough to understand that Oliver is treading in dangerous waters.

"Oliver," I start. "How old are you?"

"Sixteen, Ms. Rivera."

"Do you know how old my daughter is?"

"Fifteen—"

"I'll be sixteen in November!"

I hold up my hand. "Fifteen. Lucy is fifteen years old. Which is *not* old enough to be up here alone with you in her *bedroom*."

"I know, and I'm really sorry."

"I bet your mother would like to hear how sorry you are," I bluff, eyebrows raised. I've never met Oliver's mother, and over my dead body will I allow her first impression of me to include such lack of supervision on my part.

"Mom, no!" Lucy begs. "This was my fault. I know the rules, and I broke them."

My cell phone buzzes from my shorts pocket, and I pull it out, thankful for the minor interruption. Daphne's face smiles up at me from my home screen, and I hold up a finger at Oliver and Lucy as if to say, "one minute."

"Daphne, hi," I say, not taking my eyes off the trembling teenagers.

"Hey, girlfriend," Daphne croons, "We still on for drinks?"

I check the time on my Apple Watch and look from Oliver to Lucy. "Yeah," I say, rubbing my eyes with my fingers. "Can you meet me here first? I've got to take care of a few things."

"Be there in ten."

I stick my phone back in my pocket, relieved to know that within ten short minutes, I'll have reinforcements. Daphne is a good friend to have in your corner. I met her during my freshman year of college, and we've been inseparable ever since.

"Was that Aunt Daphne?" Lucy asks, eager to change the subject.

"Meet me downstairs," I say to my daughter. "And it's time for you to go home, Oliver."

"I'm really—"

"You can go home now, or you can be subjected to a mortifying lecture on condoms and teenage pregnancy. Your choice," I say with a smile.

***

Twenty minutes later, Daphne, Lucy, and I are perched around the kitchen island, inevitably deciding Lucy's fate. My son, Max, stands by, leaning against the fridge with a bag of blue Takis and enjoying every second of his twin sister's demise. While Max and Lucy are obviously not identical, their resemblance is uncanny. My father was from Mexico and my mother from France, leaving me with warm golden-brown skin kissed with a hint of olive undertones and eyes so sapphire blue they seem to sparkle like a crystal-clear sky. My twins inherited these characteristics, too, but also benefited from my ex-husband's French Canadian and Dutch descent, giving them defined cheekbones, lighter hair than mine, and the ability to tower over me by a solid five inches each. That's not hard to do as I stand at five feet *nothing*. I cannot help but feel proud of their heritage and all the unique features that set them apart.

"So let me get this straight," Daphne says, her elbows perched against the marble countertop. "You and Oliver were *doing it*?" She asks casually, like she's asking her about the grade Daphne received on an algebra test.

"Gross! No!" Lucy wails.

"They don't call it that anymore," Max chimes in.

Daphne stares at him in disbelief, her oversized blond messy bun bouncing in all directions and taking on a life of its own. "Come on, buddy," she says with a chuckle. "I think the term *doing it* has always been and will always be a universal term for having *sex.*" Her emphasis on the word "sex" might just put my daughter over the edge.

"We didn't have sex," Lucy whines.

"Well, what do you call it, then?" Daphne asks Max, turning her back on Lucy.

"What do we call having sex?" he asks between bites. "Smashing, hooking up, clapping cheeks—"

"Enough!" I say, holding my hands up to both Lucy and Max.

"What? Mom, you need to know this stuff for your books."

"I write young adult mystery and suspense, not teenage erotica," I argue, rolling my eyes and shaking my head. "And this is about Lucy and Oliver, and I need to focus."

"Sorry," he says, munching on his Takis and running a hand through his thick tresses.

"We have rules," I say to Lucy, trying to keep my tone firm but more than ready for this conversation to be over.

"It won't happen again, Mom."

"Damn right it won't. No more boys at the house."

"Ever?"

"Ever."

"But when will I see Oliver?" Lucy asks, wiping a tear from the corner of her eye.

"Listen," I say, placing a loving hand on hers. "I was a teenager once too. I completely get it."

"Yeah," Max chuckles. "Like in 1980."

"I was born in 1989," I correct.

"Same thing."

"No, it isn't," Daphne and I say in unison.

"It sort of is, Mom," Lucy chimes in. "How old are you now? Forty?"

"Watch yourself, young lady. I'm thirty-five," I snap, meaner than intended.

"Sorry."

"Listen," Max says, finally approaching us around the island. "Yeah, sure, Mom, you were a teenager once, too, but you have *zero* idea what it is like to be a teenager in 2024."

"I get what you're saying," I agree, assuming he is referring to the social media platforms I was never subjected to when I was in high school. "But relationships are relationships. I know what it is like to date boys, to be curious about sex…" My voice trails off because my children are looking at me like I'm an alien from another planet.

"Whatever, Mom," Max says, rolling his eyes. "I've watched your nineties shows, and it's just different."

"You have?"

"*Friends, Dawson's Creek, Gilmore Girls*—"

"You watch *Gilmore Girls*?" I ask him, eyes wide.

"He has a thing for Alexis Bledel," Lucy explains.

"I do not," Max says, throwing a blue Taki at her and hitting her square in the face.

"Whatever," Lucy sighs. "So how grounded am I?"

"No phone, for starters. And no Oliver."

"But, Mom—"

"But, Mom, *nothing.*"

"Ugh," she grunts. "I feel like you are overreacting."

"Are you still breathing?" I question with a smile. "And does Oliver still have a pulse?"

Lucy nods her head slowly, eyes downcast. "Yeah."

"Then I guess I didn't overreact."

Lucy adjusts her hair into a ponytail, placing it on top of her head while rubbing her eyes. "Fine. How long?"

"Let me sleep on it, okay?" I wrap my arms around her just as I have done so many times over the years, feeling the warmth of her body against mine and the familiar scent of her coconut-oil shampoo that always reminds me of home. I feel a surge of love and pride swell up inside me and decide, in that moment, not to kill her no matter how much trouble she has caused. I'm surrounded by the comforting notion that even though I've made a million and one mistakes in my life, I am totally crushing this single-parenting thing because no matter what—I will always be her mom, and she will always be my baby girl.

***

Two hours later, Daphne and I are seated at the bar of our favorite Mexican restaurant in Scottsdale on our second round of prickly pear margaritas, and all is well with the world. We are surrounded by bright, authentic décor, and the smell of freshly cooked tacos permeates my senses. The laughter of other patrons fills the air as we talk about the Lucy-and-Oliver scandal, as well as my interaction with Pest Control Guy.

"I told you to lay off the Botox," Daphne says with a chuckle when I tell her that he asked for my mom or dad.

"Like I said," I mumble between bites of taco, "Botox is for migraine prevention."

"Sure it is," she says, sipping her margarita and stifling a laugh.

"It is!"

"So forehead lines, under the eyes, crow's feet... all migraine prevention?"

"Actually, yes," I state firmly, though I'm not so sure.

"All I'm saying is if you're sick of people treating you like a teenager, then maybe lay off the Botox."

"It doesn't happen all the time," I say, gesturing to the bartender for two more margaritas.

"Yes, it does. Don't you get sick of being carded?"

"Sometimes," I say, crunching the taco shell between my teeth. "But I guess it's just who I am." Daphne nods in agreement, and I wonder if she's thinking about the year we met in college that we often reminisce about. "Besides," I say, gesturing to my skinny jeans and black halter top, "I can look older when I want to."

"Crushing it," she says sarcastically before changing the subject to my newest book release, *Only Human*, the sixth and final installment in my *New York Times* best-selling series, the Cat Rose Collection, which I have authored anonymously and successfully adapted into a major motion picture. "Any word on the reviews?" she asks.

I sigh deeply and shake my head, rubbing the base of my neck with the back of my hand as we wait for our drinks to arrive. "Reviews never get easier, but it's part of the job. I guess we'll just have to wait and see," I say with a shrug before clinking glasses with Daphne in a toast to whatever comes next.

"It will be great," she reassures me. "It always is. But I totally get it. Being in the fashion industry has its ups and downs too."

"Yeah, but you're badass," I say with a wink.

"Hell yeah, I am."

"Thanks for your help today with Lucy."

"I didn't do anything," she says, taking her drink from the bartender and gazing over my shoulder. "Hot guys, two o'clock," she says like an amateur ventriloquist.

"Ugh," I moan. "I never know which direction to look when you do that."

She bobs her head sideways, and I can't help but laugh. "You look like you're trying to get water out of your ear."

"Screw you." She chuckles. "They are hot."

I try to act casual, but that never works, and the group of men she's referring to are all completely aware that I am checking them out. I turn back around quickly, wondering when, suddenly, it got so hot in here. "Cute," I say.

"Hot," she argues.

"You're married," I remind her.

"You're not."

"I'm not interested," I say with a shrug.

"You never are."

"I date," I say, gathering my brunette tresses over my shoulder.

"Travis?"

"Yeah, Travis."

Daphne makes a face that I don't recognize, and I am suddenly offended. "What's wrong with Travis?" I ask, thinking of totally sexy six-foot, dark-skinned, chiseled abs, super-sweet Travis Mullins.

"Nothing is wrong with Travis, he's hot… but… he's your booty-call guy."

I hit her playfully on the shoulder. "No, he isn't!" I gasp.

"Oh yeah?" she challenges. "Tell me about Travis."

I think about this for a beat, and when all I can think of is *the sex is fabulous*, I realize that she's on to something. "Travis is great," I say reassuringly. "We have a lot of fun together, and he's always there when I need him. He's been a great friend to me, and he's really supportive of my career."

Daphne nods in agreement, but her expression still says she doesn't quite believe me. "But you don't want a relationship with him? You just want to keep it casual? That's okay too," she quickly adds, noticing the look on my face.

I take a deep breath and let it out slowly as I consider her words. "I just don't want a relationship right now," I say finally. "I'm happy with the way things are." But as the words fall from my lips and I utter them exceedingly joyfully, I cannot help but wonder if I am trying to reassure Daphne or myself.

Chapter Two

Then (2008)

As my fingers brushed swiftly against the keyboard of my new Dell laptop, and "Umbrella" by Rihanna rang out from my iPod on a drizzly day in April, I could not help but wonder—how many Starbucks Frappuccinos are too many Starbucks Frappuccinos? Indeed, there must be some sort of pass given to college students who are struggling to finish an essay on the Great Depression for a history project that, let's face it, was making me overly depressed. I had already gone through two large plastic cups of the frozen creamy beverage and was starting to feel the effects of the caffeine coursing through my veins. I knew I should probably take a break and get some fresh air, but I was so close to finishing the essay that I could not bring myself to stop. I could feel the pressure of the looming deadline and knew I had to finish it before midnight, or I would fail the class.

Starbucks in downtown Tempe had become a refuge for me during my time at Arizona State University. I loved my roommate, Daphne, to death, but let's face it. Daphne was the girl you wanted around when it was time to let loose and have fun, not when academics needed to take priority. I didn't mind working in the coffee shop. My laptop had been a Christmas present from my parents, and Starbucks had recently started offering free Wi-Fi, so for me, it was a win-win situation. I would order my favorite Frappuccino, find a seat near the window, and get lost in my work. The hustle and bustle of the cafe was comforting, and frequently, I found myself surrounded by other students just as dedicated to their studies as I was. Taking a deep breath, I pushed away from the table and stood up, stretching my arms above my head and releasing a long yawn.

Then I tucked my iPod into my jeans pocket and made my way back in line for just one more. Since the line was now more than six people deep, I decided it might be a good time for a bathroom break.

I glanced around, eager to find someone I could trust to watch my belongings while I used the restroom. Though I could be trusting and assumed the best in everyone, the idea of someone taking off with my laptop was too much to even imagine. To my left was a woman seated next to an angry toddler. While I didn't know much about children, I knew enough to assume that the child was probably overdue for a nap, and I didn't have the heart to bother them. To my right was a couple that appeared to be on a first date. They were smiling and laughing as they sipped their drinks and shared stories about their lives. I momentarily thought about asking them but reconsidered.

Just as I was about to leave my electronics to the fate of the Starbucks gods, I saw him. A Tempe police officer, someone who had caught my eye many times before. He occasionally came in and always left with a large tray of frozen beverages. Today, he was third in the long line of Starbucks patrons. I casually made my way toward him, noticing for the first time just how handsome he was—not cute or hot, as Daphne liked to say, but genuinely handsome—as in a Channing Tatum-meets-Leonardo DiCaprio sort of way. Since he was at least six feet two, I giggled to myself as my neck strained while I stared up at him. I felt my heart skip a beat. His blond hair and blue eyes were a striking contrast against his tan skin. I removed my headphone from my ear and cleared my throat.

"Hi," I said in the coolest, most confident tone I could muster.

"Hi there," he replied, his tone both raspy and smooth simultaneously. He placed his hands on his belt and smiled, lips curling up into a smirk that revealed a dimple on his left cheek and a boyish grin I hadn't expected. Suddenly, I was interested in way more than his security detail.

"I was wondering," I stammered as the blood rushed to my cheeks and my heart skipped a beat. "Would you be able to watch my things?" My words came out jumbled and awkward, and I wished more than anything I knew how to be chill.

"Yes, ma'am," he said with a wink—at least I think he winked. His eyes sparkled in the light of the cafe, and I felt my stomach do a flip. Then my eyes shifted to his bronze name tag, which read Cote.

"Thank you… sir," I said, self-consciously tucking a strand of hair behind my ear and locking eyes with him longer than probably was appropriate. He nodded, and I quickly strode off to the restroom, my cheeks feeling flushed as I walked away.

I used the restroom faster than humanly possible, but after washing my hands, I couldn't help but take a few moments to check out my reflection with the hopes of more conversation with Officer Cote. I swept my brunette tresses up into a bun on the top of my head, quickly reapplied a layer of clear lip gloss, and adjusted my Arizona State T-shirt over my shorts. I only wished I could rewind the day and redo my outfit. Then I spritzed a quick burst of Bath & Body Works Cherry Blossom spray over my collarbone, took a deep breath, and exited the restroom. To my chagrin, Officer Cote was nowhere to be found. What the hell? I screamed under my breath.

I scanned the room for any sign of him, but he wasn't there. Had he forgotten about me? I felt a wave of disappointment wash over me as I slowly made my way back to my table, hoping against hope that he had just stepped away for a moment. Then, as I rounded the corner, I saw him leaning against the wall, arms crossed, and a wicked smile on his face. He was waiting for me. I waved a somewhat dorky wave and followed his gaze to my table, where a new and freshly made Venti

Operation Superglue

Frappuccino sat beside my Dell laptop. I looked up in surprise, not able to hold back a nervous laugh, and made eye contact with him. He winked—*definitely* winked this time—but then, to my shock and disappointment, he turned and exited the coffee shop with his usual tray of coffees.

I shook my head, baffled by the events that had just unfolded. I tried to process what had happened, but all I could wrap my mind around was that Officer Cote—the handsome and hot officer Cote—had bought me a drink. That could mean he was interested in me, right? I wasn't the kind of girl to go out of her way to meet guys. Since my breakup with my high school boyfriend, Sam, I had rarely shown interest in another relationship. But there was something about this guy, something about Officer Cote, and I was determined to learn more. But, unfortunately for now, it would just be me and my Dell as we finished our essay on the Great Depression. Still, I was feeling less depressed by the second.

I unwrapped my straw and stuck it through the whipped cream and into the frozen coffee. It wasn't until my second sip that I noticed something interesting. There, on the side of the plastic cup that usually read Venti Frap Whipped, I saw something entirely different. My heart skipped a beat, and my breath caught in my throat. It read: Jon Cote 480-121-1516 CALL ME.

Chapter Three

Now

I sip my last bit of lukewarm coffee and massage my aching forehead with my fingers, beginning to regret my fourth margarita more than I regret marrying Jon Cote. Max slams the dishwasher loud enough to wake a sleeping giant, and I swear that Lucy's voice is an octave higher than usual as she accuses me of taking her favorite leggings by mistake.

"I don't have them," I argue for the hundredth time. "The bus is coming in twenty minutes... check under your bed or find something else to wear."

"Mom!" she shrieks. "I have *nothing* else to wear."

"You know that isn't true. It's hot outside. Grab a pair of shorts or something."

I can feel her rolling her eyes at me without turning around as she frantically jogs up the stairs to her room. "You have zero idea what it's like to be me," she hisses.

I shake my head and rub the back of my neck, deciding this is a battle I will surrender for now. "Are you getting school lunch today?" I ask Max, who is wrist deep in a jar of pickles. "*Pickles?*" I shriek. "Maximus Jonathan Cote, pickles are *not* breakfast."

"Why not?" he challenges between crunchy bites. "Technically, a pickle is a cucumber, and cucumbers are vegetables."

"Because..." I start but stop as my cell phone buzzes from my back pocket. My agent's number flashes across my home screen. "Just... eat something healthier for lunch, and don't miss the bus," I say, kissing his cheek and answering my call.

"Ana, hi," I say, hoping against all hope that she has news regarding the reviews on my book.

"Catalina," she says, her Russian accent thicker than usual as she somehow manages to make my full name five syllables. She is the only person on the planet, other than my mother, who uses my full name, Catalina, and she only seems to do it when she has bad news. I brace myself against my kitchen island with my eyes focused on Max as he finishes off the jar of pickles.

"What is it?" I ask, rubbing my tired eyes. "The last time you called me Catalina was when you broke the news about the second movie deal falling through." I wince, thinking back to the day producers pulled back their offer, leaving the Cat Rose series a one and done in the movie industry.

"Well…" Her voice trails off, and I can tell she is hesitating.

"Give it to me straight, Ana," I beg. "Is it bad?"

"It's not good, Catalina."

I pull a stool out from under the island and sit as Lucy flies down the stairs, shoving Max away from the fridge. "The reviews?" I ask Ana. "Are they bad?"

Lucy mouths a concerned, "What's wrong?" I shake my head and hold up my finger.

"The *New York Times* was pleased with your storyline," she starts. "The plot twists, the suspense, all on point."

"Okay," I say, breathing a sigh of relief. "So, what's the problem?"

"The problem," she says, clearing her throat, "is that they are being a bit critical of your character development. They say, and I quote, your protagonist is a sixteen-year-old girl with the personality of a middle-aged woman."

"What?" I shriek, pounding my fist on the countertop. "That's insane!" Max and Lucy jump from my sudden outburst. "What does that even mean?"

"It sounds like they are saying you are out of touch with what it is like to be a teenager, Catalina."

I glance at my two teens, the irony of the situation not passing me by. "I *have* teenagers," I argue. "Are they the only ones suggesting this?"

"Unfortunately, no."

"No?"

"Other sites, younger reviewers are saying the same thing."

"This has never happened." I grunt, more to myself than to Ana. "What are they saying?"

Ana is quiet until she says, "Ah, yes, right here. It says, who is this author in real life, and exactly how old is she anyway? *Eighty*? She has her antagonist showing up to class in a Mario T-shirt and her characters posting on Facebook." She pauses to clear her throat or for dramatic effect. I'm not sure which. "And the use of *Netflix and chill* is completely inaccurate."

"What?" I moan. "Netflix and chill? My character had her crush over to watch Netflix and chill out! What could be wrong with that?"

Lucy lets out a chuckle as pickle juice almost comes out of Max's nose. I threaten their lives with my pointer finger, and they stand straight like soldiers during roll calls.

"And what is wrong with a Mario T-shirt?" I whisper, trying to ignore Lucy's judgmental stare.

"Let's sit down this week and go over it all," she says. "They liked the book. They simply think you have become disconnected from your audience. That's all, darling. Nothing to worry about."

"Nothing to worry about?"

"Nothing to worry about, Catalina. I will see you tomorrow. Lunch at that Italian place I like in Old Town at noon."

"Okay," I sigh.

"Maybe stay away from the reviews," she suggests.

"Yeah, maybe," I say, an unfamiliar wave of panic rushing over me. I've never had a bad review like this before. I hang up my phone and slide it back into my pocket, forcing myself to look up at my children.

"What's wrong, Mom?" Lucy asks, sliding onto the stool next to me.

I glance up at the clock above the stove. "It's fine," I say, not sounding overly convincing. "You need to get your shoes on because the bus is coming soon."

Lucy leans her head on my shoulder and wraps her arms around mine. Her sweet gesture warms my heart, but her Hollister perfume is too much for my hangover. My stomach does a sudden flip-flop. "I'm okay," I say, kissing her head. "Some of my reviews say that I am out of touch with teenage life," I confess.

Max secures his baseball cap backward over his head before grabbing his black Nike backpack. "Lamers," he says, rolling his eyes.

"Yeah, it is. Lame, isn't it?" I agree. "Don't you have a Mario T-shirt, Max?"

"Like two years ago, bro. I don't wear it anymore."

I sigh, wondering when I went from Mommy to *bro*. "So, what? If you wore it, you would get made fun of?"

"You can't wear that to high school, Mom." Lucy chuckles, standing from the seat and kissing my cheek.

"Yeah, in elementary school, that shirt is drip," Max adds.

"Drip?" I ask, realizing that up until this moment, I have written off his teenage lingo as Max's language. I never stopped to consider that other children spoke this way.

"Yeah, like cool."

"Oh. And Netflix and chill?"

Max shakes his head, turning ten shades of pink, and heads for the door. "Not going there right now. Love you," he says, heading out the front door into the morning heat.

"Netflix and chill are an invitation to come over and hook up," Lucy whispers into my ear.

"What?!" I shout louder than I mean to.

"You heard me," she repeats, gathering her hair over her shoulder. "Shouldn't your editor have picked up on that?" she asks, rolling her eyes and shrugging her shoulders.

I picture my editor, Dottie, well into her mid-seventies, with her adorable ginger perm and the vintage pearls she sports daily, and realize that yes, my editor would have most definitely missed the meaning behind Netflix and chill and the misuse of a Mario T-shirt not being *drip* enough. "I guess not," I say with a shrug. "It will be fine," I say to Lucy but also to reassure myself.

"It's just a couple of reviews, Mom. Don't let it get you down. Hey, isn't today your coffee day with Dad?"

"Yes, it is," I say, trying to shake the pit that has formed in my stomach. If there were ever a day to cancel my coffee with Jon, this would be the day.

"Are you going to tell him?"

"About the reviews?"

"About Oliver?" she asks, eyes wide.

I consider this, realizing that this is indeed a lose-lose situation. If I tell Jon about Oliver, he will murder him. If I don't tell Jon about Oliver and he finds out, he will surely murder me.

"I don't know yet," I say because I don't know.

"Please don't, Mom," she begs.

"Go to school, girly. It will be fine. It will all be fine."

"Okay, Mom."
"And Lucy?"
"Yeah?"
"What's wrong with Facebook anyway?"
"Oh, Mom," she sighs. "Only *old* people use Facebook."

***

The Starbucks in downtown Tempe has served as a meet-up point for Jon and me since Max and Lucy were ten. It was then that our children, especially Lucy, started experiencing some social difficulties with bullies at school, and it was becoming harder and harder to stay on top of it when I only had her fifty percent of the time. It was also around the same time that Max began having difficulties in school. His grades started slipping that December, resulting in more and more meetings with his teacher. Jon quickly agreed that meeting up once or twice a month at the Starbucks in Tempe was way more beneficial than staring wide-eyed and clueless at Mrs. Adams while she talked at us about things we didn't know were happening in Max's world.

I slide my red Honda Civic beside Jon's Camry, cursing under my breath at his ability to be punctual. Indeed, he's already inside, perched at his favorite corner booth, sipping on his black iced coffee with a Frappuccino waiting for me. I will fake my usual gratitude and have no choice but to be on my best behavior. In the past, I found his grand gestures romantic. However, after all we have been through, I can now only see them as manipulative because let's face it—he buys my coffee. Therefore, I can't be an asshole.

I adjust my brunette tresses into a messy bun atop my head and brave the Arizona heat. My clothing is minimal—a short pink-and-yellow floral sundress with spaghetti straps that I'm pretty sure was purchased when the twins were in kindergarten—but I still feel like I am going to melt into a puddle when I step out of my car and into the Starbucks parking lot.

I am convinced that I am already in perimenopause at the age of thirty-five. Daphne thinks I am crazy for assuming this, but the truth is, my mother was through menopause before she turned forty. My doctor brushed off my concerns at my last appointment, determined to find something else that could contribute to my hot flashes, but there are no other culprits, as it turns out.

I let out a relieved sigh as the Starbucks air conditioning welcomes me. Jon sits perched against the wall in his favorite booth, eyes glued to his laptop, researching his latest case, I'm sure. My ex-husband traded his badge with the Arizona Police Department for a private investigator's license shortly after an undercover operation went south. Although I am out of the loop regarding Jon's cases, the general consensus from clients and the raving reviews on his website prove that he is, in fact, good at what he does. If only he could have been good at marriage.

Jon annoys me for many reasons, but he gets better looking with age, and this is the most irritating. He has traded his original polished buzz-style haircut and clean shave for a trendier fade with scruffy-looking facial hair that gives him an edgier vibe than in years past. However, as he glances up at me through his deep and concentrated stare and his baby blues meet mine, for a moment, I am provided with a nostalgic sense of comfort that both soothes and aggravates me simultaneously.

"Thanks for the coffee," I say as I sit across from him, my bare legs sticking to the wooden chair, and I curse the hot weather again under my breath.

"No problem," he says, his fingers typing briskly along the laptop's keys.

"It is freaking hot out there," I say, shifting uncomfortably in my seat.

"It's *Arizona*," he replies.

"I *know* it's Arizona," I say, rolling my eyes.

"Just saying," he sings, matching my tone. Jon shuts his laptop and reaches for his iced coffee. "How are you?"

I dig my straw through the layer of whipped cream and poke at my frosty beverage, considering for a moment how much I should get into with this man. Jon has a way of showing up for me emotionally that I haven't been able to find with anyone else. The problem is when I let him in and give him a piece of me, he always seems to find a way to look for something in return. Boundary setting has been vital in our relationship post divorce. I have consistently kept these meetings about Max and Lucy, and my gut is screaming at me to stay strong and not fall apart now. "I'm good," I say, not sounding overly convincing.

"That's crap." He chuckles.

"It's been a day."

"The kids?"

"Sort of," I reply between sips.

"Everything okay?"

I stare up at him wide-eyed, trying to read his mind. I should tell him that I caught Lucy and Oliver in bed. The right thing to do is admit that I caught Lucy and Oliver in bed. But if I report this information to my private investigator ex-husband, there is no telling what he will do. So instead of being the responsible parent I should be, I take one for the team and make it about myself.

"The kids are fine... great, even."

"So what's going on?"

I inhale deeply and sigh. "It's my new book," I say, my words catching in my throat.

"What about it?"

"The reviews. They aren't great."

Jon raises his eyebrows and throws his head back in surprise. "That's... unusual."

"No kidding!" I say, flinging my arms over my head, overly grateful to hear him say this.

"What do the reviews say?"

"Well, they liked the *actual* book. It's the characters... They are claiming that I'm disconnected from my target audience."

"Teenagers?" he asks through a playful snort.

"I know, I know. I *have* teenagers. But did you know that other kids talk like Max?"

"Well, yeah. I mean, I assumed so."

"I didn't," I admit.

"So they are basically calling you old?"

I kick him under the table. "If I'm old, you're ancient."

"I'm only five years older than you."

"Ancient," I repeat, checking my cell phone. I have three missed texts from my friend Ryker, one from Daphne, and four from Travis. I turn my phone over on the table as the heat rises to my cheeks. After all this time, it's silly being worried about what Jon might think of me dating. We have been divorced since 2011, which feels like an eternity, yet neither of us has settled down with anyone new. Jon could be seeing dozens of women for all I know. He keeps his private life locked up tighter than a bank vault.

"What does your agent say?" he asks, ignoring my jab.

"She's not telling me much but doesn't want me freaking out."

"Then don't freak out."

"Easier said than done. Hey, do you know what Netflix and chill means?"

Jon's phone buzzes on the table, and he stares at the number on the home screen. "I would assume it means watching Netflix?"

"Ha!" I shout louder than I mean to. "Wrong!"

Jon holds up a finger as if to say *one minute* and answers his call. "Cote Investigations, Jon speaking." Jon stands up from the table and scurries outside.

"Saving the world one investigation at a time," I mutter sarcastically. I retrieve my own phone from the table and begin answering my texts. Ryker is interested in hearing about my book reviews, and Daphne wants to know if I am as hungover as she is. I efficiently text my friends until I pull up the thread from Travis, who has decided that today will be a good day to break our usual relationship pattern. By this, I mean I usually only text him to come over when I want to see him, and I usually text *him* to go out when I want to go out with him.

Travis: Hey babe, I hope you are having a good morning. I know it's Thursday and we don't typically do much on weeknights, but I was hoping tonight might be a good night to stay in and watch a movie? Smith is with his mom tonight. Sorry about how we left things.

I realize, at this moment, that I have just been asked to Netflix and chill, and I choke on my Frappuccino at the irony. I glance over my shoulder at Jon, pacing back and forth in the parking lot. I love my time with Travis. Really, I do. Daphne might be right. What if Travis is my booty-call guy?

Lina: Rain check? I've got some work stuff I need to sort out.

I swipe out of my text thread with Travis just as Jon returns to the table. "Everything good?" I ask.

"Not great," he admits. He joins me back at the table and wipes beads of sweat from his forehead. "That was the Tempe police returning my call. I thought I had a lead on something and was wrong."

"Sorry," I say, genuinely meaning it. Jon puts everything into his cases and puts much pressure on himself to get the job done right.

"It's fine," he says, rubbing his eyes. "So, your reviews… is there anything you can do about it?"

I think about this for a beat. "I don't really know. Learn their language?" I ask, letting out a laugh.

"What do you mean, their language?"

"What I mean is, kids today are way different than when I was in high school. They talk differently. It's like a completely different language. They communicate like this," I say, waving my phone. "I wish I could be a fly on the wall in a high school." I might be on to something. "I wonder if the twins' principal would let me shadow," I add, relaxing my shoulders.

Jon's eyes narrow, and a muscle in his jaw tightens, his expression one of pure concentration. I wave my hand in front of his face to distract him from whatever idea he's concocting in that mind of his. I've seen this expression a few times throughout our relationship. It usually means he has cracked the code on a case or has an over-the-top idea. "Huh," he mutters chewing on his straw.

"What's going on up there, Detective Cote?" I sing. When he remains silent, I check the time on my phone. "I have to head out soon," I say. "I need to start brainstorming ways to think like a teenager in—"

"Wait," he says. "Hear me out."

"Hear what out?"

"You need to learn what it is like to be a teenager today, right?"

"Yes," I reply, my patience growing thinner by the second. "If I want to keep my job, yes."

"Well... What if you *were* a teenager?"

"What on earth are you talking about?" I ask with a heavy sigh.

"An undercover operation," Jon says, not missing a beat. "You, undercover as a high school senior."

I bolt upright in confusion. "Are you serious right now? I can't be a teenager. I *have* teenagers."

"Lina, you could pass for a teenager, and you know it."

"You're being absurd," I say, grabbing my purse from the back of my chair and placing it on my lap. "Even if I could, what? Would I just enroll in the kids' school? No, I will do some shadowing, and it will be fine. Plus, there is always Google, YouTube, ChatGPT..." My voice trails off as I tuck my phone into my purse. I stand from my chair and begin to turn away.

"Wait," he says, his tone one that I have become familiar with. Jon stands and reaches across the table, placing an eager hand on my shoulder.

"I've seen this face before."

"Sit, Lina. Please?"

I slump back in my seat with a thud. "What's your big idea?"

"I'm going to tell you something, and you have to promise me that you won't tell *anyone.*"

"Anyone?"

"Anyone."

"Okay," I agree, intrigued.

"I've been working on a case since last year. Three high school teens have gone missing from a private school in Tempe."

I think about this for a minute. "Emerson Academy? The runaways?" I vaguely remember seeing something about this on the news.

"They aren't runaways. I believe all three of them were kidnapped. We may be looking at human trafficking."

"That's… That's just awful," I say, rubbing my neck and thinking about my own daughter. "What is your involvement in the case?" I suck down my drink, suddenly very interested in what my ex-husband has been doing for the past year.

"I've been undercover at Emerson Academy, posing as the school's art teacher."

I try to stifle a laugh, but it is hopeless. I choke on my coffee, and in my attempt to take a breath, I spit it out all over Jon's face. When I finally get my coughing under control, I look up at him, and his Frappuccino-covered facial hair sends me downward spiraling once again.

"Here," a woman says as she passes me a napkin. "For your dad."

This sends me into another fit of laughter. "Thank you," Jon says, taking the napkin from her and wiping his face as he mouths the word "dad" as if to say *told you so*.

"I…I'm sorry," I say, still eager to catch my breath. "Did you say *art teacher*?"

"Why is that so funny?"

I gawk at him like he has ten heads. "You can't even color without breaking the crayon."

Jon tosses a crumpled-up napkin at me. "I'm a sub. The teacher leaves stuff for me, and I hand it out."

"So, you are undercover as a sub, trying to find the missing girls?" I ask, finally able to compose myself.

"Yes, the dean hired me last year. It's so frustrating, Lina. I've got nothing."

"I'm sure you have a lead or two."

"Nothing. I thought I was on to something, but I was wrong." Jon gestures to his phone with one hand and rubs his scruffy chin with the other. "I think the only way to find these girls is to infiltrate their social circles."

"You need a teenager," I say, the realization washing over me.

"I need a teenager. I even… I even thought about asking the kids for help, but I could never…"

I shake my head and agree that asking our kids for assistance is out of the question. "Look, I can see why you think this might be a good idea, and I know I can seem younger than thirty-five, but I don't look seventeen or eighteen," I say, gesturing to my mom dress.

"When was the last time you bought a scratch ticket?" Jon interrogates.

"I don't know what you mean," I say, looking down at my feet.

"Yes, you do."

"On my birthday, like every year," I confess.

"And?"

"I got carded."

"Exactly. Do you trust me?"

I furrow my brow and crinkle my nose at him. "I'm not answering that."

"Come on, it's been years."

"Still not answering that."

"Do you trust that I'm good at my job?"

"Yes," I confess. "I trust that you are good at your job."

"Think about it?" he asks, his blue eyes piercing my soul.

"I'll think about it," I sigh. "But Jon… Don't hold your breath."

Chapter Four

Then (2008)

It had been two days since Jon asked me out via message on a Frappuccino cup. Against Daphne's advice to play hard to get, I called him that evening, eager to accept his invitation for dinner at Rick's, the hottest date-night spot at ASU, and also proceeded to talk to him for hours, only stopping when the battery on my Motorola flip phone blinked warningly at five percent.

It turned out that Jon was a rookie cop, still in his first official year with the Arizona Police Department, which explained why he was constantly in Starbucks, fetching iced coffees for his colleagues. He had graduated from the police academy the previous year and was living in a one-bedroom apartment in Tempe, getting his feet wet as a cop and enjoying rookie life. He was passionate about his job, which made me passionate about him.

"I can't believe you aren't even playing hard to get just a little bit," Daphne scolded over my shoulder as I adjusted the length of my white spaghetti strap tank top and pulled at the waist of my low-rise skinny jeans. I studied my reflection in the mirror, gathering my dark tresses over my shoulder and dismissing her comment entirely. "Seriously, Lina. You met him less than forty-eight hours ago. You gossiped with him on the phone like a needy little teenager looking for an invite to prom, and the second he asks, you agree to go? Guys like a chase. They don't want to *be* chased."

"He's not like other guys," I shrugged, making eye contact with her in the mirror.

Daphne's curly blond tresses bounced to the beat of her increasingly annoying rant. "Hate to say I told you so," she said with a yawn, turning and flopping down onto my unmade twin bed in a seated position, crossing one gray sweatpants-covered leg over the other. "It's just you don't get out much. You *never* get out, so I want this to work out for you. Besides, how on earth do you know he isn't like other guys? Or are you saying that he isn't like Sam?"

"I just know, okay?" I ignored the implication that I was comparing him to my last relationship—my only relationship. "I've got this," I said as I applied my fourth layer of lip gloss. "But it's sweet that you worry… or analyze me… or worry." I shrugged, bent forward, wrapped my arms around her shoulders, and pulled her close in a friendly embrace. "Explain to me why you can't wear your own clothes?" I asked, gesturing to my gray Arizona State hoodie.

"It's easier to steal your stuff than to do laundry," she huffed, as if this response made taking my clothes okay.

"Of course it is," I exclaim. "I'm heading out to Rick's. Don't wait up," I sang, grabbing my crossbody purse off my doorknob and tucking my phone into my back pocket.

"I can't believe you are bailing on me on a Thursday night," she whined. "Thirsty Thursday is our thing. Now what am I supposed to do?"

"Do laundry?" I suggested, eyebrows raised.

"Why do laundry when I have you?"

"You're a lost cause," I said, rolling my eyes and heading for the door. "Don't wait up," I repeated, reaching for the doorknob.

"Hey, Lina?" Daphne called from my bedroom.

"Yeah?"

"Have fun but be careful."

"I love you, too, Daphne," I called from the hallway, allowing the apartment door to close behind me. "I love you too."

***

I arrived ten minutes early to our date, and to my surprise, Jon was already in the restaurant, seated at a corner booth and sipping a beer. He stood from his chair upon my arrival at our table, brushing his hands on his jeans and smoothing the front of his baby-blue polo shirt with his palms. He looked different out of uniform, much taller than I remembered, and for a moment, I felt like I was staring at a stranger. I chuckled under my breath because I *was* staring at a stranger. I studied his face for signs of anything familiar, but even his blond buzz cut seemed foreign and out of place here in this restaurant and out of Starbucks. I stared nervously around me, my heart pounding, wondering if Daphne was right. This might be too much too soon. I should have played harder to get. But when my gaze fell on his eyes, with their hints of blues and flecks of silver, and they stared confidently through me, lighting every part of me on fire, I knew with my entire being that I was where I was supposed to be.

"Thank you," I said to the hostess, my words catching in the back of my throat and coming out in a hoarse whisper.

"Enjoy your night," she sang, eyebrows raised in approval.

My cheeks flushed, and I gathered my hair over my shoulder, biting my top teeth down on my bottom lip, a nervous habit.

Jon pulled my chair out for me as though he had done it dozens of times before. "Hey," he said, his tone smooth and confident.

I slid into the chair and nodded awkwardly. "Hey!"

Jon sat back down and took a swig of his beer. "I was going to order you a drink, but I…" His voice trailed off.

"You don't know what I drink." I laughed nervously.

"Right."

" 'Cause we don't know anything about each other," I added, sassier than I intended.

"Well, Lina," he said, reaching his hand across the table and wrapping it around mine. "I would like to change that if that's okay with you."

I wasn't sure when my heart stopped beating. It might have been when Jon held my hand, but it also could have been when he leaned forward, locked his gaze on mine, and somehow shook the innermost parts of my soul. The pieces I kept locked up and protected to avoid the hurt and heartache I had experienced in the past. The side of me that I purposely left alone, being careful to leave conveniently numb and focused on my simple responsibilities. Tasks like going to class, completing assignments, and doing everything correctly. *Don't do anything stupid, Lina.* Those were the last words my parents said when they dropped me off at college. But then… his hand. His hand was on mine. His eyes were on mine. I realized at that moment that I couldn't go back. That I would never again be just Lina. That this was one of those moments like in movies—the climax. I had met my person. After meeting this man, I would never be the same.

"Okay," I said in a choked whisper.

"Hey there!" An overly cheerful voice sang and interrupted my downward spiral of emotions. "My name is Jill, and I will be your server this evening."

I shimmied my hand from Jon's and wiped the sweat from my palm on my jeans. "Hi!" I said, my tone matching hers.

"Can I grab you something to drink?"

"Coke, please," I said. "With a lime."

"Sure thing," she said, turning away.

"I'm not quite twenty-one," I said, gesturing to his beer.

"Damn," he said, slapping a frustrated palm to his forehead. "I didn't even think of that."

"How old are you?" I asked, surprising myself.

"Twenty-five," he said, searching my eyes for approval. "How about you?"

"Twenty," I said, shifting uncomfortably in my seat. "Prickly pear margarita."

"Excuse me?"

"That's what I would have ordered. Anything prickly pear."

"How very Southwestern of you."

I chuckled at his comment. "It's a family thing," I said, wondering how much I should get into it since I hadn't even looked at the menu yet and it wasn't even 6:00 p.m.

"Nice. I'll keep that in mind. Prickly pear…" he said, his voice trailing off.

Jill returned with a Coke and placed it on the table before me. "Can I get you another beer?" she asked Jon.

"Actually, I'll take a prickly pear margarita," he said with a wink.

"Coming right up."

Jill strutted away with Jon's empty beer, and I stared at him wide-eyed. "Officer," I said in my best excuse for a Southern accent, "I'm a law-abiding citizen. I can't drink alcohol at this here establishment with you."

"I ordered it for myself." He smirked. "I've always wanted to try it." Jon took my hand in his once again, and this time, his boldness overwhelmed me. I almost pulled my hand back in surprise, but instead, I settled into the moment comfortably. I couldn't remember the last time anyone held my hand. Sure, it was a bit awkward that he was treating me like he had known me forever, but maybe… just maybe… "Maybe when she isn't looking, you can steal a sip or two," he winked.

Something about Jon's wink activated *Alter-Lina*. Daphne came up with the name to describe my alter ego, the part of me that knew how to relax and have a good time without being worried about everything under the sun. She didn't come out much, but when she did, she was a force to be reckoned with. "I have a better idea," I proclaimed, rubbing my fingers over his. "I make a mean margarita. I can swing into the store down the street and grab supplies if you know anywhere we can make them?" I considered inviting him back to my place, but Daphne would have way too much fun with that. And besides, Alter-Lina wanted to be alone with Jon.

"My place is five minutes away," he said, obviously surprised by my suggestion as he reached into his pocket for his wallet.

"Want to just head to your place and order pizza?" I suggested.

"I thought you'd never ask."

***

"I hope you tipped her well," I chuckled, harking back to our empty table at Rick's and hoping our server wasn't too upset with us for bailing. Jon had chugged half of the margarita and slipped it my way when it appeared nobody was looking. I wasn't sure if it had been my first-date jitters or if I hadn't eaten all day, but half a prickly pear margarita had me feeling decent. "I feel kind of bad for bailing." I sliced the lime and pierced it with the corner of my glass and Jon's.

"My grandmother was a waitress," he explained, picking up his margarita glass. "I always tip at least twenty percent."

"Perfect," I said, raising my glass to my lips.

"Not so fast," he said, motioning to my glass. "We need to toast."

I cringed for a moment, wondering what in the actual hell I was supposed to say in toast to a man I knew nothing about but genuinely *needed* to know everything about. "Cheers," I said, skittishly clinking my glass to his.

"To us," he said, his tone weighty and distinguished.

"To us," I repeated, locking eyes with his. I took a long and eager sip of my drink before loosening my stare from his. "Your place is nice," I affirmed, gesturing to the space around me.

Jon's apartment was a one-bedroom in downtown Tempe, and I must admit it was nicer than expected. Daphne and I mostly ate off paper plates with plastic utensils and drank from red keg cups, as college students routinely did. Jon had ceramic plates and real utensils and a variety of actual drink glasses that wouldn't need to be recycled after use. This reminded me that he wasn't a college kid like me but a man with a *career*, and this made me overly jittery. Jon had more maturity in his pinky than the guys I had been dating.

"It's okay," he said, gesturing around him. "The kitchen is a decent size, and I love having a bar in the middle of the room, but there isn't space for a kitchen table with it being open concept and all."

"Well, I like it," I said with a shrug. I studied the white leather sectional, which surrounded a glass coffee table and the large television on the wall. "It's bigger than mine. I share a room with Daphne, my roommate."

Jon nodded in understanding. "I had a roommate all through the academy," he said with a smile. "I totally get it." Jon sipped his margarita and thought about this for a beat. "It's nice, though, living with someone, right? It can get lonely at times."

I slurped my drink and perched against the bar with my elbows. "I wouldn't know," I said, considering this. "I've never actually lived alone. But Daphne is about as good as roommates can get."

"Is Daphne from around here?"

"She grew up on the East Coast," I explained.

Jon finished his drink and gestured to me for another. I nodded in understanding and reached for the bottle of tequila. "Who did you live with before Daphne?"

I bit my lower lip and tried to hold back my smile as I mixed our drinks, adding a splash of soda water at the top, just as my dad taught me when I lived back home. "Is that your way of asking me if I was in a serious relationship?" I asked, cracking a flirty side smile.

"Maybe."

"That's a second-date question. Slow down," I joked.

"Maybe. But technically, our date started at Rick's, and now we are back here, so this could be considered our second date, right?"

I reached for his glass and refilled it, sliding another slice of fruit on its rim. "I had a serious boyfriend in high school," I confessed, sipping my second drink. "His name was Sam. I dated him from freshman year all the way through to junior year, when he broke up with me and took my best friend to prom."

"Ouch."

"Yeah, it wasn't awesome. I took Sam back senior year, but it didn't work once we started at separate colleges."

"Copy that," Jon said, nodding in understanding.

"So, the last people I lived with before my roommate, Daphne, were my parents. And life with them most definitely wasn't lonely." I smiled for a beat, thinking fondly of my mom and dad, and for a strange and unanticipated moment, I wondered what they would think of Jon. "How about you?" I asked. "Former priors?"

Jon snickered at my joke, making me like him even more. "Nobody to write home about," he said, smiling. "I've always been really focused on my career. Being a cop, it's all I ever wanted."

"What made you want to be a cop?"

Jon reached across the bar and rubbed his fingers over mine. I wasn't sure if it was the two margaritas I was feeling or just the mere fact that Jon was touching me, but the unexpected zing from my toes to my fingertips caught me off guard. "You really want to know?"

"Of course. Why wouldn't I want to know?"

"I don't know," he said, suddenly bashful. "Usually, I just tell people it's because I want to make a difference or because so many of my family members are cops."

"And that isn't the reason?" I asked, sliding closer to him.

"Yes and no. I didn't want to go into the field at first because I felt like I had to. But then…"

"I can see that," I said, thinking of my parents and their restaurant business. "My parents really want me to work for their family business, but I want to be an author."

"Are you majoring in English literature?" he asked, sliding closer to me. The heat from his arm radiated onto my exposed skin, and I gravitated toward him like a magnet on metal.

"Nope," I said, mulling over him. I couldn't take my eyes off those damn iridescent baby blues. "I'm an education major. I'm going to be a teacher."

"Why?"

I snorted at this and choked on my drink. "What do you mean, why?" I asked, catching my breath.

"Sorry." He chuckled. "If all you have ever wanted was to be an author, then why are you going to school to teach?"

I traced my finger over the rim of my glass and again found myself wondering just how much was too much for a first date. I inhaled deeply and decided to go for it. "My parents," I sighed. "They are paying for my prestigious education, and they don't see how writing books will put food on the table, support a family, pay health insurance..." My voice trailed off as Jon traced my arm with his fingers, and suddenly, all I could think about was Jon touching me.

"How do you feel about that?" Jon asked.

I twirled a strand of my brunette tresses around my pointer finger. "I guess he has a point," I said thoughtfully.

"About the food on the table, the stability, or the health insurance?"

"Probably all of it," I admitted, sipping my margarita. "Teaching has more job security, so I guess I see his point."

"*His*?" Jon asked. "So, more so your *dad* than your mom?"

My cheeks flushed at my Freudian slip, but there was also something so vulnerable about that moment. I'd never met anyone like Jon before. He was paying attention to every comment and word, so much so that he picked up on the fact that I wasn't sharing the whole truth with him. Then again, he was a trained police officer. This was, however, anything but an interrogation. "Busted," I sighed. "I'm a daddy's girl of the worst kind."

"What kind is that?" he asked, his hand now grasped around my fingers.

I studied his fingers and how they seemed to fit perfectly around mine. Was he like this with all the girls? His confidence could be misunderstood as overly arrogant. But coming from him, it just seemed business as usual. "The kind that needs approval at all costs," I said, surprising myself with my honesty.

"Even at the cost of your happiness?"

I jerked my hand away from his, overwhelmed by his sudden assumptions. "I'm happy," I rebuked, sterner than intended. "I love my dad."

Jon held his hands up in front of his face in surrender. "I didn't mean to overstep."

"It's fine," I said, finishing off my drink. I stared down at my glass and poked at the wedge of lime.

"I never meant to imply that your dad is anything short of fantastic."

"Sorry," I muttered. "I'm really close with my parents, and I just... I don't like when people talk about them. Sure, they were strict. I had the earliest curfew of anyone I knew, and I was the only one in my friend group without a tattoo."

"You really don't have a single tattoo?" he asked, eagerly attempting to change the subject.

"None," I said again.

"Piercings?"

"Just my ears. My cousin got her belly button pierced last year, and Dad told me he would drop dead if I ever did such a thing."

"You must be an only child."

"Bingo."

"I have one," he said. Without warning, Jon lifted his shirt, revealing chiseled abs and a red, white, and blue American flag sketched under his pectoral muscle, following the natural curve of his body, starting at his shoulder and ending under the center of his breastbone.

With all the willpower I could muster, I forced my stare to hold steady on the tattoo, but I failed miserably. Maybe it was the drinks. It might have been the instant connection I felt with Jon. Either way, I felt myself crumble inside as the emotional barriers I had worked so hard to construct disintegrated at the speed of light. I reached my unsteady pointer finger to his chest and traced it over the American flag, the heat from his skin radiating on to my finger and sending electricity through my body. "God bless America," I blurted, my words catching in my throat.

Jon smiled at my joke, clearly amused, and I should have laughed, too, but I was so busy thinking about him and his V-shaped waistline that I couldn't focus. More than anything, I wanted to run my fingers over his exposed chest and abs. My eyes traveled to his belt, and I shuddered, embarrassed at how badly it needed to be unbuckled. "So, you like it, then?"

"Like what?" I asked, louder and more defensive than intended.

"The tattoo. What else would I be asking about?" he asked, raising his eyebrows in pure amusement.

"I love it," I admitted, retracing my fingers over the fifty stars, mesmerized at the tattoo's beauty *and* Jon's. "Who is RJA?" I asked, noticing the initials in cursive in the center of a star.

Jon cleared his throat and stared up at the ceiling. He released his shirt from his fingers, letting it drop back down. I removed my hand from underneath it and studied his solemn expression. I gathered my hair over my shoulder and bit down on my lip. *Way to kill the moment, Lina.* RJA could be anyone from an ex-girlfriend to a dead grandparent, neither of which Jon would be excited to explain on a first date.

"It's okay," he reassured me, sitting back on the barstool, opening his legs, and pulling me between them. Jon was taller than me by almost a foot, and although I had noticed this at dinner, it surprised me how far he needed to bend down to hold me. He wrapped his arms around my lower back and nuzzled his face in the crevice of my neck. My heart rate increased, as did his, tremendously, because I could feel it pounding against my chest. Who was this person? He was acting like he had known me for years, forget minutes.

"We don't need to talk about it," I affirmed. "It's okay."

Jon inhaled deeply, followed by a long exhale. His breath smelled of prickly pear and lime, but the faint smell of his cologne ignited my senses and turned my knees to jelly. Was that sandalwood? Cedar? I wanted to bottle it up and keep it forever, whatever it was. "I usually don't want to talk about it," he admitted. "But I feel like I want to with you."

I pulled back and studied his expression, both serious and thoughtful. His enigmatic blue eyes had secrets to tell, and they were locked on mine, and for a moment, I got it. A warmth spread through my chest, and a surge of emotions washed over me, contrasting with the tough exterior I'd taken years to build. With every breath and every blink of his eye, Jon was deconstructing my emotional barriers, causing me to feel as though I had known him my whole life. I traced my thumb and pointer finger over his freshly shaved chin. I wanted to pull him close to me and kiss him. I wanted to rip his clothes off and yank him into his bedroom, wherever that was. But even more than that, I wanted to be there for him, to listen to him about RJA and the American flag tattoo. "I'm listening."

"My friend Russ… We were friends since kindergarten… He…"

His voice trailed off like it was too painful to finish his sentence.

"He died?"

"Yeah."

"I'm sorry," I said, pulling him back to his spot in my neck's crevice. "Was he sick?"

Jon drew back and shook his head. He sipped the rest of his drink before looking back at me, at least ten seconds passing before he spoke again. "He was working in New York City on September 11," he said, turning his attention to the floor. "He was in the towers."

I gasped as a chill ran through me. I had never met anyone with a family member or friend who passed away that day, but it was still one of the saddest days I had ever endured. "That's… That's awful. I'm so sorry."

"Yeah, it's pretty awful," he agreed, laughing nervously. "He loved our country. Fourth of July was his favorite holiday. That's why I got the tattoo."

"And... it's why you became a cop?" I stated more than I asked.

"It's why I became a cop."

We stood in silence for minutes that seemed like hours, and I caught the hint that it was time to change the subject. "Did it hurt? The tattoo?"

"Nah. I've felt worse."

"What does it feel like?"

"Cat scratch on a sunburn."

"Huh?"

"It's like getting a bad sunburn and then getting scratched."

"By a cat?"

"Yeah."

"Huh." I giggled. "I guess I wouldn't know."

"Daddy's girls don't get tattoos," he teased.

I pulled away from him, reaching for the tequila bottle. "Do you have any fancy shot glasses in that cabinet?"

"Why? Are we taking shots?"

"Was that a tattoo parlor on the first floor of your building?"

"Yes, ma'am. My buddy owns it."

"Are they still open?"

"They should be. Why?"

"Because you and I are taking a shot of tequila, and I'm going to get my first tattoo."

***

Jon threw open his apartment door and led me back inside. I couldn't remember the last time I had this much fun, laughed so hard, and was so not dull. Alter-Lina was in full effect, and I liked her. I thought Jon did too.

"I can't believe we went through with that!" I shrieked, stumbling over my own feet.

"I can't believe we did either."

I reached for the bar and braced against it, trying to ignore the spinning room with all my might.

"Feeling okay?" Jon asked. I wasn't sure if he was referring to my off-balanced moment or the tattoo I had gotten a mere twenty minutes prior.

"Cat scratch on a sunburn," I lied, trying with all my might to ignore the burning sensation, gesturing to my lower back and reaching for the tequila bottle. I had gripped Jon's wrist hard enough to cut off his circulation as the needle touched my skin for the first time. Aside from almost passing out and only crying for ten minutes, my first tattoo was a success. "We need a celebratory shot."

"One more," Jon said with authority. "Then no more tequila."

"There is no such thing as too much tequila," I said, carelessly pouring the alcohol into the shot glasses. I passed Jon a shot glass and held mine in the air. "To Jon and Lina and our new tattoos. My lower back and his left shoulder will never be the same. And here's to my dad. May he not suddenly die when he sees it."

Jon clinked his glass against mine, and I shot back the tequila. It burned a bit, but the adrenaline flowing through my veins at lightning speed made me feel like I could rule the world.

"I owe you an apology," Jon said, wrapping his hands around my waist and pulling me close.

"For what?" If he had done something wrong, I couldn't recall. I could barely remember my name between the too many drinks and with him holding me that way.

"For assuming daddy's girls don't get tattoos," he sighed, running his fingers through my hair and tucking it behind my ear.

"Mhm," I moaned softly, closing my eyes and taking in the moment. I liked this feeling.

My body felt weightless as I stumbled closer to him.

"You okay?" he asked.

"I'm more than okay," I said with a smile, and I meant it. I stood on my tiptoes, pulling Jon's face down toward mine. "I like you, Jon Cote—a lot."

His lips curled up into an amused half smile. "I like you too, Lina. I..."

Jon's voice trailed off, and his lips, centimeters from mine, rubbed together awkwardly.

"It's Rivera," I finished for him, rubbing my nose against his, my skin feeling cool against his, which seemed impossible because my insides were on fire. Jon kissed the top of my nose and the side of my cheek and gently tipped my chin upward, kissing that too.

"Lina Rivera," he whispered. "I really, really like you."

I wanted to stay in that moment forever as his mouth gently danced along my forehead, one cheek, and the other. Goose bumps flooded my body as his breath teased me in all the right ways until I couldn't take it anymore. My hands took on a life on their own, reaching up and pulling his face to mine. When our lips touched, an overwhelming sense of relief washed over me. He kissed me slowly at first, gently biting my lower lip as he pressed his hand on the back of my head as an unexpected moan escaped from somewhere deep within me. I parted my lips, and his tongue slid inside my mouth, and when it did, my knees grew weak and I crumbled against him, almost falling to the floor.

"Whoa," Jon laughed. "You okay?"

"I... I'm." I struggled between breaths. "Where's your bedroom?" I knew I was being forward but lost all sense of caring.

Jon smiled, kissing me again, nibbling at my earlobe with his teeth. "You sure?"

I threw my head back, struggling to open my eyes. "Yes."

Jon moved his mouth back to my chin, over my neck, and toward the seam of my tank top, kissing over the white cotton fabric. Jon's hands were grasping my sides tightly, the tips of his thumbs teasing around my chest and on my abdomen. "Are you sure?" he asked again, his tone full of concern but his touch and body language completely contradictive.

"Jon," I scolded. "Show me where your bedroom is, or I will find it myself."

"Well," he snickered, scooping me up in one sweep like a groom carrying a bride across a threshold. "I'm horrible with directions, so I will show you myself."

"Deal," I agreed, kissing him forcefully as he carried me down a short hallway into his bedroom. I didn't open my eyes as he tossed me onto his bed, and I kept them shut as he unbuttoned my jeans, and I shimmied out of them. I ignored the brief sting of my tattoo as it rubbed under the bandage and against his comforter.

"You're so beautiful, Lina," he whispered in the darkness as he removed my shirt and unclipped my bra. I kept my eyes closed as he kissed my neck and chest and drifted over my stomach. When he shifted back up toward my face, I opened my eyes, only so I could study him again before collapsing back on the bed.

Jon traced over my stomach with his fingers, flooding me with surges of butterflies, chills, and waves of electricity. "Yes," I whispered as his fingers teased the seam of my underwear, and I gasped when he finally pressed them against me.

"Lina," Jon groaned as he touched me in all the right places, and my body responded without resistance. "Lina," he repeated as he slid my underwear off me and continued kissing me where his fingers had left off.

"I want you, Jon Cote," I begged, my fingers clawing at the back of his head. "I need you."

Whose words are these? I wondered. This situation was over the top, even for Alter-Lina. Alter-Lina didn't sleep with guys on the first date. Alter-Lina didn't beg for anything, especially sex. But I was out of control and overcome with a thunderstorm of feelings I had never experienced. Never in my life had I needed someone like I needed this man, and I needed him *now*.

I opened my eyes as Jon removed his shirt and jeans. I eased him to me, running my fingers over the American flag tattoo until I couldn't resist. I began kissing it, sliding my tongue over all fifty stars while scratching my nails along his back. Jon moaned and shuddered as he wiggled out of his boxers. "I need to get my wallet," he groaned, struggling to get his words out between breaths. "It's in the kitchen, I think."

Jon hurried into the kitchen and came back without his wallet. "Shit, Lina," Jon growled. "I think I left my wallet at the tattoo parlor."

Unbeknownst to me, I found this hilarious and began laughing, shaking my head from side to side. "It's like two in the morning," I laughed. "You aren't getting that back now."

"Nope," he sighed, rubbing his hands through his hair and tightening his jaw. "You don't have anything on you, do you?"

"Me? No," I huffed, laughing even harder now. "I don't carry condoms in my purse. I don't sleep with guys I just met." I covered my naked self with my arms and stared at him, wondering what he was thinking and suddenly aware of how naked I was. I didn't know him well enough to figure out what his expressions meant, but as he studied me, lying there in his bed, there was something in his eyes that I will never forget. Did he think I was crazy? No, he didn't think that. Was it desire? Sure, it could have been the desire, but even more than that—it was love.

Jon leaned over me, one hand pressed inches from my face. "So," he started, his voice coming out sexier and raspier than I had heard it thus far. "If you don't sleep with guys on the first date, what makes me so special?"

"Tequila?" I asked with a coy smile.

"Oh yeah?" he asked, relaxing a bit. "Just tequila?"

I traced my fingers over his chest, studying him like a masterpiece. "I got my first tattoo tonight," I suggested. "A night of firsts?"

"Maybe that's what it is," he said in agreement. "How is it feeling… really?"

"Hurts like a bitch," I laughed.

"Oh no," he said. Jon rolled onto his back and pulled me on top of him. "Take some pressure off it."

I straddled Jon with my naked body, surprising myself with my boldness. I inched down, kissing him gently and harder with more angst than expected. My hair fell freely around him as I continued kissing him. He gathered it around the back of my neck and held it there as his tongue circled my mouth and swallowed my moans. Now that I couldn't have him, I wanted him more. I traced his jawline with my lips and paused next to his ear. "Or it's because you make me feel completely incredible," I uttered quietly. "Nobody has ever made me feel this way," I shared under my breath.

Jon stopped kissing me and held his gaze on mine. "I believe you," he whispered back, kissing me harder. "Because I couldn't agree with you more."

Jon's hands traveled over me in all the right ways until I couldn't take it anymore. "I want you, Jon," I moaned. "More than I've ever wanted anyone."

"Just... just let me touch you," he murmured between breaths. "Tomorrow, when I get my wallet."

But I ignored his attempt at adulting, and instead of pausing for a brief intermission so we could be responsible, I pinned him down to the mattress. I positioned myself on top of him like I had done this a million times before. I hovered over him, kissing his face and running my fingers through his hair, and at that moment, my eyes locked on his. Jon nodded. "Okay," he agreed, his voice heavy and breathless. And with that, he gripped my hips and pressed himself into me as if we had done this millions of times before. My body took over as I gripped Jon's shoulders and arched my back, feeling sexier than I had in my entire life. "Jon," I cried out repeatedly, wanting and needing only him.

Jon pulled me closer, and I couldn't get close enough if I tried. I interlocked our fingers and pinned his hands hard on the mattress, moving in rhythm to his heavy breath. And it was in that moment, with Jon Cote, that I lost myself in ways I had never done before. It seemed ridiculous, like an R-rated Hallmark movie, but it was true. I fell in love—so profoundly in love—and I knew, in that instant, that I would do whatever it took to be stuck to this man, in this way, over and over again for the rest of my life.

Chapter Five

Now

My shoulders quiver, and my body begins to tremble uncontrollably. My back starts to ache, and I shift forward on my elbows, inhaling profoundly and biting my lower lip. "How much longer?" I grunt.

"One minute," Ryker says nonchalantly.

"Are you timing me? Or are you on Facebook?" I snap.

"I'm timing you." He chuckles. "It's only a low plank. You've got this."

"A low plank with one hundred pounds on my back."

"It's ten pounds. And it's only a minute. You can do anything for a minute."

"I can think of a shit ton of things that are more fun than this that I could do for a minute," I whimper. My heart rate increases, and I squint my eyes shut. "And by the way, ten pounds is a lot. My twins were over six pounds each, and it was no picnic pushing them out my—"

"For the love of God, breathe. Thirty seconds," Ryker demands.

"I think I hate you."

"You love me. And this is what you pay me for, girl."

"I do love you. But this still sucks. I just want to stay in shape. I'm not training for the Olympics. Damn, Ry. I'm not twenty anymore."

"Time," he calls out in his referee voice.

"Ugh." I allow myself to collapse to the floor, my sweaty face meeting my yoga mat in relief. "Are we done?"

"Just stretching."

"Okay, because I have to meet my agent at noon."

Ryker gestures for me to sit up, so I do. He crosses one of his legs over his other and pulls it tight into his chest, and I mirror him, doing the same, breathing a sigh of relief that my torture session is over.

Ryker is one of my best friends but also serves as my personal trainer twice a week. After giving birth to the twins and, well, just getting older, it has become harder and harder for me to feel good about myself, and working out with Ryker helps—a lot.

Ryker was the quarterback of his college football team and graduated with his master's in exercise science. He has his own business, a small gym in a Scottsdale strip mall, but we both prefer that he trains me at my house so we can gossip about everyone without them hearing—his words.

I would be lying if I said I didn't have a massive crush on Ryker upon meeting him in 2012. At six feet four and roughly two hundred pounds, with light-brown hair, chiseled cheekbones, and perfect teeth, he often passed as Tom Brady. He was the first person I crushed on after my marriage with Jon ended. It turned out, however, that Ryker was not into me, not because he didn't care about me, because he cared a lot, but more so because he was one hundred percent into men. This was a hard pill for me to swallow at the time, but I've realized over the years that I never really wanted anything sexual from him anyway. It was our friendship that I loved, and in a way, it was surprisingly comforting that it would never be more.

Ryker switches legs, and I do the same. "Have you heard from Alex?" I ask, hoping that he at least received an Instagram DM or a Facebook message.

"Not since the last time you asked." He winks.

"I'm just worried about you," I say with a smile. I reach my arm across my chest and focus on the stretch, not my best friend's sorrowful expression. "You were with him *forever*."

"Yup," he agrees. "Switch arms."

"Are you going to call him back?"

"And say what? Sorry I caught you cheating?"

I nod and peel my sorry self off the floor. "I get it," I say, thinking of Jon. Once he lost my trust, he couldn't get it back, no matter how hard we tried.

"I know you do," he says, pulling me in for a hug.

"Ew. I'm sweaty, and I smell awful," I cry as he squeezes my body and shakes me from side to side.

I love Ryker, but when he hugs me, it is awkward, as he towers over me for what feels like miles upon miles. "I love you," he says, picking me up off the ground and squeezing me again.

"I love you too," I murmur into his T-shirt.

"How's Travis?"

I pull back from Ryker and reach for my water bottle, avoiding eye contact at all costs. "Great!" I sing, overenthusiastically.

"Liar."

"He's good, really. What isn't there to like? Tall, dark, and handsome." I wink because this is also Ryker's type.

"But he's not Jon."

"Nope," I say firmly. "I've got too much going on to go there," I snap, a little harsher than I intend.

"I get it," he says. "I'm sorry about the reviews."

"Thanks."

"Good luck with the agent."

"I'm gonna need it," I groan, pulling back and rolling my eyes.

"Are you sure there isn't anything else you can do?"

"I will call the twins' school and see if I can shadow. I'm sure they will let me sit in the back of the room with a notebook, right?"

"You think that's going to be enough?" he asks, eyebrows raised.

"You don't, clearly." I chuckle, chug my water, and smile up at Ryker, and for a moment, I have this overwhelming desire to tell him *everything*. Jon had made me promise not to tell anyone, but Ryker doesn't count in that promise—does he? I pause for a moment and consider this. Currently, there is no way I am even considering my ex-husband's comical proposal. So what if running it by Ryker helps in my processing?

"Where did you go?" Ryker asks, stacking weights on the rack.

"Huh?"

"You were on another planet. You can't fool me, Lina."

"Yeah, I guess you're right," I confess. "It's Jon."

Ryker's eyes grow wide with curiosity. "Public-enemy-number-one Jon?"

"Yeah."

"You aren't giving him another chance, are you?"

"Hell no."

"Good, because I'd kick your ass," he laughs. "I'm kidding but not."

"I'd kick my ass too," I agree. "No, this is something different. It's ridiculous, but Jon has this over-the-top idea, and I don't want anything to do with it, but there is this tiny piece of me that thinks he might be on to something."

"Spill it."

I fill Ryker in on everything from the missing girls to Jon's undercover operation. I half expect his Gatorade to come out of his nose when I tell him Jon's been undercover as a substitute art teacher. He is rolling around on my floor laughing but stops dead when I explain Jon's idea for me to go under as a high school senior.

"What?" I ask. "Why are you making that face?"

"Because," he says, hopping to his feet and pacing around the room at lightning speed.

"Because it's silly, right? It could never work."

Ryker rubs his hands through his hair and stares up at the ceiling. "Lina," he says, his tone steady and businesslike. "I despise your ex-husband even more than I hate socks with sandals. But hell… he might be an effing genius."

***

It took me almost an hour to escape Ryker and his intense desire to transform me into a high school senior. He even shouted to me through the shower curtain in my bathroom while I rinsed off, listing reason upon reason as to why going undercover as a high school student was in my best interest. I had stayed strong at first, arguing that there was no way I could pull it off. Besides, I had other tools I could use to improve my books.

My original thoughts about the situation might be even further off than anticipated. After meeting with Ana, my agent, and realizing that things are worse than she was making it seem on the phone, Jon's idea doesn't seem entirely out of the question. We had been seated at a high-top table at the Italian place she loved so much. Over my eggplant parm panini and Diet Coke with lime, she informed me of her and my editor's decision to shift my attention to a different genre—women's romance, maybe romantic comedy or divorce fiction—that I could relate to a bit more. I agreed with Ana that my work needed improvement, but I asked—okay, I begged—for her to take a look at the manuscript for the final book in the Cat Rose series. I wouldn't be able to live with myself if the series were left incomplete. She agreed to look at it upon completion, giving me a deadline that almost choked me while I was eating my lunch, but I eagerly agreed.

I barely have my car in reverse before asking Siri to dial Jon's number. I agree to his undercover operation under two circumstances. First, I can tell Daphne and Ryker *everything.* And two, he and I need to remain professional at all costs. We're to be business partners and nothing more. Jon seems okay with this and instructs me to meet him at his office in Tempe within the hour.

I have never been to Jon's office. So, on this sticky desert afternoon with air so dry and hot that it is making me feel like I am burning up from the inside out, I pay my meter, run my fingers over the wrinkles of my white sundress, adjust my messy bun, and enter the front door of Cote Investigations.

A bell chimes as I enter his first-floor office. It is brighter and more contemporary than I thought, but I am still determining what I expected. The only things I know about private investigators are what Jon has told me in the past and from what I've watched on shows like *Veronica Mars* and *The Mentalist.* I pictured a dark interrogation room but instead am presented with an oversized plexiglass sign that reads Cote Investigations against white walls and a glass countertop. A door is closed to what I assume is a restroom. There is a gray metal desk on the other side of the room with papers scattered about and a handful of whiteboards with chicken scratch so messy that I can't make out the words. I see so much of him here that my stomach flips nervously. His white leather sectional and glass coffee table create a warm, welcoming vibe. How many clients has he consoled on that couch? Has he shown them photographs and *money shots* of their spouses cheating on them like they do on TV? Does it gut him from the inside out because he cheated on me? I hope it does. I hope he remembers my broken heart every time he discusses infidelity.

"Hey, Lina."

I'm not sure why I'm surprised by the sound of Jon's voice, seeing as though I know he is here somewhere. I inhale deeply, fold my arms over my chest, and spin around.

"Hey."

Jon smiles and rubs his fingers through his chin's scruff. He could use a shave and a shower. I know this look. He has most likely been eating Chinese takeout all night and burning the midnight oil to solve his case. This one weighs extra heavily on him, and I can tell.

"Welcome to Cote Investigations."

I smile as best I can, look around, and say, "It's nice, Jon."

"Yeah, it's coming along. Have a seat."

I sit on the leather sectional and hug my purse like a child holds their security blanket. I trace my fingers over the cushion, trying with all my might to forget that first night with Jon in his apartment, but I can't. Beads of sweat drip down the back of my sundress as I remember another night early in our relationship. Jon and I made love on his living room couch—this couch. Aside from our first night together, it was one of my life's best nights. I shake my head, trying desperately to erase the memory. "Furniture looks familiar," I sigh.

"Dug it out of storage a few months ago," he says proudly.

Jon sits beside me and pulls the coffee table close to him. He turns his lap to face me, ready to go, meaning business and business only, just as he promised over the phone.

"Do you meet with all of your clients out here?" I ask, wiping my sweaty palms on my legs. *Get it together, Lina!* I silently scold. I meet with Jon Cote *all* the time. Why is this so different? But before the thought escapes my mind, I know the answer. It's all fun and games when you are at a coffee shop discussing your children and only your children for ten-plus years. This... This is not Starbucks, and talking with Jon about things other than Max and Lucy is crossing a line I might not be ready to cross. We are so far from normal that I may puke.

"Yeah, we have our consultations out here most of the time. My desk is a complete disaster, so this works," he laughs.

"Nice."

"Here," he says, gesturing to a packet of papers he has stapled together. "State laws say that you can work under me as my apprentice. See. It says here that Emerson Academy is the client, and they employ us. We meet with the dean on Monday, but we have a *lot* to do before that to get you ready. What do you have going on the rest of the weekend?"

My eggplant panini rumbles from the depths of my stomach, and I begin to taste bile in the back of my throat. The idea of spending the weekend with my ex is too overwhelming to process. I ignore the papers. I am trying to behave. Really, I am. But the pain, the hurt, the betrayal… It's been years, but I still can't shake it. My knee begins to bounce involuntarily, and I press down hard to stop it. "Do your *clients* like the *couch*?" I ask, my tone even-keeled.

Jon looks up from the paperwork, clearly confused. "I think so?"

I nod, expressionless. "It's a good couch," I say, looking at the floor.

Jon shifts uncomfortably, and I can tell he knows where I'm going with this. "Lina—"

"That was a good night. Wasn't it? The night you made love to me on this couch," I say like I'm asking him to pass the ketchup.

"Yeah. It was."

I adjust my messy bun and bite my lower lip. I cross my arms over my chest and turn toward Jon. I feel the blood rise from my chest and to my face, and my stomach flips once more. "I'm sorry. I can't do this. I thought I could, but I can't."

I reach for my purse and leap from the couch, wishing more than anything that my legs could be longer. If they were, I could get to the door before Jon.

"Lina, wait," Jon begs. He positions himself between me and the door and places a comforting hand on my shoulder. "Please," he pleads. "I know this is hard. I know I messed up. The divorce was all my fault. I know it. But if you aren't strong enough to do this for your career, could you please do it for the girls? Let me show you what I have on them, Lina. They are real kids, just like Lucy and Max. You can help bring them back to their families. *Please*."

I study his unsettling expression and the tears that form in his eyes, and I realize, at this moment, that Jon does need *me* to help him solve his case, which honestly doesn't bode well for his case. If I'm the answer to three missing children being reunited with their families, we may all be doomed. "I don't know," I cry through my tears. "I thought I could, but this is just too weird. You and me—"

"Alanna, Chloe, and Teresa."

"Huh?" I ask, wiping my eyes with the backs of my hands.

"Those are the three girls. And just today, I sat here, on this couch, on the phone with Teresa's mother, who is convinced she's dead. So yeah, Lina. It's emotional, and it's hard, but it isn't about us. Keep it about the three girls."

I lean back against the door and close my eyes. "Okay," I agree, my chin quivering and my words catching in the back of my throat. "I'll help you. But promise me, please. I need fair warning if there is any other furniture we have had sex on in this office. I need to know now. No more surprises."

"Deal," he says, extending his hand for a handshake. "No more surprises."

"Deal," I reply, taking Jon's hand in mine.

Chapter Six

Then (2008)

It had been just over a month since my first date with Jon, and with each passing day, I grew increasingly more into him, or as Daphne accused, "obsessed," and she might have been right. Jon was all I could think about. During class, when I was supposed to be paying attention, I instead was doodling his name in my notebook, just as I had when I was younger with my middle school crush.

I had never met anyone like Jon Cote, and I had spent every free second trying to figure out how and why I was falling for him so quickly. So, as I sat at my usual table at Starbucks, attempting to study for an English exam, my fingers typed rapidly on the keys of my Dell laptop on a blank document I was using to journal my thoughts, trying with all my might to understand what was happening to me.

Sure, I was attracted to Jon. I couldn't complete a thought without picturing his firm, warm body moving in unison with mine. I could stare into his electric-blue eyes for hours, and his kisses were soft, caring, passionate, and firm. But this was more than attraction, so I was tripped up with my thoughts. I felt what was between us that night with Jon before I understood it. For the first time in my life, I experienced something with a man that was emotion based and not logical. The real me, Lina, had never even considered sleeping with a guy on the first date. But my connection with Jon completely took over the girl I used to be.

Our shared moments and conversations were never surface level. Mainly, we spoke on the phone, which we mostly did because Jon was working jobs nonstop. I hadn't even returned to his apartment since our first date, as our schedules needed to align, and he worked overnights. Instead, we found time together in chunks, walking hand in hand through Tempe Town Lake or grabbing a quick lunch at the marketplace. But when we saw each other, it was effortless. I felt a pull toward him that I couldn't explain, and I hoped and prayed it could last forever.

With these new feelings and realizations came some hesitations. Doubt crept in occasionally, and I couldn't help but worry that I might be falling for Jon faster than he was falling for me. Daphne was happy for me but was nervous I might get my heart broken. I was sure her questions and doubts were permeating my thoughts and raining on my parade.

I heard the Starbucks door open and knew it was Jon before I saw him. I clicked Save on my Word document and shut my laptop, my smile already reaching from ear to ear as he approached my table in uniform.

"Officer Cote," I sang. "I wasn't sure if I would see you today." I stood from my seat and wrapped my arms around his waist, his name badge grazing my forehead. Alter-Lina immediately started daydreaming about hooking up with him in uniform.

"I needed my Lina fix," he whispered into my ear.

His words sent electric jolts of happiness through my body. "Lina fix," I repeated. "Cute."

"You're cute," he said, bending forward and kissing my forehead.

It took all the restraint I could muster, but I released him and sat back down, reaching for my coffee. As a rookie, Jon was overly cautious about his behavior while in uniform. And although I wanted to rip it off in the middle of Starbucks, I respected his morals and instead sipped my Frappuccino. "Are you going to get something?" I asked, wondering how much time I would have him here.

"I have a massive order for the guys," he sighed, rubbing his hand through his hair. "You are so pretty, though."

"Unless you plan on pulling me into that bathroom over there, I will kindly ask you to refrain from flirting," I said, joking but not. "I mean, it is an individual bathroom, no stalls. Just saying."

Jon reached across the table and wrapped his fingers around mine. "You know we can't," he said with a smile.

"I know, I know," I huffed. "You're in uniform."

"Yes, ma'am, I am. But hooking up in public bathrooms isn't really my thing."

"Well, it's not like it's *my* thing." I shrugged. "But I'll take you where I can get you."

Jon blushed and studied me, amused. "I'll take that as a compliment."

"Just don't let it get to your head. What time are you off work?"

"I'm on all night again. But I'm around tomorrow night if you want to come over and keep me company?" he asked, raising an eyebrow.

"Yes! What time?"

"Seven?"

"Perfect. I'll bring stuff for drinks," I said, flirtier than intended.

A wave of nausea took me off guard, and I shifted uncomfortably in my seat.

"You okay?" Jon asked, his concern not going unnoticed.

"Yeah. Daphne and I got Chinese last night. I don't think it's settling well."

"Or you're just nervous to spend the night," he accused.

I hit him playfully on the shoulder. "Don't humor yourself, Jon Cote."

"I make you nervous," he teased, kissing my hand.

"Maybe."

He kissed my hand again, and I rolled my eyes. "Stop," I begged.

"I make you nervous, and you can't get enough of me."

"Something like that." I winked. "I'll see you tomorrow night, officer."

***

The next evening at seven p.m. sharp, I knocked on Jon's apartment door, carrying a paper bag of groceries. Jon greeted me shirtless, wearing nothing but black athletic shorts. His blond hair was disheveled and wet, and his skin glistened like magic. Clearly, he had showered quickly upon getting home from work, and I liked it.

"Hey, you," he murmured, kissing my cheek. He took the grocery bag from me and peeked inside. "What's all this?"

"I was going to make you something yummy for dinner," I said, tucking a strand of hair behind my ear and biting my lower lip. I looked him over and smiled. "But it might need to wait, because *you* look pretty yummy."

Jon shook his head and chuckled in amusement. "Come inside. I'm starving. What are you making me?"

"I brought stuff for tacos," I said proudly. "Maybe if we pair them with our margaritas, we won't get so drunk we get tattoos."

Jon placed the grocery bag on his kitchen counter and turned toward me, pulling me close. "But I like our tattoos," he whined, tracing his fingers under the seam of my low-rise jeans. I inhaled the sweet smell of his eucalyptus-and-mint shower gel, his aroma consuming my senses and relaxing me entirely.

"I like them too. But tonight, tacos and margaritas—no tattoos."

"If you say so," he said, cupping his fingers around my waist and pulling me close. He kissed me softly on my lips, pulled back with a smile, and then kissed me again. "I'm just glad you're here."

"Me too," I agreed. "Let's get cooking so we can eat the tacos." *And you can take me to your bedroom.* I wiped the beads of sweat from my palms onto my jeans.

"Yes, ma'am."

Jon began unpacking the groceries and organizing ingredients while I mixed our margaritas. After toasting to "us," just as we had on the first date, we sipped margaritas, cooked beef tacos using my father's secret recipe, and sang along to his Rascal Flatts CD. When we were finished, we sat, perched at his bar, devoured our dinner, and sucked down our margaritas.

"These are the best damn tacos I've ever eaten. Where did you learn to do this?"

"Do what? Cook?"

"Yes, cook *these,*" he said, gesturing to his mouth as he chewed his last bite, eyes rolling to the back of his head in approval. "And can you make them for me every night for the rest of my life?"

I coughed, choking on my last sip, unsure if he was proposing to me or my father's secret taco sauce. "My father, Pepito," I said, clearing my throat to stop obsessing over his previous comment. "He immigrated from Mexico City as a teenager. His family was in the restaurant business, and this is their secret sauce," I said, raising my eyebrows for dramatic effect.

"Nice," he said. "How old were you when you learned to cook?"

I thought about this for a beat. "I don't remember *not* cooking," I realized. "I guess I've just always known how. I was just expected to learn, like walking and potty training. Both of my parents are in the food business."

"Is your mom from Mexico too?"

"No, she isn't," I said. "Her parents immigrated from Paris, France. It's quite the story. I've considered writing about it someday."

"Wow." Jon smiled. "That's really cool, Lina."

"Yeah, it's pretty neat. My mother, Celeste, worked at her family bakery in Phoenix. They were popular for their prickly pear baked goods," I explained, gesturing to my margarita.

"Hence the prickly pear obsession," he teased.

"It's not an obsession."

"I'm just busting your balls. I think it's sweet."

"My dad loved *anything* prickly pear. One day, in his early twenties, he stumbled upon the bakery searching for cupcakes for his girlfriend's birthday. He met my grandmother, who not only introduced him to prickly pear cupcakes but also to Celeste. They were married less than a year later."

"That is quite the story." Jon laughed.

"So yeah," I sighed. "Family, food, prickly pear. These are a few of my favorite things," I sang.

"Am I one of your favorite things?" Jon asked with a smile. He stood from the barstool, grabbed his glass, and gestured toward the white leather sectional in his living room.

"Maybe," I said with a sigh. I followed Jon, placing my drink on his coffee table and nuzzling against his bare chest. "We have to clean up your kitchen," I sighed.

"It can wait," he said, his voice sounding bold but soothing.

"My mother says a good cook always cleans up the kitchen."

"That may be true," he said, kissing my forehead. "But I've been waiting all day to kiss you, and I think there is some unwritten rule that states when there is a hot girl on your couch, you can wait to clean up after dinner."

"You've been waiting all day to kiss me?" I asked, relieved.

"Of course I have. I told you. I really like you."

His words pierced my heart like a bow and arrow. Of course he has told me this, but to hear it again, in this way, after a month of not being able to be alone with him, all my insecurities and fears chose that moment to surface in the form of tears flooding from my eyeballs.

Jon's concerned expression made me cry harder. "Lina, what's wrong? What did I say?"

"It's fine." I smiled through my tears. What was wrong with me? Sure, I was known to be emotional from time to time, but nothing like this. Between Daphne and me, she was the one who would cry watching reality shows like *Extreme Home Makeover* and *The Bachelor*. Typically, it took a lot to make me cry. So why was I reacting this way to Jon's comment?

"It's not fine," Jon insisted, pulling me over him so I could straddle his waist and bury my tear-streaked face into his bare chest. "It's too fast, isn't it? That's why you're upset?"

"No," I cried, shaking my head. "I'm so happy you care about me so much. I… I care about you that much too."

"So then, what's the problem?"

"Nothing is the problem."

"But you're crying."

I lifted my face and studied the concern in his eyes, and my heart broke for him. I didn't like this version of him. I wanted his lips to form his usual confident smile. I was eager for his dimples and the cheerful glistening in his eyes. I decided at that moment that being honest with him was the only way to get that version back. "My high school boyfriend broke my heart. There, I said it."

"Oh," he said, thinking about this for a moment.

"He took my best friend to prom. And they slept together. I know it sounds silly, but I've just…"

"You have your hesitations," he finished for me.

"I guess I do."

"You don't have to worry, Lina," he whispered. His breath tickled my earlobe, sending a chill through me.

"I know," I said. "This isn't like me. Usually, I can keep it together better than this."

"I'm sorry."

"You didn't do anything wrong."

"And I won't," he promised.

"You can't promise that," I laughed between tears.

"Lina, you make me the happiest I've ever been. I don't know where this is going, but I know where it's not. I promise you, I will never do anything to hurt you." Jon wiped the final tears from my eyes with his fingers.

I searched Jon's eyes like a detective studying a crime scene. When Sam broke my heart, I was devastated. It took every ounce of faith for me to take him back. But the damage had already been done. Once that trust was broken, there was no going back. My imagination was my worst enemy. If he wasn't home when he promised he would be home, I would get jealous, and I hated that about myself. I made a promise that I would never let anyone hurt me like that again.

"You promise?" I sniffled.

"I promise."

"Are you doing this… you know, with other girls?" I asked, gesturing around me.

"Eating super-secret tacos and drinking margaritas in my living room? No."

"You know what I mean."

"I know exactly what you mean, and the answer is no. I'm not with anyone but you, Lina. In fact, I was hoping you would be my girlfriend?" Jon held the sides of my face and pulled me close for the most passionate kiss of my life. His forehead pressed to mine, his tongue eager, and his breath increasing rapidly.

"Yes," I answered, my voice becoming a moan more than words. "Yes, I will," I whispered as I ran my fingers through Jon's hair and pressed his face against mine. His kiss spoke volumes. Although neither of us could predict the future, it was clear that he meant what he said.

"You're my girlfriend, then?" His lips curled up into a broad smile, and his dimple poked at my heartstrings.

"Yes, sir."

Jon removed my shirt and tossed it on the floor. He rolled me onto my back, the couch's leather feeling cool against my bare skin. His fingers worked at the button of my jeans, and I slid them off as he reached behind me and unclipped my bra, tossing that to the floor with ease. I lay in my underwear, Jon hovering over me, feeling naked and vulnerable but more secure and at ease than I had ever felt with a man. It felt like our first time, maybe because the last time was somewhat of a tequila-induced haze, and because of that, I wanted to take him in and remember every second.

I reached for Jon's face, holding it steady for a beat, taking him in and engraving every part of it in my mind. The seriousness of his demeanor and the softness in his eyes. He gently traced the contours of my neck, chest, and abdomen before removing my underwear and his shorts, kicking them away briskly before lying on his side, touching me with ease.

Once again, my body responded quickly and effortlessly to him. Foreign noises escaped from deep within me as he teased and touched me. "Do you want to go to my bedroom?" he asked with heavy breaths.

"No," I groaned with authority. "Please don't stop."

And he didn't stop until I couldn't take it anymore. I reached for him, clawing my fingernails into his skin, and screamed his name like nothing else mattered—because nothing else did.

When I opened my eyes, I found Jon reaching for his wallet. "That was…" My voice trailed off because there were no words to describe what that was.

"Amazing," he finished for me. "You're amazing."

"No, I'm not—" I started to argue but stopped because Jon wasn't finished. He was just getting started. He climbed on top of me and, without hesitation, pressed himself into me. With a deliberate but unhurried rhythm, our bodies glided together in unison.

"Lina," he repeatedly groaned, our souls connecting like they had that first night. We had an unspoken connection, our heartbeats in sync, when his mouth found mine and his body trembled over me.

I wanted to lay there forever, but my stomach did an unexpected flip, and the super-secret tacos were suddenly not settling well. "You're incredible," Jon said with admiration. He exhaled, releasing his listless body on mine.

"I… I'm sorry… I need to…" I squirmed from beneath him.

"What is it? Are you okay?"

I shook my head, covered my mouth, and made a mad dash to his bathroom, where I barely made it before kicking the door closed and vomiting my dinner into Jon's toilet.

"Lina?" Jon called from the doorway; his voice filled with concern.

"Mhmm," I responded, flushing the toilet and curling up naked on the cool tile floor. But I wasn't okay. Not because I wasn't feeling great but because I was already starting to feel better. But as I lay there on Jon's bathroom floor, I realized that not only had I been unusually queasy for the past week, but my breasts had also been sore and tender.

"Can I get you anything?"

"No," I insisted. "I'm okay, really."

But as I said the words aloud, I knew they were lies. Because I was anything but okay. And as I did the math in my mind and realized, without doubt, that my period was indeed very late, I didn't know what was worse. The idea that I could be pregnant with Jon's baby and ruin everything we had going for us, the start of something new and carefree being tarnished by this sudden involuntary shove into adulthood, or the harsh reality that my father, indeed, was going to kill me. And then he would most definitely kill Jon Cote.

Chapter Seven

Now

I tap my pen against my notebook to the beat of "Who Let the Dogs Out" by Baha Men, a song often stuck in my head, especially in nerve-wracking situations. And sitting here across from Jon at his desk is a nerve-wracking scenario, to say the least.

"Are you sure you want to handwrite your notes?" Jon asks.

"Don't judge."

"It's just you're an author. Don't you type faster than you write?"

"I like my notebook," I say, crossing one leg over the other. "Can we just get started? We are meeting the dean of students in an hour, right?"

"That is correct," he says in his deep private investigator voice.

I glance up at Jon, running his hands over his chin's scruff and passing me a stack of papers. An entire weekend has passed since I met him here last, and the guy still looks like he hasn't showered. He is all business as he places the papers on his desk facing me, double-checking his laptop notes and hurriedly checking boxes on his whiteboard. "What is all this?" I ask, tracing my finger over the paper closest to me.

"This is your life, Gemma Mendoza," he says to me as if my name is actually Gemma Mendoza.

"Oh, Gemma... huh?"

"What's wrong with Gemma?"

"Nothing," I say, biting my lower lip, wondering how on earth I will pass for a high school senior named Gemma. "Gemma's great."

"Gemma gets the job done," he says.

Jon stands from his seat and wipes a clean whiteboard. He uncaps a dry-erase marker and scribbles *Operation Superglue* in deep-red ink.

"Operation Superglue? What's that?"

"That's the name of our operation."

"Why superglue?"

"Come on, Lina, you're the author," he says, cracking the day's first smile.

Before realizing that Superglue must be about his undercover position as the art sub, I think about this moment. "Art teacher?" I guess.

"Bingo."

"Got it. I like it."

"Good," he says, writing Gemma Mendoza underneath his heading. "Write this down," he instructs. "Your name is Gemma Lynn Mendoza. Your birthday is November 16, 2006—"

"Same month and day as Max and Lucy," I interrupt.

"That is correct. I figured you couldn't forget that."

"Good thinking."

"You live in an apartment in Tempe, Arizona. We will use a PO box number as your address, but we can stage my apartment as yours if necessary. It would be good to come over and familiarize yourself with the area if you need it for your alibi."

Over my dead body, I think to myself. Jon studies me, no-nonsense, waiting for my reply. "Sure," I say, clearing my throat. "Whatever you need." I inhale deeply and copy the PO box number in my notebook.

"Memorize it," he says, like a teacher instructing a student. "You live at that apartment with your father, Mateo Mendoza, who has recently separated from your mother, Madison Mendoza. She lives in Jupiter, Florida, where you previously resided."

"Copy," I say, wondering how I will remember all this. When I mentioned my undercover operation to Daphne, she was excited, a bit jealous, but also nervous for me. Improv has never been my thing. She knows this more than anyone. I was hesitant to ask her about keeping this from her husband, Mal, but she said that wouldn't be an issue, and besides, he will be working in Boston for most of the summer.

"You run track—"

"*Run?*"

"You ran track in high school, Lina."

"Yeah, like a million years ago," I gasp, eyes wide. "Jon, I'm thirty-five years old. I will die running track."

"Don't be dramatic."

"Don't be an asshole."

"Lina, I need you to cooperate, or this isn't going to work." Jon's jaw tightens, and his cheeks flush.

"Fine," I huff. "I'll sprint the hundred or run the mile. But *no* hurdles. I'll pee my pants."

"That's between you and the coach," he says with a sly smile. I rub my eyes with my hands, making a mental note to ask Ryker for help with endurance.

"So, what? I'm supposed to tell the track coach that I can't hurdle because I birthed twins?"

"So, like I was saying," he continues, ignoring my valid concerns, "you run track, you play the violin—"

"The violin?!" I explode.

"You told me you played the violin."

"When I was twelve!"

"Well, there is always YouTube."

I stare at him wide-eyed. "You want me to learn violin on YouTube?"

"Nobody says you have to be good at it. You like to write short stories and poems."

"I can work with that," I say, jotting it in my notebook.

"And you love cats."

"Why?"

"Why not?"

I assume the cat thing is a joke, so I shrug it off and continue note-taking. "Fine," I huff. "I like cats."

"And you like to cook."

"Thank you," I say, grateful for these tiny microfacts aligning with my identity.

"Listen closely," he says, pointing to the board. "Dean Elizabeth Downing," he says, placing an eight-by-ten photo beside my notebook. "She's the only one at Emerson Academy that knows our true identities."

"Okay," I say, studying a picture of a woman who looks to be in her mid-sixties. Her dark hair is pulled back in a tight bun, and her smile is stern and distinguished.

"If anything goes wrong, if somehow you are made, head directly to her office and tell her secretary that Gemma Mendoza is here to see her. Tell her you miss your mom, and you need to go home."

"Got it," I say, writing *I miss my mom* in cursive, getting distracted momentarily and making a mental note to call my mother, who hopefully has my middle school violin tucked away in her attic.

"You will be strategically placed within the social circles of the missing teens. Alanna Foster," Jon says, his words coming out sharp, businesslike, and firm. He places a photograph of Alanna next to Dean Elizabeth's picture, and my heart drops. Alanna Foster is stunning. Her petite features and sky-blue eyes smile at me from her school photo. Her blond wavy hair was over her shoulders for a traditional back-to-school headshot. I think about Alanna's mother and that first day of school. Had they taken photos at their house and posted them on Facebook? Who could have guessed that when this photo was taken, it would be used to locate her in a missing person's case?

"She has been missing since October 23," Jon says. "She never came home from school. She is the oldest of three children, an honors student, commuted to Emerson from Scottsdale."

This is when I burst into tears, and Jon passes me a tissue before he continues. "She had a fight with her mother earlier that morning, and because certain items were missing from her bedroom and there was no evidence of foul play, Tempe PD assumed she ran away."

Jon rolls his eyes and shakes his head before placing two more photos before me. "Chloe May," he states. "She has been missing since January 24. Police are convinced she ran away as well. Chloe was the captain of Emerson's volleyball team. She has a brother with special needs and was heavily involved with the Special Olympics. Again, she fought with her parents the morning she went missing."

"She's gorgeous," I whimper as a tear falls on Chloe's school photo. In her picture, Chloe wore a light-pink shirt, creating a beautiful contrast to her dark skin and black wavy hair.

"You're crying on my pictures," Jon says, tossing me another tissue and continuing. "Get it together, Lina."

"How are you *not* thinking of Lucy?" I snap, more accusatory than intended.

"Of course, I think of Lucy," he says calmly. "Why do you think I'm so invested?"

"You're talking about them like they are… I don't know… lost dogs or something."

Jon places his hand on mine, and I shift back nervously. "I'm not a monster, Lina."

"Well… that's subjective," I retort, blowing my nose into the tissue.

"My head is in the game, that's all. You need to do the same. Crying over these girls won't bring them back."

I nod and toss my tissue in his trash as Jon places the last photo on his desk. "Teresa Vargas," Jon says. "Teresa went missing on March 24."

"Let me guess," I say, tracing my finger over yet another beautiful teenage girl. Her brown eyes smile with what seem to be thoughts of endless possibilities. Her chestnut hair was pulled atop her head in a high pony. "She had a fight with her parents the day she went missing?"

"Nope." Jon shrugs. "Everything was great. She was a lead in the school's recent production of *The Sound of Music*. She had high hopes of performing on Broadway."

"This is *so* sad," I whimper, reaching for another tissue. "But I get it. I understand why we are doing this, and I'm going to pull it together… for the girls," I say, motioning to the photos.

"Good," he says. "Get your things. We have to meet Dean Downing, and we need to pick up lunch on the way."

"How can you eat at a time like this?" I shriek, gathering my sweater and my purse. "There are three missing teens, Jon. We need to get to work. Geesh."

***

Dean Downing is just as I expected from her photograph. She sits perched behind an oversized mahogany desk, with a number two pencil piercing the peak of her slicked-back bun. I can't find even one wrinkle on her burgundy suit dress, and her pearl earrings and necklace set match her gleaming white teeth.

I am overly thankful for Jon, who didn't wait for this meeting to brief me on the missing girls. Stopping for sandwiches and the short drive were enough to ease the tears from flowing, at least for now. Dean Downing informs us that the application Jon submitted with my false info was expedited and approved by the dean of admissions, Dean Orson Turner. Gemma Mendoza—age eighteen, straight out of Jupiter, Florida, with a single-parent father—is set to be a senior at Emerson Academy. She also hands me a printout of my course schedule, explaining that I will begin school next week.

"You won't be too far behind," Dean Downing reassures me. "School only began a short two weeks ago, and most of that time is review work and syllabus review," she says, waving it off like it's no big deal when it's a huge deal.

"We operate on a rotating A-B schedule," she explains, gesturing to the schedule. "You have eight blocks on your schedule. On an A day, you will have blocks one to four, and then on a B day, you will have blocks five to eight. See here, you have lunch and then study on an A day, but on a B day, you have study then lunch."

"Okay," I gulp, feeling my heart rate increase. A few major red flags are glaring up at me from my schedule. Chemistry and algebra are what I notice first. "It's been years since I've had to study any kind of science," I say.

Jon sits motionless, probably annoyed with me for complaining to the dean.

"You will be okay," she reassures me. "Stay on top of the coursework and simply ask the teacher, if you have questions."

I nod, cringing as I give this advice to my children, and I'm not sure how much it will help me now. "Thank you," I say.

"You're welcome. I'm sure Jon has informed you that the schedule was created based on patterns he identified regarding our missing students. He will review this with you, but I want to emphasize that you must form friendships during your time here. If I've learned anything in my twenty years as dean, it is that if you want to know what is going on, ask the students."

"Yes, of course."

"Do you have any questions about your schedule, Gemma?"

She drops Gemma like it's no biggie, but again, it is. I glance over the schedule once more. PE, psychology, AP English, and drama all seem manageable. "What is FCS?" I ask, scrunching my nose in confusion.

"Family and consumer sciences," Jon says. "It used to be home economics."

"Why did they change it?" I asked, genuinely confused.

"By using family and consumer sciences, we aim to highlight the practical and relevant nature of home management, focusing on preparing students for *life* and providing them with valuable skills beyond the confines of the home."

"Oh," I mutter. "But it's still cooking, managing finances, organization…"

"Yes."

"Okay," I sigh. "Sounds like home economics to me."

"Thank you," Jon says, rolling his eyes at me. "Art is on her schedule, correct?"

"Yes. Art is on your schedule, Lina, because Jon—or Mr. Jacobs, as he's known around here—will be here at least one day per week, covering one of our art classes, and you must be in art to utilize his office hours."

"Mr. Jacobs," I repeat. "When are office hours?"

"You will visit Mr. Jacobs for help in art during your study hall when he is in the building. This will be when you can brief each other on findings or concerns of any particular nature. Occasionally, I might pop in and join you as well."

"Do many students utilize the art sub's office hours?"

"You, my dear," she snorts, "need to be *really* bad at art."

"Not hard to do," I say, a slight laugh escaping for the first time today.

"Also," she says, rising to her feet and smoothing out the front of her dress, "I'm confident this is going to work. Jon and I have been working closely on this, and I'm sure you are our missing puzzle piece. But I do want to caution you both. I strongly suggest you stay out of the public eye during this operation. Meet only during Jon's hours or at your homes. The fact that you live in Scottsdale is helpful, Gemma, but this whole thing could crash and burn in seconds if you are spotted together or even with your kids. Simply... lie low."

"Understood," Jon and I say in unison.

"Looks like you're Ubering home, Gemma." Jon chuckles, rising to his feet and shaking the dean's hand.

"Wait, what? It's *Sunday*. Nobody is here."

"I'm just kidding," he says. "Geez, lighten up, will you?"

Chapter Eight

Then (2008)

When Daphne called, I was perched on the white leather couch with my swollen ankles elevated and a box of Cheez-Its propped on my baby bump. I was surprised to hear from her since she would typically be out frat-house hopping late on a Saturday night as I would in my former life. I flipped open my phone and stuck a pillow behind my aching back. "Hey," I sang. "House of the pregnant, unwed, bedridden college dropout."

"*Stop* talking about my friend like that," she scolded.

"Well, it's all true."

"So, yeah. You are pregnant and unwed, on bed rest, and your parents forced you to drop out of ASU because of it. But You *love* Jon, and he *loves* you."

"Tell that to Pepito and Celeste."

"You've been pregnant for seven months, for the love of God. Are they still being assholes?"

"They aren't assholes," I say, crunching the Cheez-Its between my teeth. "They're just… disappointed in me, I guess."

"I get being disappointed. I don't understand monetarily cutting off their only child when she needs them most."

Her honesty burst my optimistic bubble like a pin popping a balloon. I pressed my hand against my stomach, breathing through what I had been told were Braxton Hicks contractions. "Yeah," I agreed, thinking back to the afternoon Jon and I told my parents about the pregnancy, which, ironically enough was the same day I introduced them to Jon. I was just shy of eight weeks when we broke the news. We were pregnant… with not one but *two* babies. *Twins.*

"Are you really *not* finding out the genders? I think you are both insane."

"We want to be surprised," I said, rubbing my hands over my belly. One of the twins rolled inside me, and I watched in awe as my belly took on alien-like form. I rubbed my baby bump, silently wondering what they would look like when they came out. "What do you think they are?" I asked her.

"How am I supposed to know?"

"It's a guess, Daphne. You aren't supposed to *know* anything."

"Girls?" she asked more than said. "Boys? One boy, one girl?"

"You suck at this, Daph."

"Yes, I do. But does that surprise you?"

"Nope."

"I miss you," she sighed. "It's not the same without you on campus."

A wave of sadness washed over me as I missed Daphne and our time together. My carefree days of sharing our on-campus apartment seemed like another lifetime, ultimately. But as quickly as that dreadful feeling consumed me, it dissipated just as fast because I thought of Jon. Jon had been nurturing and supportive since I tested positive on the pregnancy test the morning after our taco night. It was also Jon who consoled me evening after evening as I sobbed into my pillow, feelings of guilt and shame surrounding my actions, as I hated disappointing my father more than anything, and in this case, disappointment was an understatement. When my parents asked us what our "plan" was for raising the babies, we both shrugged, acknowledging that we didn't have a plan, had just started dating, and hadn't landed on a real solution. What we did know was that we loved each other very much.

Operation Superglue

That must have felt like salt in an open wound for my father, because he took it upon himself to make the plan *for* me. He insisted I take the next year off from school, demanding that he wasn't funding a college education for a daughter who couldn't make logical choices. He would revisit college tuition if I could prove him wrong. Heartbroken, I informed him that I wouldn't be living at home, but I would be living with Jon. Needless to say, I hadn't spoken to them since.

"Want to come over?" I asked. "Jon's working overnight, and I sleep like crap when he's not home. Plus I can show you the crib. We set it up yesterday, and by *we,* I mean Jon."

"I love that guy." Daphne chuckled. "Aside from knocking you up, he's decent. Give me an hour. I'll be over."

"You're the best," I said, prying my oversized body from the couch and heading toward the bathroom. Another Braxton Hicks contraction caught me off guard, taking my breath away.

"Can you pick up snacks? What's open this late? I'm dying for a hot dog. I know I'm not supposed to eat them, but I feel like at this point..."

"The ones from the sidewalk vendor?"

"Yeeesss," I said, already drooling.

"I'll see what I can do."

"I'll leave the door unlocked—"

But my words were cut short because of the immense pressure I started to feel in my belly. A cramping sensation followed by aches in my lower back. I braced myself against the couch with one hand and reached down, grabbing at the crotch of my sweatpants with the other, only to find they were soaked. "Oh my God!" I shrieked.

"What? What is it?"

"I think I'm peeing my pants," I started. "And I can't stop. It's not stopping!" But as the words escaped my lips, I knew that wasn't true. My water had broken. I was in labor. "Daphne, I think my water broke."

"You think? Or you know?"

"I know." I moaned, studying the puddle of amniotic fluid staring back at me from the beige carpet. I gripped the couch with both hands, forcing myself to breathe through what I assumed to be contractions, the pain coming on so severe and so forceful I began to panic.

"I'll be there in twenty," she said, calmer than I could have ever anticipated. "Call Jon. Tell him to meet us at the hospital."

"I don't know if I have twenty minutes," I whimpered, my knees buckling beneath me.

"It's okay," she sang. "We've got this. I'll call 911 and give them Jon's address."

I once read that the people you assume to stay calm in an emergency are the people you would least expect. I never would have suspected Daphne to be one of those people.

"How are you calm right now?" I cried. "It's freaking me out."

"Because, Lina, I know you're going to be okay. I'm hanging up now so I can call you an ambulance."

The word "ambulance" sent me further into panic. "I'm only seven months, Daphne," I whimpered, wiping tears from my eyes.

"You're going to be okay. Call your doctor, and then call Jon."

"Okay." I sniffed. "Daphne, these babies… They *need* to be okay," I whimpered, overwhelmed by my first rush of maternal-instinct overload.

But as I flipped my phone shut and scurried over to the fridge, where my ob-gyn's number stared back at me, I didn't call my doctor or Jon. Instead, I flipped my phone open, fingers trembling, pulse increasing, and called the only person who could ease my anxieties. The only person who could help me through something as petrifying and increasingly painful as this. I flipped open my phone and called my mom.

***

I was having an out-of-body experience when Jon called Daphne and promised her he was on his way. I looked down at myself from the hospital room ceiling, observing my face as it glistened with sweat and strands of damp hair stuck and matted to my skin. My eyes squinted shut, and my face turned various shades of red and pink as I breathed through each contraction. My mother stood at one side of me, rubbing my back and pressing in all the right spots to ease some discomfort, while Daphne sat across from her, holding my hand. Two nurses worked around my bed, monitoring heart rates and examining my progress.

I wasn't sure how much time had passed since the paramedics picked me up. It might have been an hour, or it could have been several.

"You're doing great," one of the nurses reassured me. "It's almost time to start pushing."

I snagged my mother's hand and held her stare with mine. "Where's Jon?" I yelled louder than intended. "I need Jon."

"He's almost here," Daphne reassured me. "He was handling a case when you went into labor."

"I can't do this without him," I sobbed.

My mother brushed my hair from my eyes and softly kissed my forehead. "It's going to be okay," she said.

"It's not," I cried, shaking my head from side to side, fear taking over me. "I want my epidural."

"It was too late for that when you arrived at the hospital," Mom repeated for the millionth time. "We missed that window."

"I don't care," I wailed, pulling back from her, another contraction bursting through my insides. I squeezed both of their hands and breathed through it, deciding that this was the day I was going to die. "I want it anyway," I roared directly at the nurse. "Please," I begged. "I need drugs. I'll take anything you can give me."

"You're doing great," she said again.

"Nobody is listening to me!"

"The doctor will be here shortly," she replied with a smile. "Keep breathing, Lina!" she encouraged, separating my knees and examining me once more.

"Where is Jon?" I asked again. "I'm not doing this without him."

"He will be here," Daphne reassured me, squeezing my hand harder.

"This is all his fault. I wouldn't have had sex with him on the first date if he weren't so hot, charming, and perfect."

"Well, sweetheart, that's what birth control is for," my mother said. Daphne, the nurse, and I shot daggers of warning at her. "It's true," she said with a shrug.

"It's because he forgot his effing wallet at the effing tattoo parlor after we got effing tattoos," I wailed.

"Tattoos?" My mother gasped.

Daphne gestured to the spot above my tailbone at my infinity tattoo, and for a second, through the stretching and ripping apart of my insides, I found peace and solace in the memory of that night. "Infinity is a long time," Jon had joked as the needle scraped across my skin. "Not with the right person." I had shrugged, knowing at that moment that I would love him forever.

"It's pretty," Mom admitted. "Don't show your father."

My father and his reaction to my tattoo were the last things on my mind as a doctor entered the room and mentioned something about ten centimeters, pushing, and not waiting anymore. "I'm waiting for him," I insisted, forcing my legs closed.

The doctor placed a hand on my knee and very seriously informed me that I would be putting the babies' lives in jeopardy if I didn't start pushing.

"I—" I started but stopped because Jon burst through the door in full uniform, beads of sweat pouring from his crimson face. "Jon," I cried, tears shooting from my eyeballs. "They said we have to push."

"Okay," he said, wiping away his tears. "Then we should probably push, then."

Jon took my mother's place, and she slowly stepped away. "No, Mom," I called between breaths. "Stay."

My mom stepped forward, tears welling as she put her arm around Jon. "I'm not going anywhere."

"I love you, Mom."

"I love you too."

"Push, Lina!" the nurse encouraged, and I did. I pushed as if my life depended on it and found every ounce of inner strength because I was surrounded by the three people I loved most. And I decided then that I wouldn't let my unplanned pregnancy act as a stopping point for my life but as a beginning. I was going to be a mom. What Jon and I had done was something other than a mistake. Jon and I had made a family. We were going to be Mom and Dad to two beautiful little babies—and I was ready to meet them.

Chapter Nine

Now

It has been a week since we sat with Dean Elizabeth. Jon and I have spent night after night at his office, studying my new identity and preparing me for my first day of school—tomorrow. I have also learned every possible fact about Alanna, Chloe, and Teresa and their connections to the students and staff of Emerson. Jon has quizzed me about their lives like a contestant preparing for *Jeopardy*. I have brushed up on my math facts thanks to an app I once used to help Max, and I have dusted off my violin and can play the basic notes thanks to YouTube. Gemma Mendoza has a fake Instagram account with two hundred followers—some real, some artificial intelligence thanks to Jon's tech guy—and I have a new iPad equipped with all my textbooks and messenger apps, thanks to Dean Downing. Emotionally, academically, and intellectually, I'm ready to go undercover. I'm prepared to be Gemma Mendoza. Now, I need to look the part.

"Like it?" I question Ryker as he awkwardly leans against my kitchen island, his eyes glued to Alex, his ex. Alex has been working diligently for over three hours on my renewed hairdo, and I'm obsessed with it. My once-familiar chocolate-brown locks have undergone a total metamorphosis.

"It's a wolf cut," Alex explains to Ryker. "The layers are trendy enough without looking too mature. See, her bangs take at least ten years off her pretty little life. I also added some honey-brown tones to warm everything up—"

"And to cover the grays." I chuckle.

"Sweetheart, you don't have grays," Alex says with a roll of his eyes.

"I had a few."

"You had like half of one," he says, shrugging me off. "Like I was saying, I also added some rose-platinum highlights. See how they frame Lina's face?" Alex runs his finger over his chin, studying Ryker for a reaction. When Ryker doesn't react, Alex runs his fingers through his own dark tresses and flashes his gorgeous brown eyes Ryker's way.

Ryker crosses his arms over his chest and nods in approval. "I love it," he mumbles, the first thing he has said to Alex all day.

"Time for makeup," Alex adds.

"This is kind of fun." I giggle, standing from the stool and grabbing water from the fridge.

When I told Ryker that I was going along with Operation Superglue and needed a makeover, he knew Alex was who I needed to help me. "Please," I had implored. "You know I can't do this myself."

"It's true," he sighed. "You desperately need help. It's time to lose the skinny jeans and the side part, Mama. Oh, and the frosted lip trend isn't really a thing anymore. It's very 2001. Get yourself a pair of cargo pants and a thirty-ounce Stanley and call it a day." And with that, he texted the man who, after five years, had broken his heart.

After insisting that cargo pants should have stayed in 1998, I accused Ryker of only wanting an excuse to text Alex, but he insisted otherwise. Either way, I was getting a makeover in my kitchen. Alex agreed to do it for free under two conditions—first, I purchase the recommended makeup products from him, and second, Ryker would go for drinks with him afterward.

Ryker agreed to this right away, which also proved my point, and I had crossed my fingers that the two of them might be able to make amends. Although I have been in Ryker's shoes, forgiving infidelity is challenging no matter how much you love someone.

My stomach does an unexpected flip, and I can't tell if I'm nervous for Ryker or myself. The first-day-of-school jitters are something I haven't experienced since college, which, at this point, feels like another lifetime.

"How did it go shopping with Lucy and Daphne?" Ryker asks.

"It was great!" I say, shaking myself out of my melancholy. "Do you know they make something called mom jeans? I've gone *out* of my way to avoid wearing pants that look like mom pants."

"Sounds rough," Ryker laughs.

"Well, the good news is they are comfortable. This generation knows what they are doing. I'll never wear another pair of skinny jeans again."

"Thank God," Alex huffs.

"Crop tops are another story, though." I cringe.

"You can pull that off, easy," Alex admits. "You're gorgeous, girl."

"Thanks." I blush. "It's just… I like my shirts as, you know, shirts."

"What did you tell Max and Lucy about all of this?" Ryker asks.

"About Operation Superglue? I told the kids I was starting a new job in Tempe, working with authors in publishing, and that I'm trying to look more youthful to fit in."

"And they bought it?"

"Well… Max had his AirPods in, and he nodded at me. Lucy wanted to know a few more details, most of which had to do with *her*. Got to love teenagers."

I had been nervous about the wardrobe aspect of this makeover, but the fact that Emerson Academy has a dress code was more than helpful. The uniform consists of khaki pants or skirts, navy-blue polo shirts, ebony blazers, Sperry boat shoes, and a required black leather belt. Cell phones are allowed between classes, but Apple Watches are not. However, Dean Elizabeth informed me that the female students like to convey their personalities with accessories, nail polish, faux hair extensions, backpacks, and handbags, which is where Lucy and Daphne came in. I had made my first rookie move by including Lucy in this project, though, because I couldn't tell her about my school uniform. Therefore, she believed that I needed new clothes for work. Jon and I decided that having casual outfits couldn't hurt, as I plan to spend time with my new friends after school.

"What do you wear for makeup now?" Alex asks.

"What do you mean?"

"You know," he says, clearing his throat. "Tell me about your daily makeup routine."

"She doesn't wear makeup," Ryker laughs. "Ever."

"Not true!" I holler, slapping him playfully on the arm. "I do too. You're my trainer. You just never see it."

"Yeah, okay," Ryker laughs, rolling his eyes. "The last time I saw you wear makeup was at Daphne's wedding."

"Liar. I wear it."

"What brand of foundation do you use?" Alex asks.

"Foundation? Ew, I don't wear that."

"Told you," Ryker sighs.

"Okay, so I don't have a daily makeup routine," I huff. "I'm an author, I work from home, and I'm, you know, swamped... but I wear it when I go out."

"Which is what?" Alex asks.

"You know," I start then stop and start again. "I do eyeliner, obviously... and a little bit of eyeshadow... mascara... and lip gloss."

Alex stares me down like I just confessed to killing my best friend. "That's it?"

"That's it."

"Well, your skin is stunning," he raves.

"Botox." Ryker snorts.

"Stop!" I say, between laughs. "It's for migraines."

"Sure it is."

"Either way," Alex interjects, "You don't need much in real life. But we have some work to do if you're trying to look eighteen. Have a seat."

I take a seat back at the kitchen island, ready for makeup. Alex rambles on passionately about my skin tone, CC creams, shades of bronzers, eyebrow pencils, and false eyelashes, but I am too busy observing Ryker watching him. The way Ryker feels right now is hitting way too close to home. His facial expressions shift from sore to melancholy and then back again. I know these emotions firsthand now that I spend so much time with my ex-husband.

Shifting my mindset has been rough. So many years despising Jon Cote, wallowing in the betrayal, and feeling overly rejected can get to a person. I would have cut him out of my life if not for the twins. It is such a catch-22. I love my children more than life; I can't imagine my life without them. I don't regret Max and Lucy, but sometimes, I wish I had never met Jon.

As if on cue, the doorbell rings. "Are you expecting someone?" Ryker asks.

"No, I don't think so," I say, wracking my brain. I was overly careful about having company today during my transformation back to my teenage years.

"Lucy didn't ask to have Oliver over, but that doesn't mean she didn't invite him. And I'm going out with Travis tonight, but he won't be here to pick me up for an hour."

"Who's Travis?" Alex asks, eyebrows raised.

"A guy I'm dating—"

"Her hookup buddy."

"Can't you go play video games with Max or something?" I ask Ryker with a roll of my eyes.

"I'll get it!" Lucy calls, hurrying down the stairs, side glancing at me as she reaches the front door. "*Yes*, Mom! Your hair! So much better. I love it! You look so boujee."

"Thanks," I say hesitantly, unsure if that's a compliment. "Hey, are you expecting company?"

"No," she says, turning the doorknob and opening the door. There is a brief pause, and then, "Dad!" she shrieks. "What are you doing here? You *never* come over," she accuses as she leaps up and wraps her arms around him.

"Nice to see you too." He chuckles. He waves at me from the doorway, wearing the same jeans and Duke's Waikiki T-shirt he wore last night, still looking like he needs to shower but somehow managing to pull this look off, which aggravates me on so many levels I've lost count.

Ryker leans forward and grazes my ear with the tip of his nose. "Who invited the dirtbag?" he huffs.

"*Shhhh*," I scold. "That dirtbag is her father. Lower your voice when you bash him. But please, keep bashing him."

"Still a dirtbag," he whispers.

Alex stiffens, probably realizing that forgiveness isn't our jam between Ryker and me, which doesn't bode well for Alex's evening. Let's face it, if we won't let Jon off the hook after all these years, why would Ryker forgive Alex in such a short amount of time?

Lucy yanks Jon by the arm into my kitchen. "Dad's here?" she asks more than says, her tone full of confusion. She may as well be announcing the arrival of Santa Claus. An overwhelming ping of guilt zaps my insides as I witness how strange it is for my daughter to see her father inside our house. But the truth is, it *is* weird.

Jon seems so foreign standing in my kitchen, his hands in his pockets, looking me up and down, clearly liking what he sees.

"Look at you!" He whistles. "What's the occasion?"

My shoulders tighten, and my back stiffens as I realize Jon has done this intentionally. He has come to my home as a test to see if I can lie to my daughter. As messed up as it is, I am thankful for the practice. This is it. I take a deep breath and prepare my speech. "I—"

"Mom's starting a new job," Lucy explains. "She's trying to be way cooler so she can fit in."

Thanks, Lucy.

"Yeah… I'm taking on a new project with my publisher. Going for a new look. Like it?"

"I love it," he says sincerely. "I'm happy for you."

Lucy says, "I took her shopping, and now she's learning about makeup. Want to stay? We can order pizza?"

My eyes shoot daggers at him, and he politely declines. "No, Pumpkin. Thank you. I have some work to do on an important case."

"Oh, come on, Dad! You can spare an hour, can't you?" She bats her eyelashes at him and pouts like a toddler.

"It's a massive case," he repeats. "Sorry."

"What's this one about?" Lucy asks Jon.

"The case?" he asks, tightening his jaw.

"Yeah, Dad, the case. Why are you being weird?"

"Missing dog," he says with a frown.

"Oh no!" she cries. *Good move.* Lucy loves dogs, which is all she needs to hear to let this go.

"What kind of dog?"

"Purebred Dalmatian," he says without missing a beat.

"Poor buddy." She pouts. "Where did he go missing from?"

"Tempe Marketplace," he explains. "Was taken from a car when the owner went into Walmart."

And there, at that moment, I am not only impressed with Jon's ability to lie on his feet, but I am also completely and utterly disgusted with him for being able to do so.

"So sad," I agree, holding my gaze on the floor.

Lucy's cell phone rings, loosening the brief tension in the room. "It's Oliver. I'm going to take it upstairs," she sings. "Goodnight, Dad. I love you."

"I love you too." He kisses her on the forehead and squeezes her close.

"You stink, Dad. Take a shower, will you?"

"I will," he laughs as she jogs up the stairs with her phone, slamming her door behind her.

"Time for eyes," Alex says. "Look up."

I look at the ceiling while Alex applies my fake eyelashes.

"Are you sure I need these?"

"Yes," the three men say at once.

"Okay, okay," I sigh. "I know they are trending, but they just seem so... I don't know, fake."

"Are you ready for tomorrow?" Jon asks, pulling up a stool next to me.

"As ready as last time you asked," I sass.

"Let's go over the plan for the morning."

"Again?"

"Again."

"I am getting ready for the day like normal. I'll say goodbye to the kids before their bus leaves the house at six a.m." I gag at the thought of leaving that early. "I will then drive to Ryker's gym, where I have rented a locker and keep my school uniform. I'll change and leave for school before Ryker's first client arrives, being careful not to put my blazer on until I get to school. That way, if anyone recognizes me, it won't blow my cover."

"Good," he says, nodding. "Then what?"

"Then I park in the student lot with my parking pass and head to chemistry class, my homeroom."

"Excellent."

"I'm good," I say reassuringly.

"I know you are," he agrees. "I'm just trying to ensure we don't forget anything."

"I think we thought of everything," I say, blinking my eyes and adjusting to my new lashes. "Can't we just do mascara?" I whine. "There is no way I can do this myself."

"Practice," Alex says. "You will get it. They look perfect."

"What about when you change for PE?" Jon asks.

"I have my gym uniform," I say. "Stop worrying. It's stressing me out."

"Just try to change in the bathroom stall or something. You are kind of young for an infinity tattoo," he cackles. Jon glances from me to Ryker and back to me, allowing the awkward silence to wash over him. I bite down on my lower lip and hold my breath.

"What?" Jon asks. "Why are you guys being so weird?"

"Dude," Ryker sighs. "Lina had her tattoo removed like a million years ago. You don't have to worry about it."

***

My makeover has Travis all sorts of flustered. My new job has been the focus of our conversation since we arrived at his place, as he can't seem to wrap his mind around why I would need to go through so many physical changes for this position. "Don't get me wrong," he says, handing me a piece of pizza and smiling, his dark eyes soft and tender. "You look beautiful. But you were beautiful before too."

"You always know what to say," I say, leaning into him for a quick kiss. "Come on, let's watch the movie. I have an early morning."

But watching the movie lasts less than twenty minutes before Travis puts the moves on me, and I'm faced with the true meaning of Netflix and chill. We are in his bed together ten minutes later, and I have the usual mind-blowing sex I always have with Travis. And now, as I lie next to him, completely naked under his 1,200-thread-count sheets, I am comforted by the brief pause from my new and chaotic way of life. I run my fingers over Travis's dark buzz cut and kiss his forehead, cursing Daphne and Ryker for calling him my hookup buddy. Travis is way more than just sex to me. Sure, we have lots of sex, and it's genuinely fantastic, but none of that is the issue. I wish, more than anything, I could let my guard down with him emotionally. He is constantly ready to move forward with our relationship, and I keep shutting it down. And now, my world is full of lies. I will lie to my children and Travis about my entire day. Everything I do will be as Gemma, not Lina. And even though I would like to have more with this man, I know the timing isn't right—not now, at least.

"What are you thinking about?" he asks, grazing fingers over my cheek.

"Just work tomorrow," I lie. "Big day."

"Yes, it is," he says, pulling me in for a kiss. His mouth is warm against mine, and I'm overwhelmed by how good he feels. He pulls back and studies me intently. "But is that really what you were thinking about?"

"You're too smart," I say with a smile. "I figured being a pharmacist and all, you are book smart. Just didn't know if socially, your intelligence would match up." I wink, climb on top of Travis, and wrap my legs around his torso.

"Harsh," he declares with a smile. "Is it my looks? You think I'm just a pretty face?"

"That's got to be it," I agree with a shrug. I recall describing Travis as tall, dark, and handsome to Ryker, and I couldn't have been more on point. Travis is tall and muscular. He spends at least two hours a day at the gym, and it shows. I run my hands along his dark, defined biceps and smile. "You caught me," I confess. "I was thinking about us."

"Us? That's not like you at all. What about us?"

"You know." I giggle awkwardly. "Us."

"I told you," he whispers, pulling me down and squeezing me tightly. "No pressure to be serious."

"I know," I sigh. "And I'm thankful for that. But... maybe... when things settle down with work, maybe we can do something special? Just the two of us?"

"I would love that, Lina. Whenever *you're* ready."

His words send chills to my core. Maybe it is because his voice is super raspy, sexy, and deep when he says it. Or perhaps it could be because I genuinely care about him, and he truly cares about me. But the underlying anxiety that flows through me stems from the fact that deep down inside, I might never be ready to trust again and love again. And more than anything, I hope beyond hope that this is simply a fear and nothing more.

Chapter Ten

Then (2009)

When the instructor at the YMCA announced it was time to sing a song, my one-year-old Max had just gotten comfortable in the pool during Mommy and Me swim. Surrounded by the eager voices of new parents and their somewhat-frightened babies, I floated Max on his tummy, encouraging him to kick his feet and blow bubbles until I located my mother, who was doing the same with Lucy.

"Thank you for coming, Mom," I shouted over the commotion.

"Of course!" she hollered back, kissing Lucy on her tiny forehead.

"I'm sorry Daddy couldn't make it," she sang in her best baby voice, smiling at my daughter. "But Grammy is pleased about the invite!"

I adjusted Max on my hip, his body slippery against mine from the pool's water. It was a letdown that Jon couldn't come to the first day of the class, but I understood. It would have been nice to have him here with us, but he had been working on a significant case and left for work unexpectedly in a hurry. "Mommy's happy too," I agreed, smiling at Max. "Mommy and Me swimming lessons are great but pretty tough with twins!" I slipped my hands under Max's armpits and lifted him out of the water with a cheer as the instructor sang "Pop Goes the Weasel," and I dunked him under the water and back up again. "Yay! "I cheered as he emerged from the water with a bittersweet expression.

"Did he like it?" Mom asked.

"I can't tell," I said between laughs. "You okay, buddy?"

"More," Max said, his little voice melting my heart. Max's laughter bubbled forth and echoed around us.

"Again!" I cheered, lifting him up and back down under the water.

I cast a side-glance at my mother as she navigated her way around the pool with Lucy, sporting her new yellow-and-pink polka-dot swimsuit with a ruffle bottom. "How is she doing?" I called over the strained voices of parents singing to their children.

Mom faced Lucy toward me and bounced her up and down. "Pop!" Lucy cheered, clapping her little hands together and smiling brightly. "More pop!"

Mom dunked Lucy under the water and back up until the song ended, and the instructor began scattering small bath toys around us. The noise in the pool subsided as the babies gnawed at their toys. Lucy was mesmerized by an orange crab, and Max, a green octopus.

"Want to switch?" Mom asked.

I nodded and planted a kiss on Max's wet, slimy face. "Who wants to swim with Grammy?" I cheered, hoping he would be okay with the shift. I took Lucy from my mother in exchange for Max, who grabbed on to her eagerly.

"How old are they?" a quiet, meek voice asked from behind.

I spun around, one hand on Lucy and the other on her orange crab. A petite woman with curly ginger hair balanced a little boy with red hair and freckles. "They will be one next week!" I said proudly, hardly able to believe it myself. "Can you believe it, Lucy? You're going to be one!" I said, kissing the top of her head. "How about your son? How old is he?"

"He just turned three," she said with a smile. "Twins?" she asked, gesturing toward Max and my mother.

"Yes," I said. "This is Lucy, and that is my son, Max," I said, pointing. "And that's my mom, Celeste."

"This is Henry," she said. "Over there, that's my other son, William."

"You have twins too?" I asked.

"Sure do! That's my husband over there with William," she said, smiling and waving across the pool.

"Nice," I said, wishing Jon were with me. Part of the reason I signed up for swim was to meet other parents, and it would have been nice for Jon to meet a friend too. I was a young mother and longed for a friend who could understand what it was like to raise babies. "My… boyfriend, their father, is working today," I said awkwardly. "He's a police officer," I said, tripping over my words. "I'm Lina."

"That stinks he needs to work on Saturdays," she said with a pout. "I'm Penelope. It's nice to meet you."

"Nice to meet you too."

We chatted for a bit, mainly talking about babies, swim diapers, naps, and sleepless nights before the instructor announced that the class was over and collected the toys from our children.

"It was so nice to meet you, Lina! Your children are beautiful."

"Yes, see you next week," I said with a hopeful smile, wondering if I might have a potential friend in Penelope.

***

Later that evening, after a day filled with many adventures, including the twins trying banana yogurt for the first time—Lucy loving it, Max spitting it on my face—and neither child napping, Daphne and I were finally out for a night on the town for my birthday. It was my first night out in the city post pregnancy, and I was determined to live it up.

I had been nervous that Jon would get called into work, so I sent the twins overnight with my parents, Celeste and Pepito, to be proactive and not miss my big celebration. Both were overjoyed to have the babies for the night, but leaving them had been more complicated than I had anticipated. Packing them up had taken most of my day, and my father's face upon my arrival was priceless. "What on earth do we need all this for?" he had asked, eyeing the Pack 'n Plays, cans of baby formula, packages of Puffs, bags of diapers, Max's elephant, and Lucy's lion.

"You're going to need all of this stuff. Trust me, Dad," I said with a kiss.

"We didn't need all of this when you were a baby," he said, his accent thick. "What the hell does that do?"

"It's a video monitor."

"A what?"

"It's a video baby monitor."

My dad's face was priceless as I set up the playpens and hooked up the monitor. After an hour of conversation and going over instructions with my parents, I was ready for my big night. I had hurried back to my apartment, thrown on a red baby-doll top that covered my postpartum belly, and was taking shots with Daphne, all before six p.m.

I was flying high after feeling the effects of my first drink since taco night. Daphne and I were at Club Red, an up-and-coming spot for ASU students, and tonight, my favorite cover band was performing.

"I miss this!" I shouted.

Daphne bounced to the tempo of the music, her blond spiral curls dancing around her. She looked stunning in her black miniskirt and matching halter, and the guys around us began noticing.

"I miss you!" she hollered back.

I shut my eyes and swayed to the music, relief flooding over me, finally feeling like myself again. When I opened my eyes, I was surprised to see a good-looking guy behind Daphne with his arms around her. She closed her eyes. She leaned her head back against his chest as they rocked to the beat of the music.

A wave of gloom flowed over me as I observed my friend. How different would my life have been if I had been more careful in bed with

Jon? Daphne would go home to her on-campus apartment tonight and easily sleep off her hangover. On the other hand, I would need to wake up at a decent hour and collect my children from my parents, ready for another day of changing diapers, teething, napping, and who knows what else… which wouldn't be so bad if Jon were with me, but he would most likely be working.

I jumped, startled, as someone pressed against my back and gripped my waist. I strained my neck and looked behind me, but the lights were bright, and my vision was beginning to blur. The guy, whoever he was, smelled of Axe body spray, cigarettes, and vodka, and my stomach turned as he attempted to shift my hips back and forth. I drew back, put some space between us, and turned to face him.

He was handsome. He looked about my age, a little taller than me, and wore an ASU T-shirt and matching cap. He smiled an enticing smile, reaching for my waist again, but this time, I removed his hand from my body, releasing it down by his side.

"What?" he asked with a pout. "You don't want to dance?"

"I like to dance," I said, slurring my words. "It's my birthday."

"Happy birthday," he said, curling his lips into a soft smile. He tugged me close again, and this time, I allowed him. He seized my waist, moving my hips in small circles, then drove me closer, bending his knees and pushing me against his leg. I gasped, alarmed at first, but my new friend was great at moving his hips, and I liked it as the beat quickened and so did his movements. He took my hands in his, sliding them up around his neck, damp with sweat, but I liked that too.

"What's your name?" he asked over the music.

I peered over my shoulder at Daphne, who was making out with her dance partner, her back arched as he ran his hands over her chest. "Daphne," I lied, because that night, I didn't want to be Lina, mother of two, I wanted to be Daphne, mother of none.

"I'm Mark."

But I didn't want to talk. I closed my eyes again, allowing every musical note to flow through my veins and each drumbeat to change my reality, one eight count at a time.

"You're pretty," he said, tickling my ear.

Stop talking, I silently begged. I nodded, allowing the cute college boy to trace my sides with his fingers until they landed back around my hips, pressing me down against his leg again, holding me there for longer than probably appropriate. When a soft moan escaped my lips, I realized what I was doing, and a tidal wave of guilt hit me like a ton of bricks. Without hesitation, I leaped back like I was stung by a bee or bit by a mosquito. I took his hands in mine and removed them from my body, silently disappointed that this had to end. Jon was many things, but he couldn't dance, especially like *that*. I squinted my eyes closed and shook my head from side to side.

"What?" he asked, clearly confused.

"I'm not single," I confessed.

"So what?" he asked through his laughter. "Neither am I." He took a step toward me once more. "It's just a dance. A birthday dance, Daphne."

"It's not *just* dancing," I snorted. "My lady parts were rubbing against your…" My cheeks flushed. "I just… I don't want to," I said, stumbling backward, my thoughts foggy through my drunken haze.

"It's okay," he said, rubbing a sweaty hand through my hair.

"No," I insisted. "It isn't. I wish it were okay, but it isn't."

"It's not like you're married, right?"

That hit me like a lightning bolt, electrocuting me to the depths of my soul. He was right. I wasn't married. *Why* wasn't I married? Why hadn't Jon proposed to me? I had one-year-old twins, and I wasn't married to their father. *What the hell, Jon?* I thought through my drunken stupor. Why were we not engaged? The realization that I had been playing housewife for an entire year with no consideration of my career, progressing our relationship, or my future as anything else but *Mommy* suddenly infuriated me.

I studied Mark through the strobe lights and the concert's electric atmosphere and thought about it for a beat. I wondered what it would be like to dance with him more, feel him against me again, and keep pretending to be Daphne. But at that moment, I thought of Jon. I remembered the way he looked when he kissed me goodbye that morning. His smile when he bounced our babies on his knee and sang silly rhymes. How hard he worked on their nursery, painting one wall pink for Lucy and the other green for Max. How funny it was when he blew on their tummies and made farting sounds, causing them to giggle, which had become my favorite sound. Jon. My Jon. Who would do anything for me, because he loved me, and suddenly, I needed to get the hell out of there.

"I have babies," I told Mark, my words coming out in a jumbling mess. "Twins. That's why I can't dance with you anymore." And with that, I made a conscious decision to not only talk to Jon about those things that I've realized have been bothering me, but I also made a promise to myself. A commitment that from here on out, I would always put Jon and the twins first—no matter how well a man could move his hips.

Chapter Eleven

Now

I adjust my Nike backpack over one shoulder and tug at my khaki skirt with the other. *Breathe.* I shake my head, desperately attempting to ignore the butterflies in my stomach, but as I file in alongside a sea of high school students, otherwise known as my classmates, I am convinced I will throw up on my new Sperry boat shoes.

So far, the morning has gone according to plan. I got the twins ready for school, set out for Ryker's gym, changed my clothes, and made it on time. I was confident as I slid into my Emerson Academy blazer and checked my reflection in the mirror. After all, I had nailed the false eyelashes on the first try. I snapped a selfie and sent it to Jon, who approved my look and wished me luck. But now, as I enter the school's brightly lit foyer alongside groups of other students, I feel like a total imposter. I am convinced that at any moment, I will be made. Visions of kids pointing and laughing at me invade my imagination, and I am one hundred percent convinced that at any given moment, I might die.

I clutch the undercover operative cell phone Jon gave me so hard that my knuckles turn white and pull away from my classmates, leaning against a wall next to a display case of trophies, eyes glued to the phone. Jon had created a contact list for me using fictional names in case my phone fell into the wrong hands. Jon is listed in my contacts as my father, which I had a good laugh about last week, but now, as my head spins and my adrenaline rushes, it doesn't seem as funny.

Gemma: I can't do this.
Dad: Yes, you can.

Gemma: No, I can't. I'm not like you, Jon.

Dad: Please refer to me as Dad.

Gemma: 😒

Dad: Go to chemistry. One thing at a time. Remember, Dean Elizabeth can always help you.

I think about this for a beat. *One thing at a time.* I lean against the wall and close my eyes, listening to the faint chatter of the boys and girls around me. Why were they so intimidating? Was my high school experience so negative that I'm allowing it to trigger old anxieties? *They are just teenagers, Lina.* I slap my hand to my forehead, smashing my thoughts away. I *have* teenagers. I think about Max and Lucy and how they have grown in many ways but are just kids in many other ways. Who am I kidding? If these teenagers are anything like the ones I have at home, they will be so wrapped up in their own crap that they will barely notice me.

"Okay," I say out loud. "Here goes nothing."

I peel myself off the wall, barely feeling the floor beneath the weakness of my knees. Chemistry is on the second floor, so I follow the crowd up the stairs, and around the corner, I am met with another series of hallways. I take a deep breath and look around, a bit thrown off at the silence surrounding me. In my old high school, students tended to gather by lockers, but that is not the case now. Instead, their heads are down, faces locked on cell phones as they write and text one another. I remember asking Max about his locker at school, and he explained that he didn't use it because he didn't have books. He had a Chromebook. I think about this momentarily and realize I don't need my locker, either. A wave of dread washes over me as I remember how I've described these scenes in my books, and this thought alone is enough to push this shell of myself to chemistry class.

The room is well lit, the fluorescent lights radiating a bright glow over rows of black lab tables, all lined with gas outlets, electrical sockets, and sinks. The Periodic Table of Elements lines the walls, along with a rack of white aprons, plastic goggles, and gloves. A strong chemical aroma smacks me in the face, and for a brief moment, I am thankful that the school nurse has my migraine medication, just in case.

"You must be Gemma," a voice sings from the front of the room.

I spin around to see a teacher standing by an interactive whiteboard, tapping the screen with her fingers until the appropriate slide is in place. I've seen these boards over the years during back-to-school nights for Max and Lucy, and I've always been impressed with them. Back when I was in high school, most classes had regular chalkboards. Only the newer rooms had boards that could be used with markers. Hell, I even remember how much fun it used to be to write on the overhead projector. "Yes," I say with a nervous smile. "I'm Li—Gemma. I'm new to Emerson."

The teacher has soft green eyes that pop against her fair, freckled skin. Her ginger hair is positioned in a messy but somehow *not* messy bun, shaped perfectly like she spent hours on Pinterest perfecting it. I hold my breath, realizing there is no way this woman is any older than twenty-five, and the pit in my stomach grows gigantic, twisting my insides and taking my breath away.

"I'm Ms. King. You can sit right over there," she says, pointing to the second row of tables.

My gaze follows her finger until I make out an empty stool between two students. One is a blond female who could pass as Lucy's twin, and the other is a male student with more facial hair than Jon. I go to my table with my head down, playing the nervous new kid with ease—because I am just that... the scared new kid.

I sit between my new friends, the boy student not looking up from his phone as I remove my iPad and place it on the table in front of me. I inhale again, but this time, a fruity smell consumes me. It reminds me of a Bath & Body Works lotion I used to use called Sweet Pea.

"Ezra," Ms. King hollers, her tone firm. "We've talked about this."

"Sorry, Ms. King," Ezra replies, tucking something into his backpack.

"Less cotton candy smell in this room," she says, eyes wide. "No more chances."

I crinkle my nose in confusion and glance around the room, wondering why the smell of cotton candy could be damaging, hopeful she isn't referring to my own perfume. Are private schools so strict that they ban various flavors of body spray? And why does Ezra want to smell like Sweet Pea?

"You okay?" the girl next to me whispers.

"Me? Yeah," I say, nodding overenthusiastically.

"You look like you're going to puke."

"I'm nervous, I guess," I say as the bell rings for the official start of class. "And at my old school, we didn't have any rules about what kinds of perfumes or lotions we could wear, so yeah, I guess I'm confused about the cotton candy thing. I don't want to get in trouble for my perfume."

The girl holds a hand to her mouth to stifle her giggles. "He was vaping," she says, gesturing to Ezra. "The cotton candy is the flavor of his vape."

My cheeks turn crimson as I realize my mistake. "Oh," I say with a nod. I recall what Jon said about thinking on my feet, and I wonder how I can get out of this awkward situation while keeping cover. As far as I know, my kids haven't experimented with vaping, so I don't know much about it. But I recall a conversation I overheard between Oliver, Max, and Lucy that I had found interesting. Oliver had mentioned that his friend had his favorite pen confiscated at school—chocolate cake. "I guess I've never tried that flavor." I shrug. "I only vape chocolate cake."

"Oh," she says, raising her eyebrows. "That's pretty specific."

"Sweet tooth," I insist.

"I love that for you. I don't touch the stuff. My parents would kill me," the girl admits. "But no judgment here. You do you."

I nod, wondering just how red my cheeks are. "I'm Gemma," I say with a soft smile.

"I'm Molly," she says, adjusting her blond ponytail, her blue eyes soft.

"I don't vape a lot," I say, suddenly needing to be a positive influence on Molly and hoping I don't spark some sudden urge for her to start vaping. "It's just, my parents are getting divorced, and I had to leave my school in Florida."

"As I said, I don't judge. What other classes are you in?"

I show Molly a screenshot of my schedule, and I'm overcome with joy to find that she is also a senior, and we have similar schedules. As we decide to eat lunch together and Ms. King begins ranting about the synthesis of aspirin, I am filled with hope that somehow, someway, I might pull this off.

***

The following two classes go just as well as the first, thanks to Molly, with whom I also share algebra class and lunch period. I make a mental note to bring my own lunch tomorrow, as the tater tots and French bread pizza do not sit well at 10:40 a.m., which is way too early to eat lunch, and I suddenly long for any sense of freedom but, at the same time, wish I could crash and take a nap. Between lying to Molly, making notes for my books, and trying to be aware of the missing girls, their patterns, and their social circles, I decide I need a nap—or a drink.

"So, I should probably tell you something," Molly says as we walk toward the art room for our second-to-last period of the day.

"What's up?" I ask as I follow her down the hallway.

"Well, I'm sure you noticed by now that I'm not swarming with friends."

"I didn't, actually," I say because I didn't.

Molly stops short and pulls me aside, her petite features animated. She is just about my height, which is strange as I'm usually shorter than everyone I know. "My last name is Turner," she declares like she's confessing to a felony.

"So?" I ask, clearly confused.

"*Dean* Turner?" she mouths, eyes wide.

"Oh," I say, remembering Dean Orson Turner from the list of admins that Jon gave me. I had yet to meet Dean Turner. Really, the only other adults I'd met were my teachers and Dean Elizabeth Downing, and I'm closer in age to them than I am my new friend. "Is that bad?"

"Generally speaking, no. But regardless, he's an admin at the school, so that makes me a total loser to most kids."

I smile, pretending to understand what she might be going through but really wanting to tell her to tell them all to go screw themselves, that high school is just a tiny blip in life, and that none of it matters. "I'm sorry," is all I manage to mutter. Because whether or not I believe this is a crisis doesn't make it less of one for Molly.

"Thank you. I thought you should know."

"I'm cool," I say, sounding like Max, just as I practiced. I give Molly my knuckles, and she reciprocates, and I can't tell if I've passed for a teenage girl or someone just impersonating one. "What are you doing next year? Are you going to college?"

"Full ride to University of California for volleyball," she says with a smile. "Getting the hell out of Arizona for good."

"I should probably tell you something too," I say as we walk toward art class.

"Spill it," she says, focused on her phone.

"I suck at art. Like really suck at art. In my last school, I failed it every quarter."

Molly laughs at this as we approach the art room and pulls me to the side again. "Bruh, you don't have to worry about that here. Our art teacher is always absent. Actually, our art sub, Mr. Jacobs, is totally hot."

I stop short, my breath catching in my throat as I stumble into art class, choking on my spit.

"What's up, Mr. Jacobs?" Molly sings, high-fiving my ex-husband. "This is Gemma. She's new. She's going to sit with me… if that's cool."

I don't know what's stranger. That sweet, little, timid Molly, who has been closed off and quiet all day, clearly feels comfortable with Jon or Jon, as he leans against the teacher's desk wearing a white apron over a black-collared shirt and blue khakis. I didn't think Jon owned a pair of khakis.

I freeze, suddenly having no clue how to behave. I want to tease him about his apron and ask him when he hit up Land's End, but I can't because I'm a senior in high school on my first day. What would Gemma do? I ask myself. I take a deep breath and channel my inner teen. "Hi, Mr. Jacobs," I say, tucking a strand of hair behind my ear. "I'm Gemma."

"Well, hello there, Gemma," he says, his lips curling into a wide grin.

"Is it okay if I sit with Molly?"

"Yes, ma'am," he says.

I follow Gemma to a table at the back of the class, and we remove our iPads from our bags. "Am I right or what?" she whispers, licking her lips. "He has two kids, is probably sixty years old but a DILF."

"A what?" I ask, eyes wide.

"You know," she says. "A dad I'd like to—"

"I get it," I interrupt, remembering the term MILF from *American Pie* and holding my hand up for her to stop, realizing that Molly isn't Miss Innocent like I once assumed.

"Are you ladies okay?" Jon calls from the front of the room. "Not sure what your last school was like, Gemma, but here at Emerson, once that bell rings, class has started."

I shrug, feeling the heat rise to my cheeks as Jon points to an assignment on the board. "Why don't you come to see me during office hours tomorrow so we can catch you up," he suggests.

I nod, giving Molly a side-glance. She taps my shoulder and coos. "Office hours with Mr. Jacobs on your first day, you lucky bitch."

Chapter Twelve

Then (2010)

I was frosting prickly pear cupcakes while Jon cleaned up dinner. Lucy, age two, sat cross-legged in front of the TV, brushing Barbie's hair, while Max bolted around the room with Buzz Lightyear wings strapped to his back, yelling, "To infinity and beyond!" while crashing into furniture and running through traces of mac and cheese on the kitchen floor.

"Max, be careful," Jon grunted as he attempted to pick food from the carpet.

"It's their birthday," I countered. "Let them celebrate."

"Whose birthday is it?" Jon asked in his Daddy Monster voice.

"Mine!" Max growled. "No Daddy Monster on birthday!"

"Birthday immunity?" he roared. "Not a thing!"

Jon picked up Max and soared him around the room. "I'm Buzz Lightyear!" he yelled again.

"Fly me!" Lucy demanded, tossing Barbie to the floor and reaching for Jon.

"I might need reinforcements from Mommy Monster," Jon cried.

I wiped my hands on a kitchen towel and swarmed in, scooping up Lucy and flying her next to Jon and Max. "I Barbie!" Lucy shouted in her tiny voice. "Barbie fly!"

I pursued Jon and Max around the room, flying Lucy over my head in her pink-footed pajamas until my arms grew weak and my stomach hurt from laughing. "Okay," I insisted between breaths. "Let's sing Happy Birthday."

I stuck Lucy into her highchair, and Jon did the same with Max. I scurried over to the kitchen, ready to retrieve the cupcakes.

"Are they ready?" Jon asked, peering over my shoulder and kissing my cheek.

"Barely," I chuckled. "It's been a week." And that it had. Not only had I picked up an extra shift at Starbucks in an effort to save for a down payment on a house, but I had also been drafting my first book. Starbucks by day and writing at night left little time for frosting birthday cupcakes, but I didn't care. Things were finally starting to come together. Jon had been promoted at work and was no longer considered a rookie, and I was doing what I loved – writing.

"They look delicious," he said, dipping his finger into a cupcake and licking the frosting off his finger.

"You're a good boyfriend," I snickered because they looked anything but delicious. "They look like a five-year-old frosted them."

"Nah," he argued. "Maybe a ten-year-old. They look like a ten-year-old frosted them."

I tapped him playfully on the arm, removed two cupcakes from the counter, I stuck a pink number two on Lucy's and a green number two on Max's. Carefully, I lit each candle, gesturing for Jon to turn off the lights. He did, and the twins cheered as Jon and I sang "Happy Birthday" to our children. Their smiles had never been bigger, and I placed the cupcakes in front of them, reaching for my digital camera just in time to snap a picture of each child before they blew out their candles.

"Yay!" I cheered as Jon flicked the lights back on. I unwrapped the cupcakes for the kids, and they accepted them eagerly. Max smashed his dessert against his face, and Lucy licked the frosting with her tongue.

"Toys?" Lucy asked between bites.

"We will do presents at your big party, remember?" I reminded her. "It's tomorrow at Grammy's house."

Lucy nodded, satisfied with my response. I kissed the top of her head and returned to the kitchen to start washing dishes, but Jon was nowhere to be found. I held my breath, hoping that he hadn't taken a call from work. I hadn't asked for much that night other than to be together. I felt the blood boil through my veins as I scrubbed and scrubbed, trying to remain calm. I washed a pan in the sink while trying to keep my cool. "Jon?" I called again as the door to our apartment swung open, and he entered, holding a somewhat-melted Frappuccino.

"Sorry," he said. "I needed to grab this."

"Where did you get that?" I asked, wiping my hands on my jeans. "There's no way you went to Starbucks and back in that short a time."

"Come here," he said, his eyes gleaming and his grin wide.

"Okay…" I said, confused, wondering why I would want a Frappuccino at this time of night.

"The neighbors let me borrow their fridge," he said proudly.

"The Connors? Let you use their fridge for a coffee?"

Jon nodded. "Yes, they did."

"But why couldn't you use our fridge?"

But I knew exactly why as Jon dropped to one knee between the twins and their cupcake crumbs. "Lina," he started, gripping my frosted beverage against his chest. "I love you. I've loved you since I first saw you typing on your Dell laptop in Starbucks. I've loved you since that first night in my apartment. I know things didn't start the way we would have planned, but the truth is, Lina, I wouldn't change a thing. I love you, and I love our family. For infinity," he said, gesturing to the tattoo on his shoulder.

"To infinity and beyond!" Max yelled, punching his cupcake in the air.

I covered my mouth in disbelief as Jon extended the coffee toward me. "Lina, would you please do me this honor and be my wife? I could never do this life without you, nor would I ever want to."

I took the cup from Jon, realizing the words *Will you marry me?* were written on it in Sharpie. "Oh my God!" I shrieked, shaking my head in disbelief because I didn't see this coming. Sure, we had spoken recently about looking at houses, and I knew we had a future together, but things had been in such chaos I was utterly blindsided.

"Is that a yes?" he asked from the floor.

"Say yes, Mommy," Lucy advised. "You're the princess. And kiss!"

"Yes," I shouted through my tears. "Of course. Yes!"

Jon leapt from the ground and punched his arm in the air as the twins did the same. "Mommy and Daddy are getting married!" Jon announced proudly to our children.

I placed the cup on the table, eager to hug and kiss Jon. Knowing I would be Mrs. Cote was enough to make me feel like I, too, could fly.

"Wait!" Jon interrupted, reaching for the coffee. "The bottom," he explained through his tears. "Feel the bottom."

I raised the cup from the table and felt the bottom of it, gasping as I realized he was referring to an engagement ring he had so cleverly taped there. I removed the tape, gasping in awe at the most gorgeous platinum diamond engagement ring I had ever seen. "It's… It's perfect," I sobbed.

"You're perfect."

"No," I said, shaking my head from side to side. "I'm not perfect. But I do love you. And I promise, I always will."

Jon slid the ring on my finger, and I shrieked again, unable to believe my eyes.

"I love you, Lina."

"I love you too."

"To infinity and beyond."

***

What felt like years later, the kitchen was clean, the twins were washed up, books had been read, songs had been sung, and Jon and I were finally in our bedroom with our door locked. I couldn't wait another second before pulling his T-shirt over his head and unbuttoning his jeans. I was overjoyed with the notion that Jon would be mine forever. I would be his wife, and he would be my husband.

Jon lifted my shirt over my head, and I worked to remove my remaining clothing until we were both naked, rolling around like wild animals on top of our bedspread. "Jon," I moaned as he moved over me, pinning my hands behind my head.

"I want to kiss every inch of you," he said, his tone earnest and sincere.

I answered with a moan as he traced his lips over my entire body. I begged him not to stop and pulled him on top of me, eager to connect to him in all the ways we had experienced before. Ways I'd only felt with Jon, my fiancé. "I love you," I whispered into his ear as he lifted my hips toward him and pressed into me and the rhythm of our breath and our bodies synched in unison.

I studied him as he drove into me, taking in every second, determined to remember every moment of this night, how he looked, his body strong and his demeanor no-nonsense. How he smelled, like cedarwood cologne, cupcake frosting, and dish soap. And how he felt as we grabbed at each other like our lives depended on it and we couldn't be closer if we tried, and I knew, at that moment, that no matter where life took us, we would always be *us*. Jon and Lina, Mommy and Daddy, and soon-to-be husband and wife.

Chapter Thirteen

Now

"Dude, you seriously have office hours with Mr. Jacobs again? You really must suck at art," Molly accuses with a roll of her eyes.

"Yeah, really bad. I even managed to mess up that project thingy due yesterday."

This stops Molly in her tracks. "The digital art project? How in the actual hell did you manage to eff that up?"

"Apparently, I didn't have the right app on my iPad," I lie.

"Why didn't you ask me? I could have helped. We are… you know… BFFs and all."

"I'm just embarrassed, I guess," I say, biting my lower lip. The fact that Molly has declared me her bestie has me downward spiraling. Sure, we have been inseparable for over a week. I fell asleep last night texting with her on my operative phone, and I actually look forward to spending time with her, but if I'm her best friend and I'm not even being honest with her about who I really am? Well, that really sucks for Molly. And what kind of person does that make me?

The past week has involved a whirlwind of emotions. I've got my morning and afternoon routines down pat. I leave my school uniforms in my gym locker, and Ryker sends them to the dry cleaner. By midweek, I had my schedule down for the most part, and by Friday, I was familiar enough with my teachers and course expectations that I could begin problem-solving Operation Superglue. The problem, however, is that I need help figuring out where to start, and Jon and I have just had a chance to talk about it outside of school, as my life at home has gone from somewhat manageable to complete chaos now that I am a thirty-five-year-old teenager.

As stressed out as I have been trying to balance parenting, a career, and my homework, it is nothing compared to what the missing girls and their families are going through, so I refuse to bail, and I am overloaded with material for my next book. Max was right—being a teenager today is light-years of a difference compared to my high school experience. I've utilized Urban Dictionary more times than I can count to understand my friends, and I'm pretty sure I received a contact high from kids vaping in the girls' bathroom.

"What are you reading?" I ask Molly, referring to the book she is balancing.

"Oh, this? I'm reading the final book in the Cat Rose series. It's lit."

"Nice," I say, hoping lit means it's good, and I hope she doesn't notice my flushed cheeks.

"Have fun with Mr. Jacobs," Molly sings, eyebrows raised.

"I'm not into him," I remind her, closing and locking the art room's door behind me.

"Gemma!" Jon greets me from behind his desk. "Back again?" Jon raises a coffee mug to his lips and sips it, and I consider ripping it out of his hands.

"*Where* did you get that?" I ask, flinging my backpack to the floor and slumping at a table in the front row. "I'll pay you fifty bucks for it."

"It's teachers' room coffee." He chuckles in amusement. "It's probably Maxwell House."

"I'll take it by IV at this point," I whine. "I need my afternoon coffee like I need air."

"Caffeine withdrawal?"

"The worst. I'm finally over the headaches. Now, I miss the experience."

Chapter Thirteen

Now

"Dude, you seriously have office hours with Mr. Jacobs again? You really must suck at art," Molly accuses with a roll of her eyes.

"Yeah, really bad. I even managed to mess up that project thingy due yesterday."

This stops Molly in her tracks. "The digital art project? How in the actual hell did you manage to eff that up?"

"Apparently, I didn't have the right app on my iPad," I lie.

"Why didn't you ask me? I could have helped. We are... you know... BFFs and all."

"I'm just embarrassed, I guess," I say, biting my lower lip. The fact that Molly has declared me her bestie has me downward spiraling. Sure, we have been inseparable for over a week. I fell asleep last night texting with her on my operative phone, and I actually look forward to spending time with her, but if I'm her best friend and I'm not even being honest with her about who I really am? Well, that really sucks for Molly. And what kind of person does that make me?

The past week has involved a whirlwind of emotions. I've got my morning and afternoon routines down pat. I leave my school uniforms in my gym locker, and Ryker sends them to the dry cleaner. By midweek, I had my schedule down for the most part, and by Friday, I was familiar enough with my teachers and course expectations that I could begin problem-solving Operation Superglue. The problem, however, is that I need help figuring out where to start, and Jon and I have just had a chance to talk about it outside of school, as my life at home has gone from somewhat manageable to complete chaos now that I am a thirty-five-year-old teenager.

As stressed out as I have been trying to balance parenting, a career, and my homework, it is nothing compared to what the missing girls and their families are going through, so I refuse to bail, and I am overloaded with material for my next book. Max was right—being a teenager today is light-years of a difference compared to my high school experience. I've utilized Urban Dictionary more times than I can count to understand my friends, and I'm pretty sure I received a contact high from kids vaping in the girls' bathroom.

"What are you reading?" I ask Molly, referring to the book she is balancing.

"Oh, this? I'm reading the final book in the Cat Rose series. It's lit."

"Nice," I say, hoping lit means it's good, and I hope she doesn't notice my flushed cheeks.

"Have fun with Mr. Jacobs," Molly sings, eyebrows raised.

"I'm not into him," I remind her, closing and locking the art room's door behind me.

"Gemma!" Jon greets me from behind his desk. "Back again?" Jon raises a coffee mug to his lips and sips it, and I consider ripping it out of his hands.

"*Where* did you get that?" I ask, flinging my backpack to the floor and slumping at a table in the front row. "I'll pay you fifty bucks for it."

"It's teachers' room coffee." He chuckles in amusement. "It's probably Maxwell House."

"I'll take it by IV at this point," I whine. "I need my afternoon coffee like I need air."

"Caffeine withdrawal?"

"The worst. I'm finally over the headaches. Now, I miss the experience."

"The experience?"

"You know that moment when everything is quiet at home because the twins are at school, and I can just sit in my favorite chair, with my favorite mug, in my favorite slippers, watching reruns of *Sex and the City*? God, I would kill to do that right now."

"Please tell me you don't talk like this to your friends," Jon teases, sipping his coffee.

"You know I don't," I say, standing from the table and going to his desk. "I'm crushing this Gemma thing."

"Yes, you are. You're doing great."

"I think I've earned a sip." I extend my hand toward his coffee mug and pout.

"You want my coffee?"

"I *need* your coffee."

"But it's mine."

"Hand it over," I order like I'm confiscating a teenager's cell phone. "Next time, bring me one."

Jon passes me his mug, and I lean against his desk, cradling the hot cup. I sip the coffee, close my eyes, and let out a deep sigh. "It's delicious," I whisper, allowing my body to relax against the desk.

"You've officially lost it, Lina. Come on, we only have ten minutes left. How's it going out there?" Jon runs a hand through his beard and looks up at me hopefully, and I hate that I am about to crush his hopes and dreams with little to no intel.

"I'm making progress," I chirp.

"That's good. Care to elaborate?"

"Molly and I are close, and her dad is the dean. She doesn't have many friends but knows everything about what happens here."

"That's good. Pick Molly's brain about the girls. Maybe her dad talks about them at home."

"Okay," I say, brushing off a pang of guilt.

"Separate your emotions," Jon warns. "I can already tell that you care about her."

I squint my eyes in confusion. "I'm fine."

"I know you. You're not okay, and this is a big deal. You can get close to Molly without getting too close."

I bite my lip and study Jon as his cheeks flush, and he sighs. "You would know," I hiss, feeling my cheeks flush and my palms sweat.

"Focus, Lina. Do you have any other leads?"

I stand from his desk and begin pacing around the room. "No," I admit. "I can't for the life of me figure it out. All the teachers seem normal… well, for the most part," I scoff, looking Jon up and down. "The only creepy one so far is Mr. White, the PE teacher."

"George White?"

"I don't know. Is he the PE teacher?"

Jon considers this for a beat. "He's quirky, but do you think he's our guy?"

"I don't know." I shrug. "I get a funky vibe from him, and I don't love how he looks at Molly. He's a little flirty with her, and it's unsettling… like if someone were to look at Lucy that way, I wouldn't like it."

"Hmm," he says, considering this. "Trust your intuition. And all three girls had PE with him, right?"

"Right. Also, Chloe played volleyball, and he's the head coach. That's a red flag, right?"

"Very true," Jon says, opening his computer and pulling up his email. "Volleyball tryouts are next week."

"That's dope," I say, sounding more like Molly by the second. "Should I stop in and watch them?"

"No, Gemma, you should try out for the team. You need to form a relationship with George. That's the only way we will be able to tell if this is our lead."

"Try out?" I cover my eyes and shake my head. "I can't play volleyball. I'm running cross country."

"So play volleyball instead."

"I haven't played volleyball since middle school."

"That's a lie, and you know it. You played on our honeymoon, and you were terrific."

"Stop right there," I snap, holding my hand up. "Don't use my honeymoon as leverage."

"But you were good. You know you were. And you need to do this, for Operation Superglue."

"I think I hate you."

"It's just volleyball."

"I can't do one more thing!" I wail. "My editor wants chapters, and I average three to four hours of homework a night. Oh, and there's the kids. I had to enlist Ryker and Daphne for help last week so they could get to their sports, and I missed their first game. And…" My voice trails off before I begin talking about Travis—sweet, perfect Travis who wants to spend time with me and grow our relationship. I've avoided him like the plague since the night before school started. It's all just too complicated. I'm growing tired of the lies by the second, and it's only been a week. I can't bring myself to go and spend time with him if I can't be honest, and that, in itself, is reason enough to stay away.

"And what?"

"It's nothing," I lie. "My personal life, it's just nonexistent. I'm starting to forget who I am in all of this."

"You mean your dating life."

"Maybe," I say, staring at the floor. "But I know that's silly. There are missing girls and books to write, so I need to suck it up, right?"

"Lina, it's—" Jon's words are cut short by the sound of the bell. "Time for you to go."

"Fine," I grunt, chugging the remainder of his coffee and slamming the mug under his nose. "I'll try out for volleyball. But you will have to pick up some slack with the twins."

"Fine," he says, matching my tone.

"Fine," I repeat with my hands on my hips. "See if you can find an in with Mr. White," I add. "You could use some friends in your life, Mr. Jacobs."

Chapter Fourteen

Then (2010)

I squeezed Jon's hand, and he pressed back, confirming my suspicion that he wasn't sleeping. I had lost track of the minutes, let alone hours, as we reclined in our lounge chairs post-afternoon mai tais. I made a mental note to stand up and apply sunblock soon, determined not to return home from my honeymoon looking like a lobster. But moving seemed like too much work. Lying there, beneath the warmth of the sun, hearing nothing but the sounds of the Pacific Ocean as its waves crashed along the shore of Waikiki Beach, was nothing short of a dream.

Lucy had been right when she told me that marrying her father would make me a princess. Jon had proposed in November, and we were married in April, leaving for our honeymoon immediately afterward. It was a small wedding of sixty guests, including immediate family and close friends. We were married at the Wright House in Mesa, a historic mansion with lush and elegant gardens, and it was everything we could have hoped for and more. Our wedding party had been small, consisting of Daphne as my maid of honor, Jon's brother, James, as his best man, and our children as flower girl and ring bearer. My father had walked me down the aisle in my blush A-line strapless wedding gown toward an overly emotional Jon Cote, who sported his police uniform, per my request, which I removed carefully, one layer at a time, when we were back at our hotel that night, leading up to a night of passionate lovemaking, our first time as husband and wife.

I had low expectations for our wedding night. I had assumed we would both be exhausted, which was true. We were emotional after leaving Max and Lucy with my parents for a week but also flying high from the excitement of the reception and anticipation of our first vacation together. There wouldn't have been much sleeping regardless, and we wouldn't have had it any other way. We made love in our hotel bed that night, Jon beneath me, his hands gripping my waist, my hands pressed to his chest as we moved together in unison, carefree, not worrying about waking up any sleeping babies, and continued in the shower immediately afterward, where we held each other under the steamy, hot water as it flowed over our bodies, his mouth on mine, my fingers gripping his shoulders as his mouth swallowed each of my gasps.

That had been almost a week ago, and Jon and I had finally adjusted to being on vacation. It was hard at first as we missed our children more than anything. It took two couple massages before we could relax and appreciate the beautiful island of O'ahu. Once we did, we had the time of our lives. Jon and I took surf lessons, hiked a volcano, became regulars at Duke's Waikiki, and even made friends with Brooklyn and Jack, a couple from Boston who were also on their honeymoon.

This was our last day as honeymooners, and we had big plans to sit on the beach with drinks in our hands for the entire day. As much as I couldn't wait to get home to Max and Lucy, it felt amazing to leave my responsibilities behind for a week and be... well... me. Being able to have adult conversations with just Jon for an entire week without worrying about work or the kids was priceless. I confessed to Jon that my biggest dream was to become a best-selling author, and he revealed that working an undercover operation was his goal. These were things we never would have shared at home with the hustle and bustle of everyday life.

"Hey there, lovebirds!" Brooklyn's voice called from behind us.

"Hi," I responded, prying my eyes open and sitting up for the first time in hours.

"Sleeping the day away?" she asked, her dark hair wet and matted from the ocean water.

"Yup," Jon responded, unapologetically in a prone position.

"No!" she wailed. "It's your last day. You can't sleep all day. You can sleep at home."

Clearly, Brooklyn didn't have two-year-olds, but I wasn't about to shove that in her face. I'm sure she had responsibilities that she needed to return to. "You're right," I agreed, rubbing my eyes. "What do you have in mind?"

"Volleyball."

"Volleyball?"

"Yeah." She shrugged. "There's a net over there, and some people have organized a tournament."

"I'm too short for volleyball," I admitted, flashes of gym-class mishaps flashing through my mind.

"It's volleyball on the beach." She chuckled. "Children are playing."

"Want to play volleyball?" I asked Jon, shaking his shoulder.

"I want to sleep," he moaned.

"Jack's already putting our names in," she encouraged. "Come on, it will make for a good story. When your twins are teenagers, and they ask you what you did on your honeymoon, you can tell them you kicked ass in a game of beach volleyball. It sounds way cooler than 'I slept on the beach all day.'"

"I think sleeping on the beach makes for a great story." I shrugged. "But okay. Let's do it."

***

It only took ten minutes on the beach volleyball court with Brooklyn and Jack to realize we were in over our heads and Brooklyn was a competitive beast. Our team dominated a family of four, a handful of locals, and a father playing with his teenage daughters. We were now in the final moments of our championship game, and Brooklyn was on fire.

"Let's go! Jack, step it up! Come on!" she scolded as the ball contacted my wrists, soared over the net with ease but just as quickly came smashing down to the sand to my right. Jon, most likely petrified of Brooklyn, dove to the ground, missing the ball, and the opposing team cheered.

"Damn it!" Brooklyn shouted, slamming her fist against her leg. "Let's go!" She adjusted her bikini top and jumped up and down, rapidly clapping her hands.

"Probably should have warned you that she played Division 1 ball in college." Jack shrugged.

"You think?" Jon panted, hopping to his feet and wiping the sand off his bare chest.

Jon tossed the ball to Jack, who served it over the net, this time scoring a point for our team immediately. The four of us cheered, knowing that we were tied.

"Game point! Your serve, Lina!" Brooklyn hollered.

I kicked at the warm sand between my toes, wishing I had stayed in my beach chair with my beverage, holding Jon's hand. I hugged the ball to my chest, taking in the situation's intensity as Brooklyn and Jack clapped their hands together to pump me up. My doubtful eyes met Jon's stare as I bit down on my lip and tucked a strand of hair behind my ear.

"What's wrong?" he asked, his tone gentle.

My stomach flipped as an anxious feeling flooded through my veins. "Nothing, except if I screw this up, I'll let everyone down."

"Everyone?" Jon asked, lowering his sunglasses and raising his eyebrows, amused that I was taking this so seriously.

"Well, yeah, Brooklyn. She's nuts," I mouthed.

Jon wrapped his arms around my bare shoulders, pulling me against his warm chest. "They don't matter," he whispered. "When we go home, it's just me, you, Max, and Lucy. We're a family. *We're* what matters, Lina. Not some stupid beach volleyball game with a couple of strangers we will never see again."

I thought about this briefly, realizing he was one hundred percent right. I would do my best, and that was all that mattered. This was my honeymoon, and I would have fun, win or lose. "You and me," I repeated with a nod. "Okay."

"You and me."

"Okay," I said again, inhaling, exhaling, winding up, and serving the ball over the net. The ball soared, and an opposing player sent it back over the net to Brooklyn, who set it in the air for Jon to spike. He did, but it came back, right at Jon, who set it to me, only it landed a bit too far in front of me. An overly dramatic somewhat-athletic roar escaped from somewhere deep within my soul, and I dove forward, just as I had done in middle-school gym class. The ball contacted my wrists before I hit the sand with a thud. I closed my eyes, absorbing the shock of the ground against my half-naked body, when I heard it. "Woo-hoo!" Brooklyn cheered. "We won!"

I pulled myself to my knees and wiped the hot sand off my face, and the next thing I knew, Jon's arms were around my waist, guiding me up to him. I jumped onto my husband, wrapped my legs around his waist, and buried my face into his neck, overwhelmed with emotion.

"You're amazing," he laughed, flooding my sandy cheek with kisses.

"No," I said, pulling back. "You are. Thank you."

"For what?"

"For believing in me," I responded, wiping a tear from my eye. "For reminding me what's important. For having my back."

"I'll always believe in you. You're my family now." And with that, he carried me to the water, where we collapsed into one of the biggest waves I'd ever seen and kissed each other like elated and giddy teenagers until the sun set over the Pacific, and we were ready to head back home as Mr. and Mrs. Jon Cote—husband and wife.

Chapter Fifteen

Now

My kitchen looks like a war scene. My center island consists of Post-it notes, highlighters, crumpled-up notebook paper, whiteboards, and empty cans of Coke. Ryker, who has just returned home from football practice with Max, sits across from me at the kitchen island with a box of Cheez-Its. Aside from being my personal trainer, Ryker also works with Max and helps out on his team from time to time. Although I love his company, I am overwhelmed by everything I need to finish, and more than anything, I would love some peace. But as I sit perched at the kitchen island, typing away on my laptop, both cell phones dinging up a storm with incoming text messages I am too busy to care about anything but the tasks before me.

"So," Ryker asks between bites, "Is all this work, school, or investigator stuff?"

"All of the above," I moan, reaching for my burner phone.

"And the kids think…"

"The kids think this is all for work."

"Even the whiteboard?"

"What about it?"

"It's about the missing girls."

"I write about crime," I say with a shrug. "They don't notice things. They're teenagers," I say, reaching for my burner phone. "Why is Jon texting me on this *now*?" I ask out loud. I had been mid-text with Molly when Jon texted me as *Dad*. I pick up my actual cell phone and text him.

Lina: Why are you texting me on that phone?

Jon: Sorry, my bad.

Lina: It's okay. I'm just in the middle of a hundred things. What's up?

Jon: Have you heard anything about the results?

Lina: Not yet. I'll keep you posted.

"He's so annoying," I mutter to Ryker.

"Who?"

"Jon."

"I could have told you that."

I continue typing on my laptop, making notes about high school and my experiences as a senior. After-school sports aren't much different than they used to be. The same competitive and territorial girls, eager to prove themselves and projecting insecurities at each other like grenades. But as much as I want to get myself out of the situation, I can't because Coach White was even weirder on the court than in PE class. With this idea in mind, I reach for the dry-erase marker and scribble *Mr. White is a perv*, toss the marker down, and continue typing.

"What is he asking about?" Ryker asks.

"Who?"

"Jon."

"Oh, he wanted to know about tryouts."

"How did they go?"

"Good," I say, my fingers tapping away. I close my laptop, reach for my iPad, and open up my chemistry textbook app. "Is it hot in here?" I ask, wiping beads of sweat off my neck, annoyed more than ever that my hot flashes have worsened.

"Nope," Ryker says, chewing away. "Did Max tell you about his math grade?"

"What about it?" I snap, eyes wide.

"Dude, you need to chill out," Ryker says, mouth full of crackers.

"Listen, *dude*. Cut me some slack, will you? I'm a perimenopausal teenager with two children who needs to cook dinner and study for a chemistry final, for heaven's sake! And I'm sore from volleyball try-outs," I whine.

"Want me to DoorDash dinner?" Ryker asks, his tone softening.

"Yes… no… I don't know." I sigh. "I'm sorry, I just feel like I'm losing my mind."

My cell phone dings at the same time as my burner phone. Molly has texted me, and so has Travis.

Travis: Did you give any more thought about tonight?

Lina: No, I'm sorry. I can't tonight. I'm swamped with work. I need to make the kids dinner.

Travis: Why is it so hard for you to let me in?

Lina: It's not that easy for me, Travis. My last relationship ended horribly, and I don't trust people easily, okay?

Molly: I'm going to fail this exam tomorrow. FML.
Gemma: You and me both.
Molly: Did you do the practice quiz?
Gemma: Doing it now.
Molly: Slay.

I toss both phones to the side, retrieve my crackers from Ryker, and face my iPad toward him. "Quiz me," I demand.

"Huh?"

"Just… ask me those questions."

Ryker begins quizzing me on the periodic table of elements while I spit back answers while texting on two devices.

Molly: BTW, what do you think of Bill Gallagher?
Gemma: Who is Bill Gallagher?
Molly: SMH. F2F

I roll my eyes and type SMH and F2F in my app, only to realize that Molly could have just as quickly told me that she's shaking her head because I'm a freaking idiot for not knowing who Bill is and that she will just talk to me about it in person.

Gemma: K

I quickly answer Ryker's chemistry questions as I multitask my teenage social life in true adolescent fashion as Lucy scurries down the stairs toward the kitchen. I hold my hand up for Ryker to stop quizzing me, and thankfully, he gets the hint.

"What's all this?" Lucy asks, leaning against the counter in only a sports bra and shorts.

"Work stuff. Put some clothes on. We have company."

"Um, it's only Uncle Ryker," Lucy argues, rolling her eyes and adjusting her ponytail. "This is what I wore to cheer practice. Besides, he's gay."

"Truth," Ryker agrees, stealing the Cheez-Its and kissing Lucy's cheek.

"This is all for work?" she asks, approaching me from behind me and staring at the whiteboard.

"Yup," I say, lying easily because faking my life has become second nature.

"Missing girls?" she asks, eyes wide. "Wow, Mom, sounds like something Hallmark might pick up," she says sarcastically. "And why the two phones?"

"One is for work," I say as she reaches for it.

"Why do you need a phone for work?"

Lucy picks up my operative phone from the counter and studies it. Of course she has picked this moment to take an interest in my career. She flashes the phone at me, activating facial recognition, and my heart drops. "That's mine," I say, my tone firm. "Give it back, please."

"Who's Molly? Who's Gemma? What exam?"

"Molly is my colleague," I say. "Gemma is the new pen name my agent wants me to write under, so I'm trying it on for size. We take a personality test tomorrow. It will determine if we are working in the appropriate departments. Can I have my phone back now?"

Ryker chomps away on my crackers and raises his eyebrows, approving my lie. "Sounds boring," he chimes in.

"It is," I agree.

"Why is she talking like she's my age?" Lucy asks, scrunching her nose up and swiping out of the text.

"Because I work with twenty-year-olds, remember? Can I have it back now, please?"

"Whose Dad? What results?"

"Oh," I say, pulling the phone from her hands. "That's my boss. The girls I work with call him Dad because he's old as shit."

Ryker chokes on his crackers, and Lucy gasps. I slam my hand against my forehead, realizing that in all the chaos, I have channeled my inner Gemma, not my inner Mom.

"Mom! What is going on with you?"

"I'm sorry," I huff. "I'm exhausted," I admit. "But he is… old as shit," I say again for dramatic effect.

"I'm DoorDashing Five Guys," she says, shaking her head. "You should get some sleep. You're scaring me."

"That's fine. Just check the delivery address and make sure the app says Desert Willow Drive and not Cactus Willow," I instruct. "Max ordered something to Cactus Willow, and now it keeps coming up as our current location."

"Okay," she agrees. "Yup, good catch."

"Okay," I say, reaching up to kiss her forehead. "I love you. I'm sorry I haven't been around."

"Love you too," she says, running back up the stairs.

"That was close," Ryker sighs.

"You're telling me. I'm putting this stuff away." I say, snapping a photo of my dry-erase board before wiping it clean.

"You coming to the gym at all this week?"

"That was another life, Ry," I sigh. "Going to have to put the workouts on hold until Operation Superglue comes to a close."

"You sure?" he asks just as the doorbell rings.

"What now?" I ask Ryker like this is somehow his fault.

"Expecting anyone?"

"No," I huff, wondering who would be coming over on a Thursday evening, unannounced.

I rise and make my way to the door, my breath catching in my throat because Travis stands there, looking as sexy as ever, gripping a paper bag full of groceries. "Travis, h-hi," I stammer. "What are you doing here?"

"I came to make you and your family dinner," he says boldly. "And I'm not taking no for an answer. Smith is with his mom, and I have nothing better to do."

"I—"

"Not taking no for an answer," he repeats, moving past me and stopping when he sees Ryker seated at my kitchen island. "Oh…" he says, his demeanor shifting immediately. "You have company."

I press my hand to my forehead, realizing that Travis has never met Ryker and knows nothing about him. I sigh, wondering how this night can keep from getting any worse. "Ryker, Travis. Travis, Ryker," I say, twisting my ponytail into a messy bun and wiping the sweat from the back of my neck.

"Hey, man," Ryker says to Travis with a nod.

"Listen," Travis says, his voice low as he pulls me outside. "If you're seeing someone else, you can just tell me."

"It's not like that—"

"There is another man in your kitchen. What's it like?"

"He's my gay best friend," I blurt.

"Huh?"

"Ryker. He's gay."

"Oh."

"Yeah, oh. Like I said, I'm swamped with work. He picked up Max for me, who is failing math," I say as my voice catches in the back of my throat and I begin to sob.

"Hey," he says, placing the groceries on the ground and pulling me close. "It's okay."

"No." I sniffle. "It's not okay. I suck at my job, and I'm a horrible mother."

"No, you're not," he says, kissing my forehead. "You're a great mom. Now, would you please let me cook your dinner?"

I nod into his chest, suddenly aware that I am starving. "What are you making?"

Travis smiles, picks up the groceries, and makes his way inside. "Spaghetti and meatballs."

"Yes, please," I say, fully surrendering.

"You won't even know I'm here," he insists as he unpacks the bag in my kitchen.

I take this opportunity to collect any items on my kitchen island that could blow my Gemma cover. I reach for my burner phone, and an email notification flashes across my home screen. I swipe it open to find an email from Coach White congratulating me for making the volleyball team as an alternate, which is the best-case scenario because I will get to be close to the coach without having too much playing time. "Yes!" I cheer, pumping my fist into the air.

"What?" Ryker and Travis ask at the same time.

"I… uh, just got some good news at work. This huge project I put in for… I got it!"

"See," Travis says, coming up behind me and planting a kiss on my cheek. "Told you, you're a rock star. Now pour yourself a glass of wine and relax. You deserve it."

Chapter Sixteen

Then (2011)

I rested my elbows against the bar in a Mexican restaurant that Daphne had suggested. I glanced at my phone, realizing she was over twenty minutes late. I had ordered a prickly pear margarita, which I was carded for before the order had left my lips.

I closed my eyes and sipped my margarita, thankful for a moment to catch my breath. Jon and I purchased our first home in late August, and exactly one month later, I still hadn't unpacked everything, purchased all our furniture, or decorated like I had intended. It was a beautiful three-bedroom contemporary modern home on 1116 Desert Willow Drive in Scottsdale. Jon and I had fallen in love with it at first glance and put an offer on it right away. I was eager to put some distance between myself and Tempe, and Jon, who was working his first undercover assignment, was also grateful for separation from work to home.

However, the problem was that Jon had been working nonstop since we moved in. The undercover operation was at ASU. Since he looked young for his age, Jon was posing as a senior in college. His team had been investigating a group of college students allegedly operating one of the city's most prominent drug rings right out of their college dorm rooms. Jon was posing as a student who lived off campus, so thankfully, he didn't need to live there. But he did have to go to classes, which he dreaded more than life itself, and most of the action on campus happened after ten p.m., which meant Jon was never... ever... home.

I was happy for him. Really, I was. It was just getting increasingly difficult. The twins had turned three in November, and whoever said two was terrible was wrong. Three seemed impossible most of the time. I could barely keep up with work, parenting the twins, and managing the household—let alone finding time to write. And the worst part was I really and truly missed my husband. I missed having coffee with him in the mornings, texting throughout the day, and our nights together. I cringed, realizing I couldn't remember the last time we had made love. This thought made my stomach turn and my knees grow weak.

"Is anyone sitting here?" a man's voice asked. There was a slight ruggedness to his deep tone that felt soothing in a way I hadn't expected.

"Actually, my friend is. If she ever gets here," I said, raising my brows and shaking my head.

"No worries," he said, running his hand through his dark curls. His eyes were onyx hued and serious but softened when he smiled. "Can I sit here until she gets here? I'll buy your next drink?"

I resisted the sudden urge to tell this mysterious stranger I was married with three-year-old twins because it felt nice to pretend I was single and hadn't gotten knocked up in my twenties. "Okay," I said. "But if you don't move when she arrives, there is a solid chance she will kick your ass."

"Noted," he said, his lips curling into a soft smile as he squeezed in beside me, his arm grazing mine. "Patron and soda with a lime," he ordered. "And another for the pretty lady."

I blushed, a wave of satisfaction washing over me because he was flirting and Alter-Lina started to surface. I wasn't sure if it was the margarita talking or the lack of sex in my life, but I was interested. I was not interested in a jumping-his-bones-in-the-bathroom sort of way but enough to drop my left hand to my side so I could hide my wedding ring.

Half an hour later, Daphne had yet to arrive. She texted me apologizing, as her final year of ASU was overly demanding, and said she just submitted her project and would be there soon.

"She's on her way," I sighed to my new friend, Kurt.

"I'll be heading out soon anyway," he countered.

I liked something about Kurt, and with every smile and brush of his arm against mine, I wanted him more, which led to guilty pangs in my gut and shameful thoughts. "Early morning?" I asked.

"You betcha. I'm a senior at ASU, and this psych professor over there is way too much to handle before eight a.m."

"I hear you," I laughed. "I was a student at ASU… in another life."

"Did you graduate already?"

"Not quite," I answered. But avoiding his question made me realize how much I liked him. I rubbed my hands over my arms and squeezed myself gently, wondering who I thought I was and how I got to this place. I was flirting at a bar with a stranger while my husband was out working hard to support my family. This action went against my morals on way too many levels.

"You cold?" he asked, gently touching my back. This sent electric shock waves through my body, and I thought I might melt into a puddle as he leaned in closer to whisper in my ear. "I bet I could warm you up," he cooed.

I sat upright, and my shoulders stiffened. "Excuse me?"

"What? What did I say?"

I blushed, wondering if I might have heard him wrong. But I knew I had heard correctly when he leaned in again and told me he could have me back to his dorm room and naked within the hour. "Dude," I hissed. "That's the lamest pickup line *ever*."

"Sorry," he snapped, hands raised in surrender. "You just seemed into me. I'm totally into you."

"You don't know anything about me," I barked, holding my left hand to his face, revealing my wedding band and engagement ring.

"What?" he asked, confused. "You don't think I saw that thing before I sat down? Made me want you more."

"Ew," I muttered, wiping a tear from my eye. This guy was a complete asshole, and I had been interested in him. But as I sipped the last of my margarita, Daphne bounced into the crowded room with an apologetic smile. It occurred to me that I wasn't into Kurt; I liked how Kurt made me feel. And I said a silent prayer that I would never allow myself to fall into a trap like that again. Jon might be busy, overworked, and utterly exhausted, but he was Jon, and he was *mine*. Sure, I could play the victim card and cry about the fact I missed out on some fun during my college years, but the truth was I wouldn't change a thing. I loved Jon, and I loved my children. And hopefully, someday, I would forget what happened in the bar that night I slid my wedding ring under my butt so that some loser could offer me sex in his college dorm.

Kurt threw a handful of cash down on the bar as I waved to Daphne. "Daph!" I called to her.

"Hey, girl! I'm so sorry."

"No worries. Daphne, Kurt, Kurt, Daphne. He's leaving," I stated boldly.

"No introductions needed," she sang, clearly annoyed.

"Nope," Kurt agreed, pressing his lips together and laughing with his eyes.

"You know each other?" I asked, my mouth gaped open.

The silence between them spoke volumes, and I shook my head. "Nice," I said to Kurt.

"Oh, I'm sure he hit on you," she scoffed as if he were invisible.

"I'm standing right here, ladies."

"Is he the guy?" I asked, eyes wide.

"What guy?" Kurt asked in confusion.

"Sure is," Daphne said, her cheeks turning pink. She raised her hand to me, held up her thumb and forefinger, pinching them together to mark one inch, and whispered, "Teeny tiny."

"I'm outta here," Kurt grunted in defeat.

"Don't hit on married women next time," Daphne advised.

"Maybe tell her not to hit on me," he said as he stormed away.

My cheeks flushed, and my eyes welled with tears. It was evident he wasn't too far off. "It's true," I sniffed. "For a moment, I was pretending what it would be like if…" My heart broke, and I couldn't finish my sentence.

"You would never do that to Jon, Lina. I know you."

"I know. It felt so nice to be someone else for a few minutes, you know? Ugh, I'm a horrible person."

"No, you're not. You're the best person I know."

"I just… I need to change… not with Jon but with me. There aren't enough hours in the day, and I want to do more with my life. There's just no time."

"I can help you with the twins."

"No, you can't." I chuckled. "You're busy too. My mom suggested day care, but it's so expensive. My parents had to help us with the down payment on our house, and I just… I feel bad asking them for more help."

"Well, day care a few times a week could be good for them," she suggested. "You're a great mom, Lina. You will know what to do."

I smiled in agreement, cupping her hand in mine, so thankful to have a friend like her. Someone who loved me unconditionally and who saw me for who I was, not who I was trying to be. And I realized then, in that moment, I had a friend for life in her. "I love you, Daphne."

"I love you too, girl. I love you too."

Chapter Seventeen

Now

I adjust the rim of my orange-and-red Emerson Academy Heat Waves baseball cap over my gigantic sunglasses as I sit perched on the football field bleachers, Molly by my side.

"Tell me why we are watching the cheerleaders, not the football game?" Molly asks, sipping from her water bottle. And why do you look like a Russian spy?"

"I don't look like a spy," I counter. "I don't want to get a sunburn," I lie. *Or be recognized by my children.* "And I'm thinking of trying out for cheer in the spring, and I'm curious."

"Curious about what? If they're any good? 'Cause they aren't."

"I can see that," I agree.

I wipe a bead of sweat from under my eyes and sigh. Stalking the cheer team had been Jon's brilliant idea, as our Mr. White lead had come up short. After stalking George White for over a week, Jon had learned that he was a member of Planet Fitness and went to the gym religiously every Saturday. Therefore, Gemma Mendoza was assigned a workout at Planet Fitness.

Jon's plan had been simple. I would work out alongside Mr. White, wearing something provocative while seeing if he would put the moves on me. After all, our working theory for Mr. White was that he may have had sexual relations with Alanna, Chloe, and Teresa.

After swiping Lucy's tiny hot-pink shorts and matching Lululemon sports bra, I paraded around that gym like a teenage girl at the mall. When Mr. White did squats, so did Gemma. When he worked his triceps, so did Gemma until it was nearly impossible for him to ignore me.

"Miss Mendoza?" he finally asked.

"Oh, hi! Wow, Mr. White, I didn't even see you there!" I lied. "I didn't know you worked out at Planet Fitness."

"I could say the same about you," he said, clearly out of breath. He wore black workout shorts and a gray tank top blotched with sweat patches, and he smelled like BO and cheap body spray.

I leaned over the bench, squeezing my boobs together as they overflowed out of Lucy's sports bra, and the man barely flinched. His eyes stayed locked on mine for the duration of my test. "Yeah, well, now that I'm on the team as an alternate, I need to put the work in," I said, just as Jon and I had rehearsed.

"Good thinking," he said, grabbing his leg for a quadricep stretch. "Don't get discouraged that you are an alternate. I had to cut ten girls. You truly have potential, Gemma."

I moved down to the ground on all fours, gliding smoothly through cat and cow yoga poses as I did often with Ryker. Only this time, I stuck my butt out a little extra. "Do you think you could help me outside of school?" I asked, batting my eyelashes.

"I'm going to need you to be more specific," he said, clearing his throat and reaching for his other leg.

"Like extra help or one-on-one coaching," I explained, sliding closer.

"I don't work with athletes outside of school. But have your dad call me. I know someone that would work with you. Have a great weekend, Miss Mendoza." And with that, he had turned away from me and headed toward the locker room, making it more apparent than ever that he was not our guy.

Jon and I had to go back to the drawing board. If Mr. White was the scumbag we thought he was, he would have put the moves on Gemma.

But he did not, which means whoever is doing this is still out there, and we need solid leads. Jon and I had spent hours in his office that Saturday night discussing other possible avenues. We ordered Chinese takeout from one of our old favorite restaurants and brainstormed for hours. Jon was impressed with my ability to place the girls in the same social circles and sports teams. For example, Alanna was the cheer team captain but also participated in the ensemble of the school's production of *Grease* during her sophomore year at Emerson. In that same production, Teresa, the most-recent missing girl, played the lead role of Sandy. Also, Teresa, Alanna, and Chloe either tried out for cheerleading at some point or managed the school's football team. Because of this, Jon and I decided it would be appropriate for me to observe the cheerleaders at the football game and to show some interest in the sport, in case I needed to get closer to some of the girls.

This seemed like a fantastic plan until I looked at my calendar for the week and realized that for the first time in the history of the twins' school, Coronado High would be playing the Emerson Academy Heat Waves. Because why not? And this would be fine if my children were not on the team. Even though Max was on JV, he still needed to dress for varsity games, and Lucy made varsity cheerleading as a freshman, so both twins would be standing on the sidelines on the away side.

I begged Jon to postpone this mission one week, so I wouldn't blow my cover and so I could support my children from their side of the field, but Jon insisted that would be risky too. It would be better if Jon sat on the away side and rooted for the kids, and I went to the game as Gemma. "We've got this," he said reassuringly. He placed his hand on my shoulder while he said it, and then I realized it had been over five years since he touched me that way. This had sent a shiver down my spine, followed by ripples of nausea through my stomach.

Operation Superglue

I hadn't expected to see Molly at the game, and when she offered to sit and watch with me, I was happy for her company. Now, as we watch the cheerleaders, I regret taking both cell phones with me. Even though they are both tucked away in my crossbody purse, it still feels risky. I can feel the pulsating of my personal cell phone from my bag, and it's driving me crazy that I can't look at it. I agreed to go out with Travis tonight, and I know he is asking for details, but the last person I want to see right now is Travis Mullins. It's hard enough to lie to Max, Lucy, and my parents, but adding Travis to the mix makes me feel like such a big, fat liar—because I am.

"Are you friends with any of them?" I ask Molly, gesturing to the cheer team.

"Not really. I've had a class with one or two, but that's about it. Hey," she says, changing the subject. "You haven't accepted my follow request on Insta."

"Oh, really? I didn't see the request," I lie. I had intentionally not accepted her request because I was nervous she would see through the faux profile. It's true that Molly isn't best friends with me as Lina, but there are pieces of me that have trickled over into my role as the Gemma who she has come to know and even love. "Give me your phone," she demands, unzipping my purse.

"I've got it," I say, pulling away from her. I reach into my purse and pull out a phone, overly grateful it's my undercover phone and not my personal cell. "Here you go."

"Why are you acting so sus?" she asks, swiping open my Instagram app.

"Who's acting sus?" I shrug.

"Here," she says, ignoring me. "I accepted it."

"Thanks," I say, taking it back. "I don't have many followers from Emerson."

"You're better off," she huffs. "Some strange walks of life here."

"Funny you should say that," I say, carefully choosing my words. "I was changing for PE on Friday, and I overheard some people gossiping about some girls from Emerson that have all run away."

"You're just hearing about this now?" she asks, sipping her water and lifting her sunglasses.

"My dad mentioned it to me once, but I didn't have the details."

"I don't think they ran away," she sighs.

Be cool, Lina. "What do you mean?"

"My dad talks about it *a lot*."

"And he doesn't think they ran away?"

"Nope. But the cops are no help anymore, and I think he's giving up. At this point, if he continues to push, it will look bad on the school," she mocks, rolling her eyes.

"Wow," I say. "That's so scary."

"My mom doesn't let him talk about it at dinner anymore. She wants it to go away. It scares her, you know? Thinking that something like that could happen to me or my sister."

"You have a sister?" I ask, wondering why I haven't asked her about this before. I know she has a very unplanned baby brother named Gavin, but I only know this because she constantly complains about having to watch him.

"I'm one of four," she says, clapping for Emerson as the team's wide receiver runs the ball into the end zone for a touchdown. "I have an older brother, Emmett, who goes to ASU, a little sister, June, a sophomore at Emerson, and a six-month-old baby brother named Gavin."

"Wow," I say, eyes wide, wondering how agonizing it would be to start over with a new baby while parenting teens. "Your mother is *busy*."

"Huh?"

"Oh," I say, shoulders stiffening. "I just mean, I am an only child. I'm sure it's busy."

"It was busy before the Broken Condom Baby. Now it's just chaos."

"The Broken Condom Baby?" I cackle hysterically.

"Yeah, my parents said they used protection, but it broke." She shrugs, disgusted.

"I guess it happens." *At least they tried to use protection*, I think but then also wonder why Dean Turner didn't consider a vasectomy.

"I bet they didn't use anything and are just trying to scare me," she explains. "Have you ever done it?"

"Done what?" I ask, eyes across the field on my daughter as she completes a perfect tumbling pass. I bite my lip, resisting the urge to clap for her.

"Sex. Have you ever had sex?"

I feel the heat rise to my cheeks at her unexpected inquiry. I hadn't considered how I would answer this question, but I should have seen it coming. The truth is, I lost my virginity senior year to my ex, so responding yes to her question wouldn't be that big of a lie. But with that decision comes a certain amount of regret. There is part of me that wishes I had waited, even though I was in love. "Yes," I say. "I have."

"With who?"

"An ex-boyfriend back in Florida."

"What was his name?"

My brain becomes machine-gunned with lists of names, from people I know to favorite movie characters, and I am again furious with myself for not preparing for this better, and for some reason, all I can come up with is Jack from *Titanic*. "Jack," I say firmly. "Jack Dawson."

I hold my breath in anticipation of her response and half expect her to laugh. "Sounds familiar," she says. "Is he hot?"

"Oh yeah," I say, reliving Jack and Rose's sex scene. "Totally."

"I haven't done it yet," she admits. "I don't like anyone enough... except—"

"Bill," I finish for her because Molly has been obsessing over a guy named Bill for weeks.

"Yup. If the moment were right, I would sleep with Bill," she affirms.

"Just... be careful," I say, trying hard to hide my mom tone.

"Why?" she asks. "Do you regret it?"

"Maybe a little," I admit. I think about my experience with men, and the truth is I'm not sure what I do and don't regret. Would I have been happier if Jon were my first? Would I be better if Jon never existed? Other than Travis, there was only one other man I had slept with since Jon, and there was no emotional connection there at all. But the times with Jon, the times with Jon *before* he ruined my life, were mind-blowing and amazing in ways I could never put into words. "Just... make sure you love him first. And maybe get on the birth control pill."

"Yes, Mom," she laughs and nudges me.

Molly and I sit in silence until I can't take the awkwardness anymore. "Did you know any of the girls?"

"What girls?"

"The missing girls."

"Not well. But I knew of them. When Alanna ran away, it was sad. She seemed like she had it all together all the time. She volunteered at the soup kitchen monthly and was starting college in the fall."

"The soup kitchen?"

"Oh, yes," she says with a laugh. "We are required to serve a ton of community service hours before graduating. But Alanna did it even though hers were done."

I resist the urge to whip out my phone and take notes. "That is sad."

"And then, when Chloe ran away, too, my dad got *obsessed*. It was all he could talk about at the dinner table. It upset my mother, probably because she was pregnant and her hormones were raging."

"Ha, probably." I snicker harder than I should.

"Chloe was captain of the volleyball team and had a brother with special needs that she helped care for. She wouldn't have just abandoned him, you know?"

"It sounds more like kidnappings," I agree, hoping I haven't taken the conversation too far. "Were there more girls? Or just the two?"

"Teresa was the third. She ran away in the spring."

I nod because this is when the school hired Jon. "Your dad must have lost it at that point," I say, realizing that we need to somehow talk to Dean Turner about this if Jon hasn't already.

"She was the sweetest of the three. She had huge dreams of being on Broadway. Why would she just up and leave? She had just been accepted to a school in NYC."

"What does your dad think?"

"He—" she starts but stops. "OMG, Gemma, it's Bill."

"Oh," I nod, disappointed that my interrogation has ended.

"He's coming over here!" she whispers.

"Hey, Molls," a tall, slender teen with red hair and freckles says as he approaches the bleachers and smiles at her.

"Hey," she says, trying to sound chill. "This is my friend Gemma. She's new."

"Hey, Gemma."

"Hey." I smile back, eyes on Lucy's team as the cheerleaders perform their halftime routine and Lucy flies in a stunt I most definitely didn't approve. I hold my breath until her feet are safely planted back on the ground.

"Good game, huh?" he says, more than asks. "Up by twelve at the half. Can't beat that."

"How's your brother doing out there?" Molly asks. "His twin brother is the QB for Emerson," she brags.

"Awesome," I sing, thinking about my twins, who are out on the field without the support of their mother.

"Want to grab some fries and a Coke?" he asks her.

"Me? Yeah, I would love to. Want to come, Gemma?"

"I'm good. You go," I smile encouragingly.

"Okay. Text me."

"I will."

I watch them walk away, and I feel mom proud of Molly. They are at most twenty yards from me before I pull my personal cell out of my bag and scroll through missed texts, mainly from Travis.

Lina: Tonight isn't going to work after all. I'm sorry. I'm swamped at work.

I swipe out of the text and open a new text to Jon.

Lina: I've got a new angle. Meet tonight? Your office?
Jon: 7:00 p.m.?
Lina: Perfect. I'll bring dinner.

Chapter Eighteen

Then (2011)

I knew parenting twins would be challenging, but nobody prepared me for how exhausting it would be when my three-year-old babies caught the stomach bug while my husband lived the life of a college kid undercover. It had never been so apparent that I had become a single mom until that night.

I had survived forty-eight hours of Max and Lucy experiencing every GI symptom possible, but it was finally over. They were tucked into their beds and were sleeping—finally and just in time for Halloween, which was the next day. My mother, who had come to help me with my sick babies, was asleep in my bed upstairs. I was curled up on my sofa, watching *One Tree Hill* on DVD, desperately needing a shower, when there was an unexpected knock at my door.

The clock on my TV read 10:30 p.m., and I wasn't planning on having visitors. Jon had a key, so he wouldn't be knocking. I adjusted my pajama pants around my waist and approached the front door. I swung it open, shocked to see Daphne standing on the other side. "What's wrong?" I asked because it was very much unlike Daphne to come over unannounced. Daphne remained silent, which was eerie on so many levels. She pushed past me, heading directly to my fridge. "Daph?" I asked again. "You're scaring me."

"I need a drink," she demanded, flinging my refrigerator open.

"I have wine," I said, gesturing to the living room.

"I need something stronger."

"Um, I have some vodka. But the only mixer I can offer you is Pedialyte."

"Funny," she muttered under her breath. "I'll drink it straight up."

"What's wrong with you?" I asked nervously, as I had never seen Daphne like this. She was pale, jittery, and meant business. Her blond hair looked messy and matted in the back, like it hadn't been brushed. I had only ever seen it like that when she first woke up. "Were you in bed?" I asked.

"Yes," she admitted, pouring vodka into her glass.

"Daphne, what's wrong?"

Daphne chugged the straight alcohol and leaned against my kitchen island. "How are the twins?" she asked.

"What? They are fine… now. Stop changing the subject. Out with it."

Daphne took another sip of vodka and passed it to me. "You're going to need this."

"No!" I snapped, my frustration growing stronger by the second. "I'm not drinking that. Not until you tell me what's going on. Are you sick? Did something happen?"

"Sit down," she said, gesturing to the barstool.

"Okay, Daph, whatever you say." I sat on the stool and leaned my elbows against the counter, adjusting the sleeves of Jon's hoodie over my hands. "This has been the longest week of my life," I sighed.

"I know. Which is why I don't want to be the one to have to tell you this."

"Tell me what?" I wailed. I rubbed my sweatshirt-covered hands over my eyes, wishing to curl back on the couch and press Play on my DVD.

"I was scrolling through Facebook," she said, her tone serious and voice shaky. "And I came across something not so great."

"Told you not to go on that crap." I sighed. Daphne had been trying to get me to open a social media account for months, and I was late to the party. I had tried MySpace and wasn't a fan. Whatever this Facebook thing was seemed like more hassle than anything.

"Let me get this out," she begged.

"Okay," I sighed with a shake of my head.

"Lina… This is… It's not about me. It's about you. And… Jon."

"Jon?"

"Yeah, your frat-boy husband."

Everything froze in that instant. As Daphne spoke, her mouth moved and words were spoken, but I couldn't hear her. This had to be a nightmare. Daphne was the only one I had told about Jon's undercover operation, and it had only been in case she bumped into him on campus, so this hadn't been about spotting him in a class or at a party. This had to be severe, and this realization sent me downward spiraling. "Wait," I said, holding up my hand. "Slow down and start from the beginning."

"I'm friends with this girl on Facebook. She lives in my building, and I have a few classes with her."

"Okay?"

"Her name is Hilary," she explained, her eyes welling with tears. "She's been talking to me for weeks about a guy she's seeing. She's… She's gone into detail about the sex. Way too much information for my taste, but I listened. I figured it was just some random dude from ASU."

A heavy pit formed in my gut as a wave of nausea flooded me. As Daphne spoke, my life with Jon flashed before my eyes. It was dread mixed with denial and anger. Lots of anger. "It's Jon, isn't it?" I asked, my words catching in the back of my throat.

"I know he's undercover, Lina. But… you're married. He's your *husband*. Did you guys talk about how you would handle this? I'm sure he's just doing his job and…"

Daphne's voice trailed off, and I reached for her vodka glass, shooting the straight alcohol down my throat, the burning sensation numbing my anger momentarily. "So, you're saying," I said, pouring more vodka into the glass, "that the guy Hilary has been having sex with could be my husband."

"Here's the thing, Lina. Hilary is one of those girls who makes everything seem more significant than it really is. She told us her dad made millions of dollars producing *BattleBots*, but the reality was that her dad made a ton of money in real estate but was a contestant on *BattleBots*."

She said this like it somehow justified something, but her attempt failed miserably. "So my husband is sleeping with a college student for work."

"We don't know that."

"What do we know?" I asked, my voice increasing in volume. "What made you think it's Jon?"

"The infinity tattoo, for starters," she mouthed more than spoke.

"Anyone could have that tattoo," I argued.

"And there's this," she said, flashing her phone at me.

My heart stopped beating, and I held my breath as I took Daphne's phone from her. There, staring back at me, was my husband with his arms around Hilary. He wore jeans and a black ASU shirt with a matching backward cap. He stared into the camera as he smiled, his blue eyes gleaming joyfully. Hilary wore a short jean skirt, knee-high cowboy boots, and a red halter top. Her long, blond hair was pulled over one shoulder, and one hand cupped the side of Jon's face, her side profile visible while she stared at him lovingly. The caption read, *Night out with my love.*

"Lina, say something," Daphne begged, placing one hand on my back. "This could all be for his case," she said hopefully. "Either way… I think you need to talk to him about it. He's coming home tomorrow?"

Blood boiled through my veins as my fists tightened and tiny beads of sweat formed on my forehead. Shock rippled through my body in long and pulsating waves. I was in pain... like someone had reached inside my body, removed my heart, laid it down on my kitchen island, and beat it with a sledgehammer, banging it repeatedly. All the while, all I could think about was trick-or-treating was the next day, and Jon promised to come home for that. We brainstormed our costumes over the phone a couple of weeks back, right around when Jon stopped coming home at night. Jon was going to be Peter Pan, and I, Wendy. Lucy was going to dress as Tinkerbell and Max, a pirate. I was devastated when the twins got sick because I had been looking forward to Halloween. I wanted, more than anything, to be a family. The four of us, together.

"What's going on tonight?" I asked Daphne, my tone steady.

"What do you mean?"

I dropped her phone on the counter. "You know what I mean. Where's the party?"

"Lina—"

"Don't mess with me, Daph. I know that Jon has been staying at a frat house. Is it the one we used to go to?"

Daphne nodded, her eyes welling with tears. "Lina—"

I bolted up the stairs, Daphne following close behind. I tiptoed around my sleeping mother as I reached for a pair of jeans from the floor and pulled them up under Jon's hoodie.

"Lina, think about this for a minute, please! We don't know the details... and Jon's operation—"

"What's there to think about?" I whispered. "I don't care about his *operation*. We're going... to the party... *now*."

"Lina, you smell like puke and Lysol."

"Give me five minutes," I huffed, whipping off Jon's hoodie and hurrying to the bathroom, knowing deep down that my life as I knew it would never be the same.

Chapter Nineteen

Now

Another week has passed, and Jon and I are still far from solving Operation Superglue. After taking my advice, Jon called Dean Orson Turner to follow up on any information he might have. Jon was careful to speak with him over the phone so he wouldn't blow his cover as the art sub.

Unfortunately, although Dean Turner had been "obsessed," as Molly put it, he didn't have any more intel for Jon about the case. He agreed that the cops hadn't been helpful, and he was convinced all three students were indeed kidnapped. He was happy to hear that someone was looking into the case, leading to our next dead end and sleepless nights trying to assemble the missing pieces, focusing more than ever on the timeline. Alanna disappeared first last fall, then Chloe in the winter, and Teresa in the spring. It couldn't be a coincidence that their disappearances were spread out like that, could it?

I was now playing volleyball as an alternate and expressing interest in cheer for the spring and the high school musical production of *Beauty and the Beast*. I was also scheduled to volunteer at the soup kitchen and on the school dance committee for the Halloween party, a holiday I've started to hate for obvious reasons.

Molly and Bill have been spending lots of time together, meaning she and I are together less. I'm determined to finish our conversation about the missing girls, but there needs to be a suitable time for that to happen naturally. Aside from that, Bill's twin brother started showing interest in me, which was creepy and inappropriate on many levels, but because of the change in my friendships, Jon thought it would be an excellent time to set Gemma up on TikTok and Snapchat just in case anyone wants to befriend me who could also be a lead.

Signing up for Snapchat has been one of the most confusing undertakings of my life. At first, I thought it was simple, like navigating Instagram or Facebook, but upon further examination, I realized I couldn't have been more wrong. I had become friends with Molly first and realized quickly that this app served more like a text message with pictures... pictures that disappeared unless you save them. I also can't quite get the hang of TikTok, and even though my Gemma profiles are private, I worry about the twins stumbling across them.

Lucy and Oliver have continued spending time together, and Max has settled in nicely with friends from football on this Friday evening, so I am taking full advantage of my free time and having drinks and dinner with Ryker and Daphne, something I haven't done in ages.

"So, how is it working with the infamous Jon Cote?" Ryker asks through bites of taco.

"It is what it is." I shrug, because I don't know what else to say.

"Do we still hate him?" Daphne inquires, sipping the last of her margarita.

"We will always hate him," I say bitterly. "But he's good at his job, he has my back, and he's a good dad. So, there's that. And he's an excellent listener for my Gemma drama," I laugh.

I poke at my refried beans and smile. True, Jon and I would never be husband and wife again, but there is this subtle peace that has come over me over the past month of Operation Superglue. Jon listens when I speak to him, like *truly* listens, which is refreshing because I sense how much he has matured over the years. And although I have found comfort through my friendships with Daphne, Ryker, and Travis, I am realizing that Jon will always have a special place in my heart. I bite into my burrito, thinking back to the taco night in Jon's apartment and remembering it fondly for the first time in years.

I sense an awkward silence, and as I look up at my friends between bites of my burrito, they gape at me, eyes wide, with accusatory stares. "What?" I ask innocently. "We work together. So what?"

"You *totally* sound like you hate him," Daphne says with a raise of her brow.

"Totally," Ryker agrees sarcastically. "How's Travis?"

"I…" My voice trails off.

"Exactly," he says, satisfied.

"I haven't had much time to spend with Travis. I'm too busy working on my volleyball serve."

"Facts," Daphne agrees. "Travis is hot. You *should* make time for him."

"I know," I concur. "I just hate the lying."

"Ask Jon if you can tell him about Operation Superglue," Ryker suggests.

"Oh gosh, no."

"That would mean talking to Jon about Travis," Ryker counters.

"Hey, Ry, how's Alex?" I ask.

"Touché."

"Exactly."

I turn my attention to my two cell phones on the restaurant's table, my burner phone dinging with texts from Molly and my personal cell with messages from Jon.

Molly: IMHO, you should give Hank a chance.

"Anyone know what IMHO stands for?" I ask Ryker and Daphne. They look at me like I have ten heads and continue a conversation they started about Alex's latest DM to Ryker, so I take out my app and learn what it means. *In my honest opinion.*

Gemma: IDK.
Molly: I'd totally ship you with him.

I stare at my phone, wide-eyed. "Why can't teenagers speak English?" I wail. "Somebody Google this," I say, flashing my screen at them.

"After careful investigation, it means she wants to set you up with him," Daphne explains. "Like, I'd totally ship you with Travis."

"So why doesn't she just say that?"

Gemma: LOL.
Molly: Party @Zack's is on. Going 2B fire. 🔥
Gemma: The quarterback?
Molly: Yes. You're coming. It's next Friday. His parents are out of town.

"Great," I sigh. "Add drinking with minors to my resume."

"Do you have to go?" Daphne asks. "It seems... risky."

I study her, knowing what she is thinking without her needing to say it. She's thinking of that night... the night we found Jon on campus at the frat house. My stomach turns just thinking about it. "It's not like that," I reassure her. "Each girl has a connection to Zack, the quarterback."

"What kind of connection?" Ryker asks.

"Teresa and Chloe both dated him, for starters. And Alanna was friends with his older sister. I would be crazy to not follow up on this."

I switch phones and text Jon, explaining that I was invited to a party at Molly's boyfriend's house. "How the heck do they even get beer? And can I be liable if we get caught?"

"Does Gemma have an ID?" Daphne asks.

"No. I don't have a Gemma ID."

"So, if the cops bust the party, just say you lost it," she suggests.

"You have a better social life than your children." Ryker chuckles.

As if on cue, my phone rings, and it is a call from Lucy. "That's strange. She never calls. She usually just texts," I say, swiping the call open.

"Lucy? Is everything okay?"

There is soft whimpering on the other end of the line and then, "Mom!" Lucy wails. "I need you. Where are you?"

I leap to my feet and grab my purse from the back of my chair. "I'm out with Daphne and Ryker. What's wrong?"

"I need you, Mom," she says between sobs.

"Where are you?"

"I'm at home."

"I'll be there in ten," I say, ending the call and tossing a handful of cash on the table. "It's Lucy," I say, my voice trembling. "Something's wrong. I have to go."

"Go," they both say in unison.

"Bye," I say, kissing them both and exiting the restaurant, saying a silent prayer that everything is okay with my daughter.

***

Lucy and I are curled up on the couch two hours later, sharing a pint of Ben and Jerry's Phish Food, watching reruns of *Gilmore Girls*, which we often do together. Only this time, we have already gone through a box of tissues.

"I can't believe this," Lucy wails.

"It's going to be okay," I say again for what feels like the millionth time. "Heartbreak sucks," I say because it does. "Are you ready to talk about it?"

"No," she says, eyes focused on the TV.

"I want to help you, sweetie. I can't do that if I don't know what happened."

"He's with someone else," she sobbed. "That's why he broke up with me."

"Oh," I say, a pit growing in the depths of my gut. I know how you feel, I think.

There is a knock on the door, and I breathe a sigh of relief because my reinforcements have finally arrived. "Who is that?" she asks.

"It's Dad."

"Dad? *My* dad?"

"Yes, your dad."

"But you hate him."

"I don't hate him. We've had our differences but…"

"So, you told him?"

"Well, yeah… You were so upset on the phone that I had no idea what was happening. It's unlocked!" I call from the couch, sitting with one arm around my daughter while the other is wrapped around a pint of ice cream.

Jon flies through the front door, a concerned expression plastered across his panicked face. "Lucy," he says, relieved she is in one piece. "What happened?"

Lucy's bottom lip quivers, and she bursts into tears. "Daddy," she wails.

Without hesitation, Jon runs over to the couch on the other side of Lucy. She reaches up, locking her arms around his neck, tears flowing freely. "Want me to kick his ass?" he asks.

"No," she sniffs. "Don't even think about it."

"What happened, Baby?" he asks, wiping her tears with his thumb and index finger.

"He cheated on me with Brooke," she moans between sobs.

"I'm so sorry," he says, holding her close and not taking his eyes off mine. His cheeks turn a crimson red, and I can't tell if he's upset for Lucy or if this is a bit more personal for him. "Did he have anything to say for himself?"

"I... I can't tell you." She sniffles.

"You can tell us anything," I reassure her.

"We went to a party last week. There was drinking... and things got physical with us. I didn't sleep with him, but I came close... and then he expected it again... and when I told him I didn't want to, he slept with Brooke... some girl he met on Snap."

"On what?" Jon asks, clearly confused.

"Snapchat," I clarify.

Jon makes a fist and pounds it against his leg. "I'm going to fu—"

I hold my hand up and interrupt Jon. "You did the right thing," I reassure her. "It's important to stand your ground. If you weren't ready, then he should have respected that."

"I'm sorry I drank at the party, you guys," she says, blowing her nose into a tissue. She snuggles up between Jon and me, and for a moment, I'm so overcome with emotion, with Lucy between Jon and me, that I myself become emotional. I steal a tissue from Lucy and dab my eyes as guilt begins to take over, and I regret not being home more.

"I really want to kill him." Jon grunts, running his fingers through Lucy's tear-matted tresses.

"Don't, Dad," she scolds. "I love him. And now you're going to ground me forever and you want to… You want to kill him."

"Listen," I say softly. "We love you. You will make some not-so-great choices, and there will be consequences."

"Am I grounded?"

"Um, yeah, probably," I sigh. "You can't be drinking. You aren't even sixteen. But no matter what… there is nothing you could ever say or do to make me love you less, baby girl."

"I love you, Mommy."

I kiss her forehead, and she cries into my neck—huge, gut-wrenching sobs. My heart breaks for her, but it isn't her pain that knocks the wind out of me. It's Jon's stare, locked on mine and holding on to every word I speak like it's gospel, and I can't help but wonder if he's wondering why I couldn't muster up that sort of unconditional forgiveness for him.

Chapter Twenty

Then (2011)

"Lina, think about what you're doing," Daphne pleaded from behind me as I trudged up the driveway of the frat house. Drunk college students in various Halloween costumes played beer pong and flip cup while others drank from an ice luge and mastered keg stands. Techno dance music blasted from the garage as half-naked coeds moved to the beat, clearly intoxicated and having the time of their lives.

"So, this is what my husband has been up to while I nurse our sick children back to health," I hissed. I hadn't seen Jon outside, so I assumed he would be inside, where he had lived for the past month, according to Hailey's Facebook page.

Stalking Hailey on Facebook on the ride over had been a mistake. I had gone from mad and confused to outright enraged. Hailey wasn't just hooking up with my husband. She was in love with him. According to Facebook, he was her world, and she was his. A small part of me assumed this was a fake relationship but only a tiny fraction. The rest of me, the part that felt betrayed, used, and left behind, was irrational. If this relationship was part of the job, he should have been more careful with social media. How selfish could he be? He had to know that this would get back to me. Was he so far under that he stopped caring? Had he forgotten about us? Or did he care more about his job and this drug bust than his children?

My fingers trembled as I opened the front door, and waves of stale beer and weed mixed with body odor and cheap cologne struck my face. "Jon?" I called out, pushing past kids my age but feeling like an imposter.

"Lina, please!" Daphne tugged at my arm. "Let's go home. Call him tomorrow. Nothing good is going to come out of this."

"What was his undercover name?" I asked her, ignoring her plea. "What did it say on Facebook?"

"Hilary posted about Mason. Mason Andrews."

"Excuse me," I said, frantically tapping drunk college kids until someone noticed me. My heart rate increased as a muscular guy with black frizzy hair and wide sideburns stopped short.

"Are you okay?" he slurred, looking from Daphne to me and back again.

"No." I laughed a bit on the hysterical side. "I'm not okay. I'm looking for Mason. Mason Andrews."

"What do you want with Mace?"

"Mace?" I chortled. "Mace?"

"She needs to talk to him, that's all," Daphne chimed in.

I took a deep breath and counted to five, something my father had taught me when I was younger. It didn't always calm my anxiety but helped me think clearly. I would have to play this right if I wanted to see Jon. Frat boys don't sell each other out, and for that reason and that reason alone, I needed to calm down. I tucked a strand of hair behind my ear and placed a hand on the frat boy's chest. "I didn't want to ruin the surprise," I cooed. "He invited me here tonight," I explained, tracing my fingers down to his abdomen and back up again. "He hired us. He said that you guys were looking for a good time?"

"Good God," Daphne gasped. I elbowed her in the side, and she stood up straighter. "Yeah," she consented. "We're the entertainment."

This caught Frat Boy's attention because he grabbed me by the waist and pressed me hard against him. "I'm Owen," he said through his drunk and seductive smile, the whiskey on his breath stale and potent. "And I'm *always* looking for a good time. Especially with someone like you."

Relieved that my plan was working, I decided to take things further. "Hi, Owen," I sang, unzipping my hoodie enough for my cleavage to peek through. I pushed against him, stood on my toes, and whispered, "I'm all yours for the night," I declared with a smile. "I just need Jo—Mason... I need Mace to compensate me."

"We get the money up front," Daphne insisted.

"Of course," he said, touching my lower back and grabbing my ass.

"Take me to Mace, then," I demanded.

"Right this way, ladies," Owen slurred.

Owen guided us down a long hallway and up a short set of stairs, where he braced himself against the railing for support. "Mace is in his room," he explained, gesturing to the second door on the right.

"Thanks," I said, pushing past him, my heart rate increasing by the second.

"I'll get him—"

"I'll take it from here," I said, my knees growing weaker and my stomach twisting in a knot. I twisted the doorknob, half expecting it to be locked, but it opened quickly, too easily.

"Jon?" I called, entering the undersized, unlit room. It smelled of dirty laundry, sweaty guys, and... sex. I hadn't realized that sex had an odor until that moment, but it did. Something stuck to my flip-flop as I tiptoed into Jon's room. I picked it up and cringed in disgust at the condom wrapper in my hand.

Daphne flicked the light on as the voice of a startled female screeched, "Close the door!"

I stared down at my feet only to find my husband laying on a rickety, filthy, extra-long twin mattress, butt naked. And underneath him was Hilary, hands gripping his shoulders, ironically enough, right smack down on his infinity tattoo. Her bare-naked legs were wrapped around his torso.

"Jon!" I wailed. I leaped forward and began pounding my fists into his back, the uninvited tears flowing harder and faster with each punch.

"Lina!" Daphne cried, trying to yank me off him with all her might.

"They said they were hookers, man," Owen shouted. "Who the hell is Jon?"

"*He's* Jon!" I cried. "He's Jon!" I repeated as I pounded my fists into him again.

"What the…" Owen's voice trailed off as Jon rolled off Hilary, grasping my wrists in his hands.

"Please," he begged, eyes enraged, silently praying for me to back off.

"I hate you!" I shrieked, punching him in the chest.

Jon released my hands and stepped backward, shaking his head. I struggled to stay focused on his eyes, not letting mine drop below his waist or to Hailey, who pulled a sheet over her naked chest. "Who is she?" Hailey demanded.

"I don't know," Jon insisted.

"You don't know? She seems to know who you are."

"She's calling me Jon!" He laughed, tossing his head back in amusement.

"Is she an ex-girlfriend?" Hailey asked, glancing from me to Daphne and back again.

Daphne took my hand and gestured toward the door.

"*Girlfriend?* Try wife," I spat. "I'm his wife."

"Wife?" Owen grunted, crossing his arms over his chest.

"We have twins," I add.

"How… How can you be married with twins if you…" Owen put the pieces together before the words were finished leaving his lips. "You're a cop? You're an effing cop?"

"What? No! I'm not a cop? Are you a cop? You brought them in here." he countered.

"No, man, but I'm not the one with some psycho chick accusing me of being someone else."

"She's nuts," Jon accused, hands in the air and backing away. He scrunched his nose up and looked disgusted, like I disgusted him. "Don't listen to her. Get her out of here."

I knew what he was doing, but I didn't care. There was a part of me that wanted to hurt him, destroy him. "Nuts? Nuts?" I crumpled to the floor, feeling the air leave my lungs, knowing I *was* nuts. I was crazy for ever falling for Jon, for believing his lies, for trusting him with me and my family, and I knew then that I would never trust him again.

"Hey, you, blond girl," Owen snapped at Daphne. "Is she telling the truth?"

"You mean… are we hookers? 'Cause—"

"You know what I mean," he shouted, pushing closer to her. "No more games."

I peered up at my nude husband, who began to look worried for Daphne. His eyes met mine as he silently pleaded with me once more. "Please," he mouthed.

"I said," Owen asked again, "Is she telling the truth?"

Daphne made eye contact with Jon and paused for a beat. She stared at the ground and then back up at Owen. "No." She sighed. "She's completely messed up. She took something, I'm not sure what, but I think she might be hallucinating. She has twins, and her husband is a total *douchebag*." Daphne stared directly at Jon when she emphasized *douchebag*.

My stomach flipped, and I swallowed back the vomit. Why was Daphne siding with him? How could the two people closest to me in the world betray me like this? Then I had an idea—the infinity tattoo. If I just showed them my tattoo, I could prove to these fools that Jon knew who I was.

I pulled myself off the ground and stood, facing Daphne and Owen, ready to end this fiasco once and for all, but the look on Daphne's face stopped me in my tracks. "I promise, she's just really messed up."

Owen stepped closer to Daphne, removing something from his pocket. She turned from crimson to a ghostly white as her eyes swelled and she backed against the wall. I tasted the vodka from earlier that night as it traveled up my esophagus to the back of my throat. "Tell me the truth, or you're dead."

Owen had a knife. And it was pressed against Daphne's throat. I couldn't help it. I bent forward and vomited on the floor, heaved forward, puking again, only this time on Hailey. I then slipped in my own throw-up, and fell on the ground by Jon's feet, vomiting again until the tears flowed freely, and I decided that this was a nightmare. There was no other logical explanation.

"See," Daphne said, gesturing in my direction. "She's freaking wasted. Now take your knife off my throat before I kick you in the nuts and call the cops myself."

"You've got nothing on me, *dude*."

"Solicitation of prostitution, *dude*."

"She's right, Owen. Just let them go. This whole thing is messed up," Jon insisted.

Owen pulled the knife away from Daphne, took two steps backward, and kicked me in the stomach. A sharp pain radiated through me, and I puked again. I squinted at Jon through tears, waiting for him to react, but he didn't. Owen looked from Jon to me and back again, gaze serious. "You sure you don't know her?"

"Don't know her, man."

"So, you won't care if I do this." *Bam.* Another kick. Shock rushed through me, and he kicked me again until I was sure I was bleeding from the inside out, if not from Owen's attack then indeed from a broken heart. "Get her out of here," Owen barked at Daphne. "I never want to see either of you around here again."

"Bitch," Hailey scoffed as Daphne pulled me from the ground, dragged me through my puke, and out the door. And I decided, in that moment, there was no way in hell I could ever forgive my husband for his betrayal, no matter how sorry he was or what excuse he would have for me. I would keep moving forward and never look back.

Chapter Twenty-One

Now

I sip my Truly Pineapple slowly to stay as sober as possible as I lean against the wall of Zack Tompkins' parents' newly renovated kitchen. Mr. and Mrs. Tompkins have taken a weekend at their vacation home on Camelback Mountain and have asked their golden-boy son to hold down the fort. When they requested this of him, I assume they didn't expect that he might invite fifty of his closest underage friends over to drink, have chicken fights in their pool, and smoke massive amounts of weed.

I'm wary about this, to say the least. Not only do I have no idea how these kids could acquire a keg, multiple packs of Trulys, and three handles of vodka, but a noise violation is almost a guarantee, and explaining this to the cops is not my idea of a good time.

Jon is parked outside Zack's house and will call me if he sees any sign of the cops. If that happens, I plan to flee out the back door, through the neighbor's yard, and out to the street behind the house and away from the cops. Of course, I would remove Molly from the house, too, but now that she has disappeared upstairs with Bill, that seems unlikely. I sigh, wondering how this has become my life. Just a hot minute ago, I was a single mother raising teenagers. I was an award-winning, best-selling author. And now, I'm posing as a high school senior in someone else's home. I would *kill* Max and Lucy if they threw this kind of party.

I take another sip of my drink and stifle a yawn. It was another long week acting as both Gemma and Lina, and if we didn't get some answers soon, we might need to call Operation Superglue a bust. It is becoming nearly impossible to keep up with my academics and after-school activities while caring for Max and Lucy, managing a household, and salvaging my writing career.

Ryker added algebra extra help to the end of Max's workout sessions, and Lucy survived a week of house arrest. And although she is still brokenhearted, she seems to feel better as time passes. Jon and I met, night after night, wracking our brains about the missing girls and their connections to other Emerson students, and we keep falling short, which is why tonight is so important. Jon encouraged me to get out there and make new friends and accused me of putting all my eggs in one basket with Molly. "You can't just act like Gemma. You need to get in the game. *Be* Gemma."

"Like when you had to *be* Mace?" I had asked.

"Lina—"

"No," I had interrupted behind my raised hand. "That wasn't meant to be bitchy. I guess... I just mean that on some level... I'm starting to get what you were going through," I noted.

"Can we please talk about that night—"

"Nope," I had affirmed. "I don't care how long it has been. I'm not talking about it. Ever."

Last night, we returned to the drawing board as we ate Mexican takeout at Jon's office. If Zack isn't our guy, our next step is to check out the soup kitchen, as all three girls served time there. But Jon is right, and I know it. I need to throw myself into this circle of underage delinquents and do it now, starting with Bill's brother, Hank. I have been wary of hitting on Hank. Sure, he's eighteen, so the possibility of going to jail is slim, but it's still all too creepy. And even though I would never allow anything physical to happen, playing with this kid's emotions feels wrong on many levels. But there are missing girls, and time is of the essence. I need more friends, and I need them now.

I take a swig of Truly and go outside to the Tompkins family's pool, and sure enough, there is Hank, bare chested in hot-pink short swim trunks, pouring beer into a red cup from the keg. His ginger tresses are curlier than his brother's, but he has broader shoulders and an athletic body type, and my face flushes as I study his muscular physique. "Hey," I sing. "Got enough of that for me?" I ask, pointing to my now-empty Truly can.

"Gemma! Hi! Of course. Here, take this one," he says, handing it to me and pouring himself another. "You look amazing," he says, eyeing me up and down.

"Oh." I blush and sip my beer; thankful I can pull off Lucy's black crop top and ripped denim shorts. "Seeing everyone out of uniform is funny." I laugh because it is.

"It's probably a good thing," he says, sipping his beer.

"Why?"

"If I had to sit behind you in chemistry class in that outfit, I would fail out of Emerson, lose my scholarship to UCLA, and my parents would murder me."

"Well, then. I'm glad I'm not a distraction," I say, tucking a strand of hair behind my ear, biting my lower lip, and raising my red cup to my mouth.

"Well, I didn't say that," he says, moving closer. "You wear that khaki skirt nicely."

I cough, choking on my beer. It takes me a moment to catch my breath.

"Are you okay?" he asks, genuinely concerned.

"Sorry," I say, my words catching in my throat. "Wrong pipe."

"My mom says that." He chuckles.

"What?"

"Wrong pipe."

"Oh. Yeah, mine too. Funny."

"Sorry if I made you nervous."

"It's okay," I sigh. "I just haven't dated since my ex… I guess talking to you does make me a little nervous."

"I got you," he says. "Want to take a dip?" he asks, motioning to the pool.

"I didn't bring a suit."

"They have them in the pool house."

"For real?"

"For real."

"I, uh, don't think so," I say, mainly because swimming with him could lead to more, but also because I've put off my bikini wax since Operation Superglue has consumed all my waking hours, and let's not forget about the stretch marks that tattoo my abdomen. I've come to accept them as battle wounds, reminders of my maternal strength, but in no way will they help me to pass as eighteen years old.

"Come on." He nudges me.

"Let's just hang out here."

"Are you on your cycle?" he asks like he's asking me if I'm going to the game on Sunday.

I choke on my beer again and nod. "Yeah, sorry," I lie. This conversation would have never happened when I was in high school. Girls, let alone guys, didn't even talk about their cycles with each other. Now they talk about it like it's no big deal. I've noticed this with Max, but I assumed it was because he grew up so close with Lucy. But apparently, I supposed wrong. It's just another crack in the age gap.

"Don't be sorry. That's nothing to be sorry about."

I am at a loss for words because eighteen-year-old Hank is handling this conversation more maturely than I am, and I've birthed children. "Thanks," I mutter. "So, UCLA?"

"Yeah, it's finally coming together," he says with a twinkle in his eye.

"Hard work pays off," I say.

"My mom says that too."

"I'm an old soul." I chuckle.

"I love that about you." Hank leans in for a kiss, and I dart to the side, sipping my beer instead.

"Did you go to Emerson for all four years?" I ask, determined to keep him talking.

"Yup," he says, raising his eyebrows and staring down my shirt.

"I... I really have yet to make many friends. Would you... Could you introduce me to some? Not sure who you... Who do you hang with?"

"Zack is my boy," he says with a smile. "He's good people."

"Oh, Zack. Isn't he the quarterback?"

"Damn straight."

"I heard about him," I say, choosing my words carefully. "I overheard some girls in gym class talking about him and how he dated two of the girls who ran away."

Hank's face drops, and his expression turns solemn. "That was very out of pocket."

"Oh, I'm sorry. It's just that I'm new and only hear the rumors, you know?"

"You're fine. It's just hard to talk about."

"Why? Was he that close to them?"

"Yeah, and I was close with Alanna too. Even when he and Alanna broke up, they stayed friends because Alanna was close with his sister, Carrie, a freshman at ASU. Zack and Carrie didn't stop trying to find her. Zack didn't eat or sleep for days. Then, when Chloe went missing, he was furious with the Arizona PD for not trying harder. He caused a huge scene in the police station and was taken into custody, but his parents begged them to drop the charges, and they did. His scholarship was at stake."

"Wow. So, he knew all three girls? Isn't that kind of…"

"Sus?"

"Well… maybe."

"Emerson is a small school. Everyone is hooking up with everyone. It goes under the radar most of the time, but everyone knows how special the girls are to Zack. It's an unwritten fact that he would never hurt them, and he would hurt anyone who did."

I nod, realizing that Zack is most likely a dead end. I need to keep Hank talking, though. And how am I supposed to do that without sounding too obvious? I take a deep breath and count to five. I need to be creative. Hank knows people. If I'm going to get further with Operation Superglue, it's time to get moving. "As sad as it is," I start, leaning against him, "I'm super into solving crimes. I find it sort of interesting."

"Really?"

"Really."

"You listen to podcasts and shit? I listened to a crime podcast once. It was insane."

"Oh yeah." I smile. "I listen to podcasts and shit. I also watch Netflix documentaries and would like to write mystery books someday."

"You want to be an author?"

"Yeah," I say, keeping eye contact and batting my lashes. "And I find this missing-girls thing really intriguing. I mean, three girls run away from the same school. Doesn't seem real."

"There is no way they ran away."

"I agree."

"I think the cops are in on it," he accuses, his eyes growing dark and his brows narrowing.

"What makes you think that—"

My words are cut short as Molly and Bill enter the pool area, beers in hand, giggling like they are up to no good. "Gemma!" Molly squeals, her words slurring. "I love you so much!"

"So, Molly's wasted," I say to Hank.

"I'm not wasted!" she shrieks. "I'm just drunk."

"I've got to get her home," I say.

"I have some Pedialyte in my cooler if you want to give her some?"

"Why do you have Pedialyte?" I ask through my laughter, leaning Molly against my shoulder.

"Electrolytes. Why else?"

"I think we are good." I smile. "I've got to get her home."

"Not so fast," Hank says, pulling me to him for a kiss. I turn my face so his lips meet my cheek. "Not fair," he whispers.

"I like to take things slow, that's all."

"Game on," he says with a smirk.

My cell phone buzzes, and I ignore it because getting lost in Hank's eyes for a split second feels good. No, it feels great. And for the first time in years, I consider talking to Jon about what really happened during his undercover operation at the college. My cell phone buzzes again. *Jon.*

"Shit," I say, pulling my phone out of my pocket to find three missed calls from Jon and a text warning me about the cops. "We need to go," I say, grabbing Molly by the hand and leading her toward the back gate.

"Time to go!" Molly cheers, pumping her fist in the air. "I'll text you, Bill... my Bill."

"Let's go," I scold.

"Gemma—"

"Bye, Hank. I'll see you in chemistry," I say, darting out the back with Molly.

"Where are we going?" Molly asks, confused. "Are we playing hide-and-seek?"

"Shh," I say, pressing my finger to my lips as I hear someone shout, "It's the cops!"

"Oh no!" Molly cries.

"It's okay," I reassure her. But my heart rate has increased substantially as I drag Molly through the neighbor's yard to the corresponding street, just as Jon and I had practiced. "Come on!" I say, glancing over my shoulder and ignoring the blue-and-red lights from down the street. "Shit!" I squeal. "Act normal and try to walk straight."

"I can't. I'm wasted."

"I know."

I pick up the pace as I hold Molly upright, and Jon pulls his car up beside us wearing sunglasses and a Phoenix Suns cap. "Uber for Mendoza?"

Thank God. "Yeah," I huff. "Mason, right?" I ask, using the only name that comes to my mind.

"Yes, ma'am."

"Thank you!" I exhale, overly thankful for my ex. "Get in," I say to Molly.

I put her in the back seat and hurry to the other side as Jon puts the car in drive and takes a left, another left, and we are away from Zack's house and the commotion.

"Thank you," I say, texting him Molly's Paradise Valley address, hopeful that she can get inside without her parents seeing her this way but also thinking it might be a good thing if they do.

"Our Uber driver looks like Mr. Jacobs," she declares through her drunken laughs. She leans her head against the window and closes her eyes.

"A little bit," I agree with a smile.

"Total DILF."

"What?" Jon mouths in the review mirror.

"Nothing." I sigh. "Just take us home."

"Don't forget my five-star rating," he reminds me.

"I won't," I say, rolling my eyes.

"DILF," Molly repeats again. "Old as shit but definitely a ten. Gemma, I'm so happy you started at Emerson. I love you. Like, I really love you."

"I love you, too, Molly."

"Gemma?"

"Yeah."

"I think I'm going to be sick."

Chapter Twenty-Two

Then (2012)

Daphne was a beautiful bride. She wore the perfect dress at the most beautiful venue on the perfect day, and I couldn't have been happier for her. So, as I sat at my table in my periwinkle strapless bridesmaid dress, freaking out about the toast I would be giving in just a few short minutes, it was quite the relief when a tall and handsome man who could have passed for Tom Brady sat down at my table. He smiled at me, and I smiled back, thanking my lucky stars that the wedding gods may have sent me someone yummy to share my best friend's big day.

Jon and I had been divorced for under a year, and in that time, I hadn't even considered dating. A part of me knew this was because it would take more than a year to pick up the pieces of my broken heart and my broken life. Other than Daphne, Jon had been my best friend. So when our marriage ended so suddenly, I not only lost my husband, the father of my children, and my soulmate... I also lost my best friend.

"Big toast coming up?" Mystery Guy asked, gesturing to the crumpled-up piece of paper in my hand.

"Maid of honor," I said because I couldn't think of anything else.

"I know." He smirked. "I was at the wedding. I saw you up there."

"It was beautiful," I said, thinking of Daphne as she walked down the aisle in her ivory, strapless, full-bodied wedding gown behind Lucy, the flower girl, and Max, the ring bearer. Lucy, four years old, wore a princess-style periwinkle flower girl dress with a wreath of white and pink roses that surrounded her blond high bun. Max had looked adorable in his tiny rented black tux and ivory bowtie.

"I'm Ryker," he said, extending his hand toward mine.

"Lina," I replied. "I'm Daphne's best friend. We met in college at ASU."

"Nice," he said with a soft smile. "I know the groom. Cousins. Not close enough to be in the wedding party but close enough to have a good seat," he joked.

"That's funny," I said, forgetting my toast for a hot minute. I liked this guy, Ryker. He was handsome, funny, and had a connection to Daphne. For the first time in a year, things started looking up.

"I think you're up," he said, gesturing to the front of the room, where Daphne and her husband Malachy shared their sweetheart table.

"Damnit," I swore, reaching for my champagne glass and swigging it back then realizing that I no longer had champagne to toast with since I drank it.

"Here." He smiled. "Take mine."

"What are you going to toast with?"

"Don't worry about me." He winked.

I rose from my seat, went to Daphne's table, faced the wedding guests, and waved to Max and Lucy, who stood off to the side of the room with my mother, who would bring them back to her house after dinner. My fingers trembled as I took the mic from Malachy's best man, James.

"Out of all the colleges in the world," I began, "and all the roommates I could have been assigned, I chose ASU, and ASU chose Daphne for me. We have been through a lot together." I paused, my words catching in my throat. "From adjusting to college life, learning impossibly difficult life lessons, and just growing up."

I smiled at Daphne, and she took my hand in hers. "Daphne never had a steady boyfriend during college. She preferred nights out with the girls, meeting new people, and doing things independently as she saw fit. Which was why, when she told me she met 'the one,' she almost had to pick me up off the floor. I'm happy for you guys." I smiled. "And for the record, I sort of set them up." I winked, wondering how many wedding guests knew that Malachy and Daphne met because he was *my* divorce lawyer. "Cheers to Daphne and Mal. May you have a long and prosperous life together, never go to bed angry, and know I am always here for you—except to do your laundry, Daph. Hopefully, your husband is better at that than you."

Daphne belly laughed at this and wiped the tears from her eyes. "I love you," she whispered.

"Cheers!" I said, raising my glass and sipping my champagne.

"Cheers!" the guests repeated, followed by applause.

"Mommy!" Max called, releasing his grip from my mother's. Max rushed to the front of the room and leaped into my arms.

"Want to say something, Max?" Daphne asked him.

I held the microphone to his tiny mouth, holding my breath because there was no telling what he might say. "Can we eat now?" he asked softly into the mic. "I want that cake," he said, pointing to the five-tiered wedding cake.

The wedding guests erupted in laughter at his question. "You heard the man. Let's eat!" Daphne cheered.

***

An hour later, Ryker and I were seated at our table, nibbling on the delicious chocolate buttercream wedding cake. We talked about everything under the sun, from his football glory days at LSU to my two beautiful children and my failed marriage. I felt like I had known Ryker for my entire life. He was an excellent listener, knew what to say during awkward silence, and kept the cucumber martinis coming. I could have sat there with him all night until the DJ played. I swear by All-4-One, and I couldn't resist anymore. I asked Ryker to dance. "Of course," he said with a smile.

So, as I swayed on the dance floor on my tiptoes and my arms wrapped around my handsome mystery man's waist, I leaned against his chest and closed my eyes, feeling like this was a sign that my love life might not be over. "I love this song," I told him over the music.

"Yeah," he said, "It's great." His voice was quieter than it had been all night, and I sensed something a bit off, and then it dawned on me. Ryker wasn't single. He was pulling back from being intimate with me because he had a girlfriend... a fiancée... or a wife, even. Why would the perfect guy be single?

"Everything okay?" I asked.

"Yeah, why?"

Because the second things progressed past casual conversation, you clammed up. "Just getting a weird vibe, that's all. Are you... Are you seeing someone?"

Ryker pulled back and smiled, brushing a loose strand of hair from my face. "No, I'm single."

"Oh, okay."

"But I should probably tell you I'm only looking to be friends."

That hit me like a ton of bricks. Of course, someone like him would only want to be friends. On what planet would someone like Ryker want to date a divorced woman with twin four-year-olds? I pulled back and released his grip on me. "Is it the divorced part? Or the kid part?" I asked with a frown. Ryker found this funny because his smile grew wide, and a soft laugh escaped him. "What's funny about this? Seriously, Ryker? I need help. I thought—"

"It isn't the divorced or the kid part, I promise," he reassured me.

"Then what is it?"

"Well, it's the female part."

"Excuse me?"

"I'm not into females."

"Oh. So you're gay?"

"Yes, ma'am."

I thought about this for a beat, feeling all sorts of confused. "You don't look gay."

"What does gay look like?"

I blushed, embarrassed, because he was right. "You know what I mean. And besides that, you were flirting with me."

Ryker took my hand in his and swayed to the beat of the music. "I find you easy to talk to. I wasn't flirting, just being friendly."

"Got it," I said, not hiding my disappointment and silently mourning the possibility of this being more than a friendship.

"But I could use a friend. And I like you," he said with a soft smile.

"I could too," I admitted, leaning against his chest and feeling thankful for him. Daphne was starting her life with Mal, and having someone like Ryker in my life might be what I needed.

Ryker bent down and kissed me softly on the forehead. "Friends?"

"Friends," I said as I closed my eyes and rested my head against his chest, relishing the overwhelming sense of peace I felt, knowing in the depths of my soul that somehow, on some level, I might have just found my soulmate in Ryker.

Chapter Twenty-Three

Now

It has been a week since Molly and I ran from the cops. Molly, who had experienced her first hangover, was ill the entire weekend and missed school on Monday. She had managed to sneak by her parents, who were asleep watching Netflix upon her return that evening, and was also able to convince them that she had a touch of the flu. Although the Gemma in me is proud of her for not getting caught, the mother in me is mortified, and I can't help but wonder if my own children have been able to sneak around like this. I make a mental note to monitor my teenagers better in the future.

That was Monday, and Molly has since returned to school, refreshed and ready to go. But for some reason, today, on a Friday, she has yet to make it to school, and it is almost lunch. I have office hours with Jon approaching, and I want to indirectly pick Molly's brain about a new development in the case. Plus it's weird not having her here. I texted her all morning, and she hasn't responded, which is unlike Molly. I decided that she must have a dentist or doctor's appointment and simply forgot to tell me, but the part of me consumed with kidnapped teens can't help but worry. What if something happened to her?

I approach the art room but realize I need to drop my tuition check at the main office. I have five more minutes until Jon's hours officially start, so I detour down the opposing hallway and head toward the stairs. I am eager to talk to Jon about my new lead, but I also need to avoid drawing attention to myself and my *dad* with late tuition.

I walk quickly to save time because I can't wait to brief my ex-husband on my findings. Just yesterday afternoon, after volleyball practice, I was grabbing my backpack from the locker room when I received a friend request on Snapchat from someone I didn't know. The stranger, Lincoln Stone, was a very handsome teenage boy with wide blue eyes and shaggy blond hair. He was charming and sexy in a Chad Michael Murray sort of way. During a colorful sunset, his profile picture was taken outside with Camelback Mountain behind him. I accepted his request immediately, considering I was grabbing at straws for any lead, and I assumed that Lincoln was a peer somehow affiliated with Hank, Zack, or any other boys on the football team. I noticed, after all, since my appearance at Zack's party, that I had become more popular with the cool kids at Emerson—mission accomplished.

After accepting Lincoln's request, however, I couldn't help but become intrigued. Lincoln was not listed as an Emerson Academy student but as a senior at Coronado High, Max and Lucy's high school. For a brief moment, I considered that social media algorithms were strange, and because of my relationship and involvement as a parent from CHS, there was a slight chance that Snapchat connected us. But once our conversations began, I realized otherwise, as Lincoln knew who Gemma was. He knew that she was a senior at Emerson, was on the volleyball team, and had moved from Florida to live with her dad.

As creepy as this was, it was just as exciting, and I couldn't wait to brainstorm with Jon. I had since been snapping back and forth with Lincoln, and I went as far as to ask Max and Lucy if they recognized him from their school, and neither of them did. I am eager to find this Lincoln Stone and know deep down that Jon's investigative skills will be more valuable now than ever.

I round the corner to the main office, open the glass door, and stop short. There, stuffing mail into teachers' mailboxes, with her ginger locks pulled into a high, curly ponytail, dressed like she stepped out of a J.Crew ad, is a very familiar face. At first, I can't place her, but I remember who she is after a few beats of staring at her with my eyes wide and palms sweaty. I scan her visitor's badge with my eyes for confirmation and read the name Penelope in black Sharpie. *Penelope.*

Shit! Shit, shit, shit. I spin around to exit the office before being recognized, wondering what the odds are that the woman I had befriended in 2011, a woman I took Mommy and Me swim classes with, would be volunteering at Emerson Academy, of all places, smack dab in the middle of Operation Superglue.

"Can we help you, Gemma?" the secretary asks.

I stop dead, gathering my hair over my left shoulder and keeping my head down. "Yeah," I say, turning my back to Penelope. "I have my tuition check."

"Thank you, dear. You can hand it to Mrs. Gallagher," she says, gesturing to Penelope. "She will take care of it."

I stand, frozen, staring at the secretary like she has just asked me to rob a bank. *Penelope Gallagher.* Penelope, the woman from Mommy and Me, shares the same last name as Bill and Hank. Bill and Hank *Gallagher.* I shut my eyes and explore the depths of my memory for evidence that I could be incorrect about this, but I come up short. I remember her as clear as day. Penelope had twins a couple years older than Max and Lucy, and their names are William and Henry. *Bill and Hank. Shit, shit, shit.*

"Gemma? Are you okay? You don't look well."

"I'm fine," I say with a giggle, wiping a bead of sweat from my forehead. "Dad told me to hand it to you. You know what a rule follower I am," I lie.

"Oh, Gemma, you can just give it to Mrs. Gallagher."

"I don't bite," her soft voice declares from behind.

"Of course," I say, inhaling profoundly and relaxing my shoulders. Surely, Penelope won't be able to place me as Lina, mother of twins, in this high school main office in this uniform.

I turn confidently, delivering my best teenage head tilt. "Here you go." I smile, handing her the envelope and turning toward the door.

"Thank—" she starts but stops, stepping between me and the door.

"You look like someone I used to know," she says, locking her eyes on mine.

"Really?" I ask with a shrug. I inhale, counting to five, eyes not shifting from hers.

"Yes, really." She scrunches her nose and looks me up and down. "You're a student here? At Emerson?"

Part of me wants to run away screaming, while the other part knows this isn't an option. One false move or one wrong answer, and this mission will be over. I refuse to let this happen, not when I finally have a lead, so I channel my inner Gemma and think about the teenagers in my life. Lucy would probably roll her eyes and keep walking. Molly might have a wise comment. Max probably wouldn't even notice someone was talking to him. So I shrug and reach for the door, but she places her hand on it to stop me.

"I'm late for something," I say, imitating my daughter when she shoos me away.

"Lina?" she mouths.

"I'm sorry," I snap. "I don't know you."

"Well, maybe I knew your mother then?"

I search my mind for answers that align with Gemma's cover. Lina's mother lives in Florida, so there is no way Penelope would know her. However, Penelope is doing the math and probably realizes I could be Lucy, Lina's daughter, based on numbers.

I clench my fists by my sides and ignore the rapid beating of my heart. "My mother—"

"Her mother lives in Jupiter, Florida," Dean Elizabeth says, coming out of her office, her tone firm.

Thank God. "It's true. I live with my dad. We just moved up here, so no, there is no way I would know you."

"I... I'm sorry, Dean Downing. It's just that I never forget a face."

"And where do you think you remember Miss Mendoza from?" she asks, arms crossed and expression stern.

A part of me feels sad for Penelope, but another piece of me is happy to watch her cheeks turn crimson and her confidence wither. "A swim class," she says confidently.

"What sort of swim class?" the dean challenges.

"A swim class I took with my twins."

"Your eighteen-year-old twins?" she asks, sticking her nose farther in the air. "Was this recently?"

"Not exactly. It was quite some time ago."

"How long?"

"Oh, about fifteen years ago."

"Gemma," Dean Elizabeth starts. "How old were you fifteen years ago?"

I do the math quickly and mumble, "Like... three?"

Penelope looks at the ground and shakes her head from side to side. "I'm sorry. I'm obviously in the wrong here. I guess I thought maybe I knew her mother?"

"It's okay—" I start, but Dean Elizabeth interrupts.

"It's not okay. This young lady just left her mother in Florida to live in Tempe with her father, and you feel the need to remind her about that in the middle of her day?"

"I'm so sorry. She just... She looks just like her."

"Here at Emerson, we have a zero-tolerance policy for stereotyping against age, sex, or race. Is this what's going on?" she challenges, narrowing her eyes.

"Oh, God," Penelope gasps. "No, that's not what this is. I swear."

"Run along, Gemma. I hope your art project is coming along nicely," the dean says with a smirk.

I hold back a snicker and mentally declare the dean my hero. "Have a good day," I whisper as I push past my old friend, Penelope, and silently proclaim Dean Elizabeth Downing my new best friend.

***

Five minutes later, I am pacing back and forth in front of Jon's desk, ranting about Mommy and Me swimming lessons and Hank Gallagher. "The guy I was flirting with at the party, no… the *boy* who tried to kiss me was the same little boy floating through the water on his tummy in bright-orange arm floaties singing 'Pop Goes the Weasel!'" I wail. "Jon, what are we even doing?"

"Take a deep breath, Lina," Jon says for the millionth time.

"I'm just so old and creepy," I mumble, wiping a tear from my eye. I sigh and perch myself against his desk as he stands and places his arms on my shoulders.

"You are not old. And you aren't creepy."

"I just don't know if I can do this anymore."

"You can, and you know it."

"No," I say firmly this time. "That was so… awful. Having to lie to her like that."

"Hey," he says, rubbing my arm. "Your cover was almost blown, but it wasn't. You're just really worked up. Take some time. It's okay."

"I know. I'm just… I'm worried about Molly. She didn't come to school today, and I… I can't worry about one more teenager, Jon." I stare down at my feet as my eyes well with tears. "And I didn't even have time to talk with you about my new lead."

"Hey," he says, placing his index finger on my chin and tilting it toward him. I want to instinctively bat his hand away from me, but I don't. I allow him to comfort me in this moment and hold his gaze on mine. I allow him to wipe the tears from my eyes with his thumbs, and when they start flowing freely, I let him wipe them up with the bottom of his dorky art teacher apron. "Molly is going to be okay," he reassures me. "You… You are going to be okay. And we are going to find those girls."

I nod, wrapping my arms around his waist and pressing my face to his torso, the familiarity of this embrace both confusing and reassuring. "Thank you."

"Let's meet tonight," he whispers atop my head. "You can tell me all about your lead then."

"Okay," I agree. "Your office?"

"Yes. Hey, Lina?"

"Yeah?"

"Why wasn't I at the swim class?"

I pause for a beat, wondering why this was important information now. "You were working."

"Oh," he says with a frown. "At the college?"

"I'm not really sure," I admit. "It was a long time ago."

"Who went with—" Jon starts but is interrupted by a fierce banging on his classroom door. "What the heck?" he asks, looking from the entrance to me and back again.

"Maybe it's Dean Elizabeth?" I ask.

"Maybe," he agrees, gesturing for me to sit at the art table, and I do.

Jon opens the door and barely has it open before a frantic student bursts into the room. "Gemma!" Molly hollers. She looks like she has been crying nonstop for hours. Her blond hair is matted to her red mascara-streaked cheeks.

"Molly? Molly, what is it?" I ask, bailing on Gemma and deferring to Mom.

"It's my little sister, June," she wails, throwing her arms around my neck. "She didn't come home from school yesterday. I don't know what to do, Gemma. The cops are at my house, my parents are beside themselves, and I can't help but think… what if she's next?"

Chapter Twenty-Four

Then 2013

I nervously bit into a very expensive filet mignon across from my date, Nick, when my ex-husband caught my eye. I coughed, startled, reaching for my napkin to cover my mouth as my eyes began to water, and I spit the piece of meat awkwardly into the freshly pressed linen.

"Are you all right?" Nick asked, his coffee-colored eyes wide and dark, bushy eyebrows raised.

"Excuse me." I coughed, my cheeks turning pink. "Sorry."

"Don't be sorry."

Nick passed me a glass of water, and I sipped it eagerly. "Thanks," I said as I peeked over Nick's shoulder for confirmation that the tall, blond, handsome man seated across the restaurant from us was Jon, and indeed it was, and he wasn't alone.

I recognized Jon's female companion instantly. She sat tall and confident with perfect posture, her black hair pulled sleekly back into a clip, her pale, petite shoulders bare beneath the silver spaghetti straps of her cocktail dress, her red-lipstick smile stunning—Max and Lucy's kindergarten teacher, Grace Tan. *What. The. Hell, Jon?*

I reached for my wine glass, finishing it off. "I'm going to need more of this," I muttered.

"Sure," Nick said, reaching for the bottle and pouring me another glass.

"Thanks," I said with a smile, inhaling and counting to five.

Of course, Jon would appear on the first date I'd gone on since our divorce, and of course, it would be with our twins' teacher. This frustrated me on many levels, mostly because I had been dying for this date and was eager to get to know Nick better. Not only had I had my hair blown out for the occasion, but I had also purchased a new strapless red dress—festive for the holiday season—had my nails done and paid a babysitter. Over my dead body would I let Jon Cote ruin this night for me.

"You were saying?" Nick asked.

"I don't remember what I was saying," I admitted.

"Your book?"

"Yes." I nodded. "I sent the manuscript to multiple publishers. I'm so excited."

"Congratulations," he said, clinking his glass to mine. "I'm really proud of you."

"Thank you. I am too," I said because I was. "It must be all my time at the bookstore." I winked.

I had managed to write my first novel while raising two five-year-olds and working mornings at Starbucks, and it hadn't been easy. I was thankful for my faithful support system—my parents, Ryker, and Daphne. They were my family, and just when I thought I didn't need a man, I met Nick Sullivan, a handsome thirty-year-old bookstore owner from Scottsdale.

It had been a rainy afternoon in mid-September, and I had an hour to kill before picking up Max and Lucy from kindergarten, so I decided to stop into Caffeine and Classics, a store I would later learn was owned by Nick. I was browsing my favorite romance books, picking them up one at a time and smelling them because I loved the smell of books, something Jon never seemed to appreciate.

So when Nick approached me and told me that he couldn't negotiate the book price based on scent, I was smitten on the spot, and for the next three months, I had made frequent stops into Caffeine and Classics, sometimes for the books, sometimes for the coffee, and mostly to catch a glimpse of Nick's soft smile.

"It's awe-inspiring," Nick said. "That you could accomplish that with two kids and a second job."

"Right? I'm awesome," I laughed.

"You are," he said, reaching his hand across the table and placing it on mine.

I couldn't help it. I glanced over Nick's shoulder once again and caught Jon's stare. I blinked his gaze away and focused back on Nick. "Thank you for taking me here tonight. It's really nice, and I know Christmastime is busy for you with the store."

"I've been trying to get you out with me since September. The store can wait." He winked. "Are you interested in dessert?"

"Um, I think I'd like to head back to your place," I said, my words jumbling together awkwardly.

Nick smiled and blushed, and I realized instantly how that must have sounded. I had meant to get away from my ex-husband, but what I said was, *Take me now, Nick Sullivan.* "Okay then. Check, please," he said through his grin.

"Sorry, I just… There is someone here I don't want to see."

"Oh? Who?"

"My ex. Max and Lucy's father."

"Check, please," he said, louder this time, and I was thankful for his sense of humor. "Hey, want to hit the bookstore after hours? Curl up on one of those germ-infested beanbags and sip decaf espresso? I'll let you have free biscotti."

"Don't say they are germ-infested." I chuckled. "My kids sit on those."

"Exactly."

"But that sounds lovely. Let me use the ladies' room, and we can head out."

"Perfect," he said, kissing the top of my hand. "Hurry back. I got a first edition of *The Great Gatsby*, and I'm sure you would like how it smells."

"Yes," I cooed like he had said something sexual. "I'll be right back."

I stood from my seat, gathering the bottom of my satin dress and my hair over my shoulder, my smile the widest in years. I strutted by Jon's table, avoiding eye contact and dismissing jealous thoughts that shot through my brain at lightning speed. So what if he was out with Miss Tan, and Miss Tan stood at about five feet nine with a twenty-inch waist and supermodel persona. My date was spectacular too. He was kind, patient, encouraging, loved books as much as I did, and looked like a young Henry Cavill. If I was going to be caught out on a date by my ex-husband, Nick was the guy to be with.

I rounded the corner to the restroom and was discouraged to find only two occupied unisex bathrooms. I sighed, cursing my bladder because running out of there and back to the bookstore and away from the nightmare of Jon Cote was what I needed more than anything... but no. I couldn't because I had to pee. And thanks to birthing twins, naturally, there was no way I could hold it for the ride. Oh, the joys of motherhood.

One of the bathroom doors opened, and a middle-aged man exited, nodding at me shyly. I squeezed past him, closing and locking the door behind me. I used the toilet, washed my hands, adjusted the top of my new favorite dress, pulled my fingers through my hair, and gave myself an encouraging smile in the mirror. I touched up my lipstick and spritzed body spray under my armpits. And I was ready. I was prepared to get out of there and continue my date.

Operation Superglue

But as I unlocked the door and turned the handle, I opened it just enough for my heart to drop to the pit of my stomach because standing there on the other side of it was Jon.

"Jon." I nodded, preparing to squeeze by.

"Lina. Lina, wait," he begged.

"Please move."

"I just need to talk to you."

"Then call me. I'm busy. And apparently, so are you. Hey, do they give grades in kindergarten? Because if they do, our children are sure to graduate with honors. Good work," I said, trying to push by. "It's always a good idea to sleep with the teacher."

"Lina—"

"Bye."

But Jon grabbed my arm harder than he probably intended, and that gesture shook me on multiple levels. "Please?"

"Please, what?"

"I really need to talk." Jon pulled me back into the bathroom and locked the door behind him.

"Are you kidding me right now?" I crossed my arms over my chest and studied my frantic ex as he paced around the tiny restroom.

"I just really need to talk to you."

"I talk to *you* at least once a week. You know because we share children together."

"I know. But we only talk about the kids."

"There's a reason for that."

"I know. But seeing you tonight, with someone else… Lina, I can't do this anymore. I miss you."

"You saw me eating dinner. I got to watch you having sex. I'd say we are even but—"

"Stop. I miss you. I miss us. I miss our family."

"Screw you," I snapped, pointing my finger in his face.

"Come on," he moaned, his eyes welling with tears. "If you would just let me explain."

"What is there to explain? You slept with someone else. End of story."

"Can't you even try to see it from my point of view? You could have blown my cover. You could have gotten us both killed. But I forgave you."

I suddenly found it hard to breathe as the bathroom walls closed in around me and beads of sweat dripped down my lower back. I clenched my fists by my sides and bit my lip, determined not to cry. "You know what," I whispered, my voice quivering. "You did get me killed. That night, at the frat party, a part of me died. And I might never get her back, but I'm sure as hell trying," I hissed, my voice increasing in volume. "You killed me, Jon. I'm not the same girl, and I'll never be, and that's all your fault, and I will never forgive you for that, ever."

"Lina," he cried, tears falling freely. "I'm sorry."

"I'm sorry too. I'm sorry that I met you. I'm sorry that I fell in love with you. And you know what? Sometimes, I regret having children with you, which hurts, but it's true."

Jon dropped to his knees and wrapped his arms around my torso, sobbing into my new dress, and at that moment, I realized that he might have killed me that night at the frat party, but a part of him died too. For a split second, I felt sorry for him. "I'm going back out there now. I will pick up the pieces of what is left of my life, what is left of this night, and I want you to leave me alone. Never talk about that night at the frat party again, never tell me you miss me, never talk to me about anything other than Max and Lucy, or I will find a way to make sure you have nothing to do with us."

Operation Superglue

I pried his arms off me, turned around, and exited the bathroom. My eyes darted around the restaurant until I spotted Nick leaning against the bar, drink in hand, talking to Grace, both of their expressions animated, smiling and laughing as they sipped their drinks. He placed his hand on her shoulder innocently. Still, I couldn't help but wonder what it might be like if I fell for Nick, started a life with him, and found him on the floor on top of Grace, in the middle of having sex. At that moment, as the tears flooded down my cheeks, my dinner crept up the back of my throat, and jealousy raged from within. I knew that I would never, ever be able to trust anyone again and that I would be better off alone. And that thought made me hate Jon Cote more than I ever allowed myself to hate anyone in my entire life.

I turned and hurried out of the restaurant, hailed a cab, and left my sexy bookstore owner behind. Because even if he could have offered me a lifetime of happiness—and endless amounts of classic first editions—the heartache and devastation that also came with falling in love with Nick Sullivan surely outweighed any of the good. And that night, I gave up on my happily ever after. I gave up on *me*.

Chapter Twenty-Five

Now

Molly's sister, June, has only been missing for twenty-four hours, but considering the circumstances, it is safe to assume she's our next kidnapping victim. This makes me sick to my stomach in more ways than I can count, but it also lights a fire under me to solve this case.

It broke my heart when Molly barged into the art room earlier this afternoon. I want, more than anything, to be there for her. She begged me to sleep at her house tonight and was devastated when I told her that wasn't possible. I wanted to reassure her that everything would be all right, but I had no guarantee that it would be.

Jon and I are convinced that my Snapchat friend Lincoln Stone is our key to solving Operation Superglue. I have been snapping with him since the end of the school day today—a selfie in my school uniform, a selfie in my gym clothes, and a locker-room selfie, all photos requested by sketchy Lincoln Stone. As a parent of teenagers, I know all too well how scary Snapchat can be, as Max once got caught up chatting with a female who ended up being a middle-aged man from outside the country. I will be careful about what I send to Lincoln, but I need to lure him in. I need him to believe that I am into him. If anything, Operation Superglue has forced me to trust my gut, and every piece of my soul knows that this is it. We are so close to finding June and the other three missing girls.

"Has he snapped you back?" Jon asks between bites of his steak and cheese.

"Not since he asked to see my boobs, and I turned him down."

"Probably for the best."

"He sent his—"

"You know what, Lina? I don't really need details."

"Suit yourself," I say, poking at my salad. "Did you know that's what people do now? Send pictures of their private parts. It's revolting."

"Are you going to eat that? You've been poking at it for an hour," he says, motioning to my salad.

"Believe it or not, I don't have an appetite. I just… I feel like there is more we can be doing."

"I get it." He nods. "But you need to eat."

"I stopped by Coronado High, you know."

"About Lincoln?"

"Yup. They don't have a student there named Lincoln Stone."

"How did you get that out of them?" Jon asks with a smirk.

"I know people." I shrug.

"Seriously. What did you say?"

"I swung by after school today. I told them that Max and Lincoln were doing an extra-credit project together, and he left something at our house. They looked him up in the system and said he wasn't a student there."

"I'm surprised they disclosed that."

"I may have offered my services as PTA president for next year," I confess with a roll of my eyes.

"Lina Rivera, look at you go." Jon chuckles. "You're actually really good at this."

"Thanks. Hey, you got any good snacks? I'm not feeling salad. I would kill for some Cheez-Its."

"You were obsessed with Cheez-Its during your pregnancy, remember?"

"Right! I think I ate a box a day."

"I thought the twins were going to come out orange," he says through his laughter.

I chortle at his comment but stop short when I realize what we're doing. Jon and I are together, laughing about a memory we shared during our lives that I pushed so far out of my mind that I almost made myself believe it never happened. "Yeah," I say, biting on my lip. "They were a little jaundiced, but that wasn't from the Cheez-Its."

"You okay?"

I nod, leaning against his desk with my arms crossed. "So, no snacks then?"

"No. Want a bite of this?" he asks, holding up the other half of his steak-and-cheese sub.

"Sure," I say, leaning forward and taking a massive bite of his sandwich. "Thanks," I mumble, my mouth full.

"You have a little something here," he says, wiping my cheek with his index finger. "Ketchup."

"Thanks. You're right. This is good."

"Steak and cheese trumps salad any day."

I nod, taking another bite and reaching for my Coke to wash it down. "Facts."

"Facts?"

"That's what the cool kids say." I smile.

"See, you know how teenagers talk now. Is it helping your writing?"

"I… I haven't written much," I confess.

"What? Why not?"

"Do you really have to ask? Operation Superglue has been all-consuming."

"I know," he says, touching my shoulder warmly. He holds his hand there longer than he should, and I know I should brush it away, but again, I don't.

I study him intently, searching his eyes for hints of his thoughts. His chin and lip are scruffy, like he needs a shave, and I like this look on him. His blue T-shirt clings to his muscles and causes his eyes to pop with shades of indigo. "Maybe we can talk sometime," I say, carefully choosing my words. "When all of this is over?"

"Talk about... that night..." His voice trails off because my cell phone begins dinging with Snapchat notifications.

"It's him," I say, leaping to my feet. "It's Lincoln. He's messaging me. He wants to meet up!" I cheer, eyes wide.

"This is good," Jon says, pacing back and forth behind his desk. "Where?"

"Messages delete after reading them, so write this down," I say, reading the address to Jon, and he types it into his laptop.

"It's a bus stop," he says, dragging his words.

"Well, that's creepy."

"Not going to happen," Jon says, shaking his head.

"What? Why not?"

"Because, Lina, you aren't bait. You didn't sign up for that."

"I did, and this is our chance. Do you think this is how it happened? To the girls? All on Snapchat?"

"Maybe. It would make sense."

"But what's the connection? Say there is some creep luring girls to a bus stop on Snap in the middle of the night. How does he know who to target? How are they connected?"

"I wonder if there are security cameras at the bus stop," Jon says, typing something into his laptop and grabbing his phone and keys.

"Where are you going?"

"To talk to the owners of the Circle K. It's adjacent to the bus stop, and they might have footage. This could be our big break."

"Let me get my purse."

"No," he insists, shaking his head. "You shouldn't come. Whoever this is just gave you the address. You can't go investigate this."

"What am I supposed to do then?"

"Go home. Be with the kids. Write your book."

"Jon—"

"I'm not putting you in danger, Lina. You are not meeting up with this dude. Not tonight, anyway."

"What am I supposed to tell him?"

"Tell him your parents won't let you out tonight. Ask him if you can meet up another night."

"But—"

"No buts. Go home, Lina."

"What about the missing kids?" I pout, crossing my arms and staring at the ground.

Jon tucks a strand of hair behind my ear and moves his hand to my shoulder. "What about our kids? They don't need a missing mom."

"You suck."

"Go home. Call me when you get there."

"Fine. Be careful," I say, taking the last bite of steak-and-cheese sub and reaching for my purse.

"And no naked photos for Lincoln."

"Yes, *Dad*."

Chapter Twenty-Six

Then (2018)

My heart pounded against my chest as I entered Starbucks in downtown Tempe. It had been years since I had a conversation with Jon Cote that consisted of more than drop off here and pick up there, etc. Occasionally, I would mention a school project that was due or provide contact info of parents for carpools and pickups but nothing more.

The meeting had been my idea, and I was kicking myself for it as I pulled the door open and entered the coffee shop—the same coffee shop I had been sitting at the day I first met Jon. It looked the same, which was eerie to me, considering all that had happened since that first day, when I had been typing away on my Dell—our first date, a pair of infinity tattoos, some homemade tacos, and a few babies, followed by a short-but-blissful marriage and a horrific divorce.

The twins were ten years old, and with that came relief from some parenting duties but heavier responsibilities with others, like trying to keep up with Lucy's social anxiety and Max's recent ADHD diagnosis. Lucy was also suddenly interested in boys, and I was determined to stay on top of things. Daphne and Ryker had questioned my reasoning for implementing this meeting, but the motives were simple. I was refusing to let my ego or my pride get in the way of the health and happiness of my kids.

Jon was seated at a table in the corner of Starbucks when I finally spotted him. I half expected him to be in uniform, but he wasn't. He wore jean shorts and a black T-shirt and was already sipping his coffee with a Frappuccino ready and waiting for me across from him. I nervously adjusted my ponytail, slung my purse on the empty chair, and slid into the seat across from him. "Thanks for the coffee," I said, removing the paper from the straw and piercing it through the whipped cream.

"Thanks for setting this up," he said between sips.

"This?" I stated boldly, holding my hand up in front of my face. "This is not about us. This is about Max and Lucy and nothing else."

"Sounds serious."

"I am."

"Need me to sign a waiver or something?" he asked sarcastically.

"Not a bad idea."

"I was joking."

"Hilarious," I said with a roll of my eyes. "You're not in uniform. Why not?"

"I'd tell you, but that would violate rule number 5,231."

"You're just a freaking comedian. What, did you get fired or something?"

Jon's expression fell flat, and I felt terrible for him for a moment. A short moment but still a moment. "Not… really."

"Oh God, I'm sorry. I—"

"I resigned."

"What happened?"

"An undercover op gone south." He shrugged. "It's fine. I'm actually studying for my PI license."

"I—"

"You don't have to worry. Child support won't be an issue. I'm technically on paid leave for a bit, including insurance."

"Oh." I shook my head. "I wasn't worried about that. I just got the next advance from my agent, and I've built up pretty good savings, so please don't worry."

"You always land on your feet, don't you?"

"Anyway," I said, sucking down my coffee like my life depended on it, "I'll start with Lucy." I opened my phone to the notes app.

"You have notes?"

"This is a meeting."

"Okay, let's hear it."

I talked for twenty minutes about Lucy and her friends' drama and her attempts to fake sickness to miss school. "I asked her if she wore her glasses to school yesterday, and you want to know what she said? She said she hadn't wanted to but needed them to see the boys better."

"Ouch," Jon grunted.

"And don't get me started on Max. He recorded his math teacher yelling at him about missed homework without her knowledge and has in-school recess detention for a month."

"For recording her?"

"For recording her and for texting it to a group chat."

"Ouch again."

"Yup. It will be critical that we communicate as they get older. Right now, it's recess detentions and schoolgirl crushes, but it won't be long before it's speeding tickets and pot."

"Speeding tickets and pot," Jon said with a smirk. "That is damn specific. Are you sure you don't mean sex, drugs, and rock and roll?"

"Jon, I need you to be serious."

"Copy that."

"I know stuff is going to happen." I sighed. "They are going to screw up, and I know that. I just don't want it to be because... well, because of our failures."

Jon considered this for a moment. "I get it. And for the record, you're a great mom, Lina."

I swatted away his compliment like I was shooing a fly. "That," I snapped. "None of that."

"I was giving you a compliment."

"No compliments."

"It was about the kids."

"Nope."

"Should I say you're a bad mom?"

I ignored this and sipped my coffee. "We need consistent rules. Right now, it's about bedtime, screen time, and nutrition, but soon, it will be more about curfews and boys in the bedroom."

"Boys in the bedroom? Don't you think you should slow down?"

"You knocked me up on our first date. Are you ready to be a grandfather, Jon?"

"Copy that."

"So, anyway, that's all I've got. And I think we should do this monthly."

"One month from now? Same time, same place?" he asked, clapping his hands together faux enthusiastically.

"Same time, same place."

"Lina?"

"What?" I asked, standing up and slinging my purse over my shoulder.

"We have terrific kids."

I turned to walk away but paused, wondering if I should agree with him. Jon and I had screwed up big time in many ways, but the truth was, we had really good kids. But I needed boundaries, strict and tight parameters, or this would never work. So instead of agreeing with Jon about how wonderful our cherubs were turning out, I raised my eyebrows and sassed, "Hold on tight, Officer Cote. It's going to be a wild ride."

Chapter Twenty-Seven

Now

My fingers tremble as I scan my key into the motel room's door. Jon is perched on the edge of the bed, fidgeting with a tiny black flip phone. "Hey," I say, shutting the door behind me.

"Did you make sure you weren't followed?"

I laugh at this, but he remains serious. "No, I wasn't followed," I say, but I have zero idea if this is true.

"Are the kids all set?"

I nod. "Ryker is bringing Max home from practice, and Daphne is hanging with Lucy, who is still eating Ben & Jerry's by the pint since the breakup. My mom and dad will be there overnight and into tomorrow. My mom does think it's funny that you and I are both on business trips. I guess she assumes something is going on with us."

Again, Jon remains serious. "What did you tell her?"

"Oh," I sigh. "I told her everything. I spilled the tea about Operation Superglue and told her we were meeting at Motel 6 to prepare for my first sting operation."

"Spill the tea?"

"It's slang. You know, like, for gossip."

"You're funny. What did you *really* tell her?"

"I need to fly to NYC to meet my publisher, and you have a nerdy PI convention."

"Seriously?"

"Yup."

"You're hopeless."

"I know."

"Are you sure you want to go through with this?"

"Positive."

Jon nods and tosses the cell phone behind him on the bed then reaches into his backpack, retrieving a necklace of some sort. "It's a GPS tracker," he says, gesturing for me to sit on the bed beside him while he clasps it around my neck.

"Thank you," I say as I clutch the fake gold necklace to my collarbone.

It has only been a few nights since Lincoln Stone first asked me to meet up with him. Jon got his hands on the security footage from Circle K, but unfortunately, the footage is automatically deleted every forty-eight hours, which didn't help us at all. All it told us was that June was not abducted from that specific spot, but that didn't rule out other bus stops. And that didn't stop Lincoln from demanding that I meet him at that location, so after days of begging Jon to let me do this, he agreed.

It was terrible saying goodbye to Max and Lucy. I kissed them goodbye and held them a little extra before releasing them, changing into my Gemma jean shorts and white tank top and heading out the door.

Saying bye to Daphne and Ryker was almost more complicated since they know what I'm getting myself into. Daphne hugged me and threatened to kill me if I let anything terrible happen, and Ryker cried over and over about how much he loved me, and I made him promise to take Alex back if I didn't make it home alive.

As much as I was kidding, a part of me knows it—I'm risking my life. I'm acting as literal bait, like a worm on a fishhook, and even though Jon will be trailing me, there is a slight chance that I might never return to my home, to my everyday life, to my kids, to… Jon.

I shake this thought from my head and scold myself for worrying about Jon, reminding myself that I hate Jon Cote, and he should be the last person I am worried about never seeing again. I should be concerned about never seeing Travis again, shouldn't I? Travis is the man I am romantically involved with. Travis would be mourning the loss of a significant other, not Jon.

"Want to go over it again?" Jon asks from his spot on the bed. His arm is pressed against mine, the heat from his body radiating onto me.

"Sure," I say, biting my lip. "You drop me off one block from the meeting location. I walk to the bus stop, and I wait for Lincoln Stone. I have my tracking necklace and my secret cell phone. I hold my Gemma burner phone in my hands. If Lincoln wants to take my phone, it is out in the open, and he won't need to search me. But do you really think it's going to go down like that? What if this guy just wants to talk?"

"He isn't going to want to talk."

"How do you know that?"

"If they put you in the trunk and you want to get out, just wait until the car stops. Do you need to watch the video again?"

"I've watched all of your stupid YouTube videos. And if they put me in the trunk, I will stay there until I find the girls."

"It's going to be scary," he warns. "And as hard as it is for me to say this, I agree. Also, don't forget that you have your Apple Watch. If they don't take that, I can track you there too."

"I've got this."

"I know you do."

I collapse and stare at the ceiling, and Jon does the same. We lie there in silence, Jon and I, hypnotized by the motion of the ceiling fan, as I ignore the voices in the back of my head screaming at me to go home to my children. Of course, I want to find the missing girls, and I realize I signed up for this. But at what point has this all become too much? I've put this before my children, career... and dating life.

As if reading my mind, Jon breaks the silence and asks, "Is there anyone else you need to call? You know, like a boyfriend? I can step out if you want to make a phone call."

"How honorable of you," I joke.

"I'm serious."

"There is no boyfriend. There is someone I've been seeing… but no boyfriend."

"What's his name?"

"Are you sure you want to hear about this?"

"I wouldn't be asking if I didn't."

"Travis. Travis Mullins."

"Where did you meet him?"

"His son goes to school with Max and Lucy. It's really nothing that serious. I mean, he wants it to be but…. You know. Do you…are you…"

"I'm not seeing anyone."

"Sorry, that was nosy."

"When did you get your tattoo removed?" he asks, clearly changing the subject.

"That's random."

"When?"

I exhale deeply. "The night you cornered me in the bathroom at that expensive steak house. I decided that night that I didn't want it anymore."

He turns his head and meets my stare. "Why that night?"

"Because that night, I had a shot with a really great guy. And I was so messed up from seeing you and what we went through… I… I just left him there. I lost the ability to trust, forget love… and I… I wanted to erase everything."

"You wanted to erase us."

"I wanted to erase us." A tear trickles down my cheek, and Jon inches closer, wiping it away. "How much time do we have?"

Jon looks at his watch and says, "We leave here in an hour. I set an alarm on my phone. I wanted to save time to order a pizza."

"I don't want pizza," I say, rubbing my hands over my queasy stomach.

"You should eat."

"I can't."

"I'll grab you a ginger ale," he says, pulling himself to a seated position.

"No," I say, bolder than I mean to. "Lie back down. We need to talk."

He does what I ask, only this time, he lies on his side facing toward me, and I do the same, his face only inches from mine. "About... about that night?"

"About that operation, that night, all of it. I... I need to hear it all before I go through with this."

"Well," he starts and stops and starts again. "You know it was an undercover drug bust."

"Like *21 Jump Street*, the movie?"

"Like *21 Jump Street*," he says with a soft smile. "Only way less exciting. I was Mace, as you know, and I was posing as a college senior. At first, things moved slowly, like how they did for you as Gemma. I tried to gain information by asking around, but I needed help to get it to work. The department was putting pressure on me. The drugs hit the streets harder than ever, and kids were dying left and right... even high schoolers."

I don't realize I am holding Jon's hand until he squeezes it tighter. "That's awful," I whisper, thinking of our kids.

"I started going out with my roommate late at night, and that's when I learned that I needed to focus my energy on the fraternity. I didn't want to, I swear, Lina. I wanted more than anything to be home with you."

I nod, letting the tears trickle down my cheeks and onto the pillow, but I remain silent, steadying my gaze on the intensity of his. "I joined the frat. I made it through every round of initiation, and it was… It was like nothing I had ever endured. There were pranks, paddles, and girls… Lots of girls."

I swallowed hard and resisted the urge to ask just how many girls because the truth was it didn't matter now.

"Are you okay?" he asks.

"Keep going."

"By the time I made it in, I was deep under. I'm not going to lie, Lina. There were times I forgot who I was. I know it's no excuse, but the partying wasn't just drinking… there were drugs too. I became obsessed with solving my case, so much so that I was doing drugs too. I wasn't Jon Cote anymore. I was Mason Andrews. And the guy you met, Owen? He was *really* dangerous. Most of the time, he carried a gun. He didn't have it on him that night… or… things would have ended a lot differently."

"Wow," I say, realizing it was a pretty dumb move to barge in on him like that. "And Hilary?"

"Owen was giving me shit for not showing interest in the girls. At first, he thought I might be gay, but something went down, and they were tipped off that the cops might be involved, and Owen and his gang grew suspicious of me. I started hooking up with Hilary to shut them up."

My stomach turns thinking about Jon hooking up with girls at college parties while I cared for our children and managed our household. I fight my anger and nod like I understand, because I recently flirted with an eighteen-year-old boy to get intel about missing girls, so on some level, I can relate. "Keep going."

"We were getting closer to the evidence we needed. It was all coming together, and Hilary started coming around more. We began spending more and more time together. I know it was wrong, Lina... and I'm so... I'm so sorry," he chokes out.

"You... You fell for her."

"No. *I* didn't. Mace did."

I start to argue, but I can't. Because even though I haven't experienced half of what Jon went through at ASU, I understand what it is like to be Gemma and switch to Lina and back again. "I understand."

"You do?"

"I guess I do."

"I didn't love her," he promises, squinting his eyes shut to hold his tears. But he fails miserably, and they flow out his eyeballs like a massive waterfall.

I inch closer to him and press his head to my neck's crevice as his tears gather on my skin. "It's okay."

"No, no, it's not."

"It has to be."

Jon pulls back and stares at me like he doesn't believe what he hears. "Really?"

"Really. And... and I shouldn't have barged in on you that night. It was stupid and dangerous, and I'm pleading insanity."

"Lina, you have to understand. If Owen realized I was a cop, he would have killed all of us. You, me, and Daphne. I had to go along with it. I knew he was going to let you go. But what he did to you, I'll never forgive myself for letting that happen. But I had no choice."

"I know."

"But we took him down, you know. That asshole is still in jail today," he says between sobs. "We got him."

"Good."

"But it wasn't worth it. I lost you. I lost everything."

"Yeah. You did."

"If I could do it over again, I would change all of it. Every second."

"But the drugs would still be on the streets," I say soothingly. "You did a good job, Jon."

"Thanks," he sniffs, pressing his head against my chest. "Do you think… Is there a way… you could ever forgive me?"

I think about this for a beat, and he cries harder when I don't answer him. "I shouldn't have asked that."

"It's complicated," I whisper because it is. "But knowing how it went down and understanding what it's like to let something like this take over your entire life helps."

"So maybe someday?"

"Maybe someday."

"I'm not that guy anymore, Lina. I'm not the same person I was back then, and I know you aren't either. I would love to get to a place where you could learn to trust me again."

"I'd like that too," I say, fingering his hair. "You're a good man, Jon Cote."

"You're not so bad yourself," he jokes.

"This is all going to be okay," I say, unsure if I'm reassuring Jon or myself.

"It has to be. I won't let anything happen to you, I promise."

"You might not be able to promise that."

"I promise."

"Just… if you can't keep that promise—"

"Lina—"

"If you can't keep that promise, tell the kids what happened here. I want them to know what a badass I am." I smile. "And then you need to take these guys down. Find the girls."

"Okay."

Jon pulls me against him, and it is my turn to ugly cry. Jon wraps his arms around my waist and tugs me tighter. He kisses my forehead, tucks my hair behind my ear, and presses his lips to my temple. "And explain everything to Molly too. Let her know that even though I wasn't who I said I was, I... loved her."

"You need to stop talking like this," he says, releasing me, pulling himself up on his elbows, and reaching for the flip phone.

"It's important."

"Okay. Take this," he says, tucking the phone into the palm of my hand.

"I'm supposed to tuck this in my bra?" I laugh. "It seems so... I don't know, Scarlett Johansson in *Lost in Translation*."

Jon removes the phone from my hand and holds his stare on mine. His face remains serious but expressionless as he tucks the flip phone into the depths of my cleavage.

"That's the most action I've had in years," I joke.

But Jon isn't laughing. "Hey, Lina?" he asks, his tone heavy and unshakable.

"Yeah?" I ask, my words catching in my throat and my palms sweaty.

"Do all your books have happy endings?"

"I mean... I write young adult suspense novels... so no, not really."

"Oh." He frowns. "Can this one?"

"This one?"

"Our story. Can it have a happy ending? Please?"

I try to process his question, but my head begins to spin, and my heart rate increases because Jon is kissing my forehead again, only this time, he holds his lips to my hairline longer than before and then slides his mouth to my cheek and farther down toward my neck, and suddenly my tears have stopped short, like a garden hose being bent in half, cutting off all water flow entirely. "Jon," I whisper into the darkness of our motel room.

Jon's lips slide over my collarbone, and a soft moan escapes me. I lie back, guiding him, welcoming his kisses and his touch as the rhythm of my breath increases, as does his. "Is this okay?"

"God, yes." I groan, catching his face between my hands and leading his lips to mine. It's different at first—his facial hair tickles my upper lip in a slightly unfamiliar way—but when his mouth fully meets mine and he gently explores me with his tongue, I am reminded of what it feels like to be with this man, to run my fingers through his hair, to feel his breath on mine, to dig my fingernails into the back of his shoulders, unable to get close enough to him no matter how hard I try, and for a second, in this moment, I have forgotten about everything. I stop thinking about Operation Superglue, the missing girls, Gemma Mendoza, Mace Andrews, slutty Hilary, and everything that has happened between that first day in Starbucks when I locked eyes with the most handsome police officer I had ever laid eyes on, and all I can think of is *yes*. "Yes, Jon. Don't stop," I beg because I want him more than I have ever wanted anyone or anything.

"Are you sure?"

"Stop asking me if I'm sure," I moan as I remove his T-shirt and launch it to the floor. I trace my fingers over his American flag tattoo as I did that first night in his apartment. "I'm a grown-ass woman."

"Yeah, you are." He chuckles. "You're a hot, grown-ass woman."

"I love this tattoo," I say because I do, and I press my mouth against it, gliding over his chest and abdomen and back up again.

"Look at it closer," he says, pointing above the corner of the flag.

"I can't see it."

"Here," he says, reaching for his cell and flashing the light between us.

"Oh my goodness." I gasp. Over his pec muscle and above the blue corner of the American flag are four birds.

"Four eagles," he explains, his lips curling into a soft smile.

"It's beautiful."

"Me, Max, Lucy, and…"

"And me?" I ask, unable to contain my surprise. Jon Cote has a tattoo of his family, me included, and I had no idea. What am I supposed to say to this? I'm at a loss for words, so instead of talking, I press my mouth to his chest and kiss it.

"Lina," he whispers between breaths. "There is so much more I want to say."

I press my pointer finger to his lips and shake my head. "No more talking."

Jon rolls onto his back and pulls me on top of him, and I shimmy out of my tank top, the flip phone plummeting down onto the mattress, a brief reminder of what we are really doing here, but I ignore it, removing my bra and pressing my bare chest down onto his, the heat from his skin setting me on fire as my hair falls over him and we continue to kiss.

He gathers my hair in one hand and traces my bare back with his other. "You're so beautiful," he whispers.

There is so much I want to say in reciprocation of this, but I'm afraid of saying too much—or not enough—so I say nothing. Instead, I pull myself off him and begin unbuttoning his jeans. He removes them, and I do the same, shimmying out of my own clothes until we are naked and intertwined and making out like two college kids in love, not a middle-aged man and his ex-wife who should be preparing for an undercover sting operation, but I've stopped caring because in this moment, in this instance, nothing else matters. Jon is like a drug, and he's numbing my fear, my anxiety, my doubt, everything.

It may be because I might not make it out of this alive. It may be because I have finally reached a point of understanding with him. It could be because, deep down, I know that I am in love with Jon Cote and will always be in love with him. Either way, this is what is supposed to happen now, in this moment. So when Jon turns me on my side, presses his chest against my back, and slowly slides his hand down the front of my body, stopping between my thighs, and touches me in a way that proves he remembers me, he knows me… I fully surrender.

"I want you," I whisper. "I want you, Jon."

Jon continues moving his fingers over me until I can't take it anymore. I'm making sounds I haven't made with anyone, not even him, and I'm begging for things I didn't know I wanted.

"I want you too," he groans, rolling me onto my back and climbing on top of me.

He pushes himself inside me quickly, and I wrap my legs around his waist, digging my fingernails into his shoulder blades, my eyes remaining open, taking in every second of this, every second of him, and he does the same as our bodies move together in perfect unison. He is calling my name loud enough for the people in the next city to hear him until our bodies explode, and he collapses onto me, and then it is silent.

We lie there, in the room's darkness, our breaths slowing, and I wrap my arms around his lower back and decide I never want to let go. "Jon—" I start but stop because the sound of his cell-phone alarm pierces through our happy little bubble and makes me want to vomit.

"It's time," he whispers into my ear.

"I… I don't know if I want to go through with it," I choke out.

"What?" he asks, his tone one of concern. He pushes himself up onto his elbows, his nose pressed against mine. "What's going on?"

"I'm just kidding." I snort. "Let's catch these assholes."

"You're crazy, you know that?"

"Maybe." I smile, kissing him again. "But I think you like it."

"Maybe," he says, pressing his lips to my forehead. "What do you say we get this over with?"

"Let's go catch some bad guys," I agree. "But do you think there is still time for pizza?"

"No." He snickers. "There isn't time for pizza. But open my backpack. I brought you a box of Cheez-Its."

Chapter Twenty-Eight

Then (2023)

I was elbow deep in a twenty-gallon tub of vanilla ice cream with a line of students eagerly awaiting their turns when I noticed the man scooping alongside me kept glancing my way.

I had always found the sensation that happens when I feel someone looking at me interesting. Like little electric pulses in various parts of my body, and I knew, at that moment, he wanted to talk to me, and I was correct. "This scooping is no joke," he said with a laugh as I adjusted my plastic glove and continued working.

"Right? I won't need to go to the gym for a while. My right bicep will never be the same. I should probably switch arms soon."

He grinned at this, and I decided that I liked his smile. He was tall, handsome, and athletic, with dark and radiant skin that caused me to do a double take. "At least the kids are happy."

"True," I said as I passed them their bowls, and they continued down the line of toppings at the school's ice cream social. "You have kids here?"

"No, I just scoop ice cream at middle schools for fun," he joked.

"Funny."

"My son, Smith, is an eighth grader."

"How about you? Are you a teacher?"

"Me? No, my kids go here."

"You don't look old enough to have kids in middle school."

"Well, I do." I smiled, enjoying the compliment. "I have twins in eighth grade. Max and Lucy Cote."

"Max plays football, right? My son tried it last year, but it wasn't his thing. He is thinking about trying out for soccer next year at Coronado."

The last students passed us by, and we were left with empty ice cream containers and messy gloves. "My daughter wants to cheer there as well," I said, avoiding the tiny voice that warned me of mixing my mom life with my dating life. I pried the dirty gloves off my hands and tossed them in the trash.

"It's hard to believe it's time for high school already."

"Tell me about it."

"What do you do for work?"

"I'm an author," I said with a smile.

"That's amazing! Anything I might have read?"

"I write under a pen name, so maybe?" I shrug. "It's just easier that way. What do you do?"

"I'm a pharmacist in Mesa."

"Nice," I said, gathering my purse from under the table. I checked my watch, realizing I would be late for drinks with Daphne and Ryker if I didn't head out soon.

"What does your husband do?"

"Excuse me?"

"Your husband? What does he do?"

"I'm not married," I said, wanting to shove my naked ring finger in his face. "But Max and Lucy's dad is a private investigator in downtown Tempe."

"Wow, that's pretty cool. Sorry, I didn't mean to get too personal."

"It's fine," I said with a shrug. "We met young. What does your wife do?" I asked, eager to change the subject.

"I'm divorced," he said matter-of-factly. "Smith's mom is an elementary school teacher."

I rechecked my watch and smiled. "I'm late to meet some friends for drinks. I should gather my cherubs so I can get them home. Nice to meet you…" My voice trailed off as I realized I never got his name.

"Travis. I'm Travis Mullins."

"Lina Rivera," I said with a smile. "Have a good night."

"Hey, Lina?"

"Yeah?"

"Here's my card," he said, slipping me a rectangular piece of heavy cardstock. "I'd love to take you out sometime."

"Oh," I said politely, holding up my hand. "I'd love to, it's just… Do you think it's a good idea? I mean, our kids go to school together."

"I think the kids will be fine." He chuckled, tucking his card in my palm and closing my hand. "Think about it?"

"You don't get turned down a lot, do you?" I winked.

"Hardly ever." He smirked. "I'm also not good at taking no for an answer."

That's because you are drop-dead freaking gorgeous. "Okay," I agreed, relishing his fingers' warmness against mine and allowing myself to again marvel at his beauty. "I'll think about it. Bye, Travis Mullins." And with that, I turned and walked out of the middle school gym, eager to tell Ryker and Daphne that I met Winston Duke's doppelganger, and I just might have a date with him.

***

Less than forty-five minutes later, I was seated at Ryker's favorite sports bar in Scottsdale with my two favorite people. Daphne sat to my right and Ryker across from me, sipping a Corona Light with lime. Daphne's husband, Mal, was in New York City on business, and Ryker's boyfriend, Alex, was behind on a big project for work, so for the first time in what felt like forever, it was just the three of us again.

We had barely ordered drinks and apps before I was spilling it about Travis Mullins and how I had the willpower to turn him down, which probably made him want me more.

"She finally gets it!" Daphne cheered, pumping her fist in the air.

"Gets what?" I asked, a tad bit offended.

"I've been trying to teach you how to play hard to get for years. Do you remember? If you had listened, you wouldn't have gotten knocked up on your second date by Jon."

"First, I like my kids, so take that back. And it was the first date. The second date, I tested positive on the pregnancy test."

"Either way, it's good you are playing hard to get."

"I don't get it," Ryker chimed in. "If you like the guy, call him."

"I don't know if I like him." I shrugged.

"She's attracted to him," Daphne said between bites of nachos.

"He's super hot," I agreed.

"Lina volunteered at the ice cream social and left with something yummier than the ice cream." Ryker chuckled, laughing at his joke.

"Cheers to that," I said, clinking my glass to Ryker's beer. "You really think I should call him? How awkward would it be if things didn't work out and I had to see him at sporting events and school functions?"

"I think you might be overthinking it," Ryker advised. "You don't have to marry the guy tomorrow, but you should at least call him."

"I think she's hesitating for other reasons," Daphne said boldly.

"What do you mean?" Ryker asked.

"She hasn't dated anyone seriously since Jon. She can't trust or commit, and she's deathly afraid of getting her heart broken."

"I can see that," Ryker agreed.

"Hello!" I shouted. "I'm sitting right here."

"We know." Daphne smiled. "Maybe Ry is right. Maybe you should text him. It's 2023. Nobody talks on the phone anymore."

"Okay," I said, pulling out my phone.

"Not yet!" Daphne shrieked.

"Why?" I asked, jumping back in surprise.

"You need to wait at least a day. Geeze, have I taught you nothing? Put the phone down and eat a nacho. Loverboy Travis needs to stew in this a bit."

Chapter Twenty-Nine

Now

I sit, perched on the bus stop's bench, the chilly-night desert breeze tickling my bare legs. I rub my hands against my arms to ease the chill, but I know it's useless. I'm not cold. I'm petrified, and I'm in this now, and there is no backing out. According to my latest Snap with Lincoln Stone, he will be here any minute and can't wait to meet me.

I rest my head against the bench and study the night sky. As scary and self-sabotaging as this mission is, I can't stop thinking about what happened at Motel 6 with my ex-husband. My thoughts are a whirlwind of emotions, like a tornado spinning furiously through my mind. Do I regret sleeping with Jon moments before I risk my life? No, I don't regret sleeping with Jon. It was, in fact, probably one of the best nights of my life. So, if I do die tonight, it was a pretty good way to go.

On the flip side, if I survive our undercover sting operation with Lincoln Stone and get back to my former life, where I can put Operation Superglue behind me, then... That's where things start to get stickier—no pun intended. I have questions for Jon and don't know where to begin. Does this mean we are back together? Is that even what I really want? Would that be going backward and giving up everything I've built for myself? Or do I trust that he has changed and grown? How can I entirely leave the past in the past?

Of course, there is also the matter of Max and Lucy. The idea of them knowing what just happened with their parents mortifies me in ways I can't comprehend. They *can't* know what happened. Only when I know more about what is happening with Jon will I mention anything.

I close my eyes and count to five, reliving what happened just a few minutes ago in the motel room. Jon, how he moved over me, touched and kissed me in all the right ways. His breath was against my ear as he called out to me in the stillness of the night, and the way he hadn't wanted to let me go as much as I didn't want to let go of him.

Afterward, I got dressed, secured the phone in my secret hiding spot, pulled my hair up into a high pony, and told him I was ready to go as if I were suggesting we hit up the nearest McDonald's drive-through for a Big Mac. I avoided making eye contact with him as I buckled my seat belt and we pulled away from our little bubble of happiness. When he pulled over a block from the bus stop, he took my face in his hands and kissed me again, squeezing his eyes closed tightly.

"See you later," I whispered, my voice catching.

"Lina..."

"Please don't," I begged. "No goodbyes. I need to stay strong."

"You are strong."

"I'll see you in a bit," I said firmly.

"I'll see you in a bit," he agreed. "But Lina—"

"I'll see you," I said again, closing the door behind me, not even turning back once before I strode toward the bus stop, ready to meet Lincoln Stone, the man of Gemma's dreams.

I stretch my arms over my head and sigh, reaching for my phone, curious about where Lincoln might be, but as I do, my breath stops short. I inhale but can't take in the air. Someone has come up behind me, and their cold hands trap my airway because they are wrapped around my throat, and I realize I'm choking. I'm actually being freaking choked. My eyes bulge wide open as my vision blurs and a figure steps closer. I flail my arms and kick my legs as I try to scream, but I can't.

I hear a car pull up just a few feet from me. *Help*, I silently beg. *Help me.* Is it Jon? Did he bail on the mission to come help me? Is it a stranger who stumbled upon the scene?

"Get her in the back," a man's voice instructs. It is deep, grave, and sounds familiar, but I can't place it. Why can't I place it? A teacher at the school? *Come on, Lina, think!*

"Not until she's out," the man behind me argues.

"She won't go anywhere, man. Just do it before someone sees us."

"Get the bat," a third voice demands. "It's in the back seat. And grab her phone, toss the SIM card, and let's get out of here."

I begin to freak out. I jab my elbows into the ribs of the person who has stood me upright and released my throat but has wrapped one arm around my waist and is tugging me toward him. "Help!" I scream through the hand covering my mouth. I bite down out of instinct, hoping to clench my teeth against his hand, but instead, my top teeth pierce my bottom lip, and I groan in pain as my purse is ripped off my body and my cell phone snatched from my hands.

I open my eyes just in time to see the car. The driver is blurry through my tears, but the metal baseball bat is not, and as it strikes me against the side of my head and my knees crumple beneath me, I think of nothing. Nothing except Jon and how I would give anything for one more chance. One more chance to tell him how I really feel. And the thought of never being able to do this hurts more than a baseball bat to the side of the head. The idea of dying without saying I love you seems worse than whatever these idiots have planned for Gemma Mendoza, and as I drift off to unconsciousness and hear the car's trunk slam shut, I know that I will do whatever I can to get my second chance. *I'll see you, Jon. I'll see you soon.*

Stacy Lee

***

Earworms. No, not earthworms. *Earworms.* I had not heard of them, either, until two weeks prior to this unfortunate experience when studying the human brain in psychology class. We've all had earworms. It's a cognitive itch that causes the brain to itch back, otherwise known as *I have a freaking annoying song stuck in my head.* Since these cognitive annoyances tend to happen more often when we are anxious or stressed out, it makes sense that "Who Let the Dogs Out" by Baha Men is powerfully belting at me from the deepest part of my soul. My fists clench tighter by my sides, thick beads of sweat trickle down my lower back, and the air inside the car's trunk seems to dissipate by the second.

I'm supposed to stay calm. Car trunks are not airtight, so the chance of running out of oxygen is unlikely. That's a lot easier to believe when you are not stuffed in one. *Think, Lina.* Jon went over hundreds of worst-case kidnapping scenarios prior to his departure, knowing that anything could happen. He explained, in rather boring detail, all of the ways to escape from the trunk of a car. I hadn't realized that automobiles produced post-2002 have an emergency lever inside, but if there is one, I can't find it. I could try to get into the car's dark interior through the back seat, but that isn't budging, either. I could kick out the taillight, but what would that solve? I chose this. I am here on purpose. Escaping is only an option if I want to quit. I should probably mention that I'm not a quitter.

I tightly close my eyes and attempt, with my entire being, to slow down my breathing and calm my beating heart which now is pounding in rhythm to my itching brain to the song's lyrics. I vividly remember the snatching of my purse and the sudden removal of my Apple Watch from my wrist. They took everything before shoving me so effortlessly into the car trunk. What am I supposed to do now? How had I agreed to something like this? How can I remain calm enough to make this work? Then I remember the small, cheap flip phone that was hidden in my bra prior to the start of our operation.

I dig my sweaty fingers into my cleavage and flip open the cell phone, wondering why they hadn't tied my wrists together. I then select the only number preprogrammed, my ex-husband's. The car swerves from the left to the right and back again as the phone plummets with a thud somewhere near my leg. I vaguely make out the sound of Jon's voice from someplace in the distance as I frantically pat around me, then finally breathe a heavy sigh of relief when my hand firmly clasps the device.

"Jon?" I whisper, grasping the phone to my ear while nervously speaking into the darkness.

"Lina." His tone is serious and gravelly, grounding me in a way I don't expect.

"Hi," I whisper.

"Hi."

"Well, this sucks."

"You're doing great."

"I am?"

"You are. How's your head?"

"My head?" I allow the confusion to settle over me but only briefly. I'm instantly aware of a pounding sensation in my left temple. I touch a quivering finger to the injured area, where I'm met with a wetness that could be blood or tears or maybe both. "I don't know," I confess.

"They got you pretty good. You probably have a concussion."

"Okay," I utter because, really, there is nothing else to say.

"Lina—"

"I'm fine, really," I whimper, biting down on my lower lip and shaking away the new memory.

"If you want to end this right now, just say the word."

I consider it for a moment, the idea of this nightmare coming to an end sounding more than enticing. But then I think of the girls…all of them. The way their families have worried and mourned and how completely agonizing it must be for them to not know their children's whereabouts. I think about Max and Lucy and how devastating it would be if something happened to them. The knot in the pit of my stomach tightens.

"Nah, I'm chillin'," I say with conviction.

"I'm serious. I'm trailing you now, but who knows where these scumbags are taking you."

"I guess we'll find out."

"Do you still have the necklace?"

I nod, securing my fingers around the faux-gold heart-shaped locket that Jon gently secured around my collarbone just hours earlier.

"Lina?"

"Yes." I'm nodding.

"It's a GPS tracker."

"I know." The car takes a tight turn, forcing me from my back to my side. From the cell phone's light, I make out a miniature pool of blood on the trunk's carpet, and I let out a tiny yelp. "Oh, God."

"What? What is it?"

"It's nothing," I lie. "I'm just getting carsick."

"You're a terrible liar." The car picks up speed then turns once more. "Damn it," Jon grunts. "I think I know where they're taking you. Listen to me, Lina. If you really… If you really want to do this, you need to understand that I might… I might not be able to help you. At least, not right away."

"But the necklace—"

"The necklace is not going to save you. If you want out, you need to tell me now." The car swerves again, and this time, I barrel roll twice before landing on my stomach.

"I'm doing this, Jon. We didn't come this far to give up now. We can do this."

"Just do what they say, and don't fight them," he says, his voice growing softer and much weaker.

"I'll be okay."

"I'm sorry for getting you into this."

"Don't be. Operation Superglue for life." I chuckle, but Jon doesn't find this funny, and his silence speaks volumes. "Jon?"

"I'm here."

"I can do this."

"I know."

"It can't be worse than birthing seven-pound twin babies."

"Actually, it probably can."

"Have *you* ever birthed seven-pound twin babies *naturally*?"

"Are we here again? Now?"

"Yes," I laugh. "We are."

"I'll stop underestimating you. Point taken."

"Just do me a favor and tell the kids I love them. I should probably save the phone's battery." My words catch in the back of my throat at the possibility of never seeing them again.

"Just… Just please be careful."

"I will. And Jon? I—"

My words are cut short since the car has come to an unexpected and abrupt stop. My body slides backward, and my head slams hard against the wall. I shake away the sharp pain that has formed at the base of my neck, do my best to power off the cell, and shove it in the back of my shorts just as the trunk swings open. I squint my eyes into focus, and gasp in horror at the unexpected sight before me. Very quickly, I realize that maybe, just maybe, there are times in life far worse than childbirth, and *this*... this is one of those times.

Travis. Travis. Freaking. Mullins. "Travis?" I choke from the depths of the trunk. "What in the actual hell are you doing here?"

Chapter Thirty

Then (July 2024)

Travis Mullins. My handsome, tenderhearted, generous, supportive, and patient *friend* sat across from me at an upscale steak house in Old Towne, sipping a dirty martini and listening attentively as I babbled on about the release of my latest book and how I was sure the reviews would be nothing short of fabulous. Travis was the kind of man who didn't half listen or interrupt sentences midway to say things like, "Oh, that happened to me once" or "That reminds me of the time..." No. Travis was the guy who listened, like actually listened, and I liked this characteristic of his best. Although his broad, toothy smile and mysterious ebony eyes were right up there. Oh, and his laugh. The way he laughed made me want to start laughing, too, even if I wasn't in the greatest of moods. Plus, he would be good in bed. I knew this because Travis was one of the best kissers... ever.

"You're so talented," Travis said, biting into his steak.

"How would you know? You haven't read the books." I winked.

"You won't let me!" he countered. "You won't even tell me who you are in the author world."

"Because I write anonymously."

"But why?"

"I don't know," I said, tucking a strand of hair behind my ear and biting my lower lip. "At first, it was because I didn't want the attention. I was worried I might not be good. But now, I don't know... I guess I like the mystery."

"You are one amazing woman, Lina Rivera."

I sipped my margarita and smiled. "You're pretty great too." I shrugged. But I wanted to say, *God, I think you're fabulous.* But I didn't, and I wasn't sure why. This was our fourth date since our first meeting at the ice cream social, and the only private time we had thus far was one make-out session in the front seat of his car that lasted a solid hour.

I wondered if our reasoning for avoiding our homes had been because of our teenagers or if we were just hesitant to progress faster. Sometimes, I sensed that Travis wanted to move things along quicker than I did, but I was cautious, and it didn't take a rocket scientist to explain why.

I knew, without a doubt, that it might be nearly impossible for me to fully trust and commit to someone else. What I went through with Jon had been traumatic, to say the least, and after finally taking my mother's advice, two years prior, I began seeing Tanya, a therapist who officially diagnosed me with PTSD from my evening at the frat house and agreed to see me weekly. I had confided in Tanya about my dating life, and she encouraged me to take things with Travis slowly but not to count him out.

Travis excused himself for the restroom, and I retrieved my cell from my purse in hopes of a response from either twin about their whereabouts, but my last two texts to both were still unanswered. I opened my Life360 App to find that neither had their locations turned on. "Great," I moaned. I had reason to believe that Lucy was with her boyfriend, Oliver, doing God knows what, and Max had made mention of a party for incoming freshmen that he was interested in checking out. I had given both of them 10:30 p.m. curfews, but I still insisted that they answer me if I texted them, and they were failing at this instruction miserably.

"Everything okay?" Travis asked, sliding back into his seat.

"Sort of. My kids aren't answering me." I shrugged. "I know it's only nine p.m., and their curfews are 10:30 p.m., but they turned off Life360."

"Smart little buggers." Travis chuckled.

"Seriously. I can't believe they are starting high school."

"You don't look old enough to have kids in high school." Travis winked. "You look like you should be in high school."

"Flattery will get you anywhere, Travis Mullins."

Our waitress returned with two dessert menus, placing one in front of Travis and the other in front of me. "Take your time." She winked. "The waffle sundae is to die for."

She turned and walked away, leaving Travis and me to decide if we were staying for dessert or if this would be the night we would either make out in his car again or go home together. "What are you thinking?" I asked. "Dessert?"

"I don't know if I can pass up an opportunity to eat a waffle for dessert in a fancy steak house."

"Want to split it?" I suggested. "It has cinnamon gelato on top."

"Sure—" he started but stopped, glancing at his phone. His eyes narrowed, and his nose crinkled as he held his breath and puckered his lips, clearly deep in thought. Travis typed back before turning his phone over on the table and smiling at me. "Actually," he sighed. "I don't know if I can stick around for that waffle."

"Everything all right? Is it Smith?"

"Gosh, no. Smith is great. He's at his mom's tonight."

Which means your house is empty? I considered asking, but I chickened out miserably and said, "Oh? What's going on, then?"

"It's a colleague of mine. I've been blowing him off for months, and he's insisting I stop by tonight for dessert and cigars."

"Interesting," I said as disappointment washed over me. "Who is this colleague?" I asked, picturing some mini pharmaceutical convention where Travis sat around discussing how to ensure patients receive the appropriate medication dosages.

"Great family guy, lives in the ritzy part of Paradise Valley. You would really like his wife," he said, flagging down our waitress and asking for the check.

"And he needs you there… tonight?"

"I promised him, but I thought he would forget."

Travis's voice trailed off as my phone buzzed. I swiped it open, hoping for some sign of life from my children, but it was Daphne rambling on about Mal refusing to redo their master bathroom because he would rather spend the money on a man cave. "I should probably get home too." I sighed. "These kids are going to give me gray hair."

"You sure? You should come with me," he said, his smile hopeful. "He's a cool guy. He runs a private school in Tempe. He's the dean of admissions. Dean Orson Turner. He has three teenagers, and his wife just had a baby. Imagine that. Starting over now."

"No, I can't," I said, sipping the last of my drink. "You go. I will wait for Max and Lucy to kill them with my bare hands for not answering their mother. But give my best to your friends for me. They sound like great people, for sure."

"Okay," he said, reaching for my hand and kissing the top of it. "I owe you one."

I thanked him for dinner, kissed him goodbye, and ordered myself a waffle sundae to go, deciding that no man, not even Travis Mullins, would decide my fate… especially when it came to dessert.

Chapter Thirty-One

Now

Travis gapes at me as he reaches into the car's trunk and pulls me out by my armpits. For a moment, I hope beyond hope that Travis is here to rescue me, but as he snorts deeply and plants my feet on the ground, holding my arms behind my back as if I'm under arrest, my longing shatters, and I am left dumbfounded, dazed, and terrified—genuinely terrified.

"Walk. And keep your head down," he demands, leading me through a large open area toward a bridge.

I ignore his request to keep my head down, and instead, I examine my surroundings as quickly and accurately as I can, just in case I have a chance to talk to Jon, as my secret phone is still in the waistband of my shorts.

"I said head down," he barks.

"Or what?" I challenge. "You going to blow up my phone with annoying booty calls? Show up at my house unannounced? Threaten me with dating ultimatums?"

"What's she talking about?" a man's voice shouts from behind.

"She's talking crazy, Slinky. Chick's insane. She thinks I'm someone else. Damn, you slammed her in the temple with a metal bat. Can't expect her to make sense."

"Screw you," I mutter.

"Shut up," he warns.

I ignore him, peering behind me, where the two other men follow. Both guys are bald and appear in their mid-thirties or early forties. They are bony and unkempt, with tattoos on their arms, necks, and faces, and I shudder at the thought of their fists around the baseball bat, or their fingers pressed to my mouth. The idea of this makes my stomach turn, and because of this and the concussion I presumably have, I turn and vomit on Travis's feet.

"Keep her moving," one of them shouts. "Or knock her out again and drag her down there."

"Calm down, Ace. I've got her," Travis mumbles.

My head spins, wondering where "down there" might be and whether June and the other girls might be nearby, and in this moment, I realize that even though they are leading me to exactly where I need to be, it would be in my best interest to act a bit more like a fearful teenager being kidnapped and less like an undercover detective pissed off at her boyfriend. "Please," I beg. "Please let me go. I… I didn't do anything."

"Shut up," Ace snaps. "You're not going anywhere. You belong to us now."

"My father will never let you get away with this," I bark. Travis looks at me like I have ten heads. "What are you looking at?" I snap. "My dad will come for you and get you for this."

"This isn't some movie, sweetheart," Ace grunts, shoving me forward as we approach an entrance.

"Where are we going?" I ask Travis as more vomit creeps up the back of my throat, and I bend down to throw up again.

Nobody answers me as I am shoved lower and lower until I realize we are underground. My knees grow weaker, and my legs turn to Jell-O as Ace and Slinky push ahead of us and march on, and I lean on Travis for support. Dizziness overtakes me, and I hold on to his arm for help, the same arm that has held me close as we kissed, the same arm I have clung to in bed while we made love. *How is this happening?*

I decide that this is a nightmare. There is always the possibility that I never woke up in the trunk, right? Travis Mullins is literally the sweetest, nicest man I've ever dated. He didn't even want to kill a spider one night in his kitchen. Something is wrong. Something is really, really wrong.

Darkness surrounds us as Travis drags me through the narrow underground hallway. It is silent except for our feet against the concrete ground and what sounds like distant voices up ahead, and I stop in my tracks as a horrific rotten-egg smell invades my sinuses, and I bend forward to vomit again, but nothing comes out. Instead, I crumple to the ground, bursting into tears, and I cannot breathe.

"Stand up," Travis whispers.

"I can't," I cry. "I can't do this."

"You need to cooperate, or they *will* kill you."

"They?" I chuckle through my tears. "Not you?"

"Look… I don't know what you're doing here or why these assholes think you are an eighteen-year-old chick named Gemma, but I won't let anything happen to you. We will get through this if you keep quiet and start moving."

"Forgive me if I think you're full of shit," I snap.

"Just keep moving," he demands, pulling me up by the armpit.

"What's that smell? Where are we?"

Travis wraps my arm around his neck and drags me forward. "None of that is important."

"That's subjective," I moan, fighting the pounding in my temple.

We round a corner, and I realize we are in some sort of underground tunnel. I see that Ace and Slinky are out of sight, so I take this opportunity to thrust my knee into Travis's groin as hard and forcefully as I can before turning and running in the opposite direction.

Travis releases my arm and falls forward, releasing an uncomfortable groan, but I don't stick around to watch. I have enough information for Jon at this point, and it is time to get the hell out of here.

"Don't do this!" he warns.

My legs move faster than I know is possible as I sprint through the underground tunnel, unable to see two feet before me. I reach into the waistband of my shorts and pull out my flip phone and manage to stick it back into my shirt while I keep sprinting, but Travis is faster, and it isn't long before he is tackling me, like a cornerback taking down the opposing team's wide receiver, and my arm hits the ground with a thud, followed by my head.

I'm not sure which hurts more, the pain that shoots through my arm or the feeling in my gut as the wind has undoubtedly been knocked out of me, but Travis doesn't seem to care as he climbs off me and picks me up in one effortless swoop, throwing me over his shoulder and continuing through the tunnel.

"Why are you doing this?" I ask, my voice coming out in a choked whisper. "Think of the kids—"

"I told you to be quiet. For the love of God, Lina, if you want to get out of this alive, you need to keep your head down and just do what I say."

"You're going to regret this," I moan as I fight the urge to close my eyes. "You are really going to regret this."

Chapter Thirty-Two

Then (2024)

Travis and I were finishing dinner at his kitchen table when a spider creepily sauntered by my bare toes. "Eek!" I shrieked.

"What is it?" Travis asked, clearly alarmed.

"It's a daddy longlegs," I chirped, pulling my legs onto the chair and hugging my knees.

"What?" He smirked. "You don't like spiders?"

"Kill it, please," I begged.

"What did it ever do to you?" Travis asked. "Those are harmless."

"Actually, they do bite."

"Where is it?" Travis asked, bending down by my feet.

"It went that way." I pointed.

"Uh huh," Travis said as he reached for an empty drinking glass and an unopened envelope.

"What are you doing? Kill it!"

"I'm not going to kill it." He chuckled as he trapped the spider under the cup. He slid the envelope underneath, creating a barrier and enclosing the daddy longlegs inside. He opened his sliding door and shook the glass until the spider was back outside where it belonged. "There." He smiled. "All better."

"I guess," I said with a shiver. "It might come back in."

"It's not going to come back in." He laughed, kissing my knee and rubbing my legs. "Besides, I was planning on taking you upstairs anyway."

My shoulders stiffened, and I sat up a bit straighter. "You've never let me upstairs before," I said, raising my eyebrows.

"Smith is at his friend's house overnight," he declared, his tone seductive and flirty. "You'd better come upstairs with me."

My heart fluttered, and an anxious chill raced through me as this would be the first time Travis and I would be alone together. Our car make-out sessions had become regular for us, and I knew Travis was eager to take things to the next level, as was I. "Okay then," I sang, matching his tone. I handed him my dishes, and he loaded them into his dishwasher. "I'm going to use the restroom," I said, excusing myself into the half bath off the side of his kitchen.

I entered the bathroom and closed the door behind me. I clutched the sink with both hands as I breathed through the waves of panic that encompassed my soul. I was not a stranger to this anxiety. I had been working through it with Tanya, my therapist, for a while now, but I had hoped I was making more progress than this. Every time things progressed further with Travis and me, I would panic. Tanya had informed me that it was a normal reaction, considering what I had been through with Jon, and it was necessary to go at my own pace and not feel pressured to move faster. But I *did* want things to progress with Travis, and I really liked him. I found Travis to be one of the most attractive men I'd ever dated, and he was a really, really good kisser.

I closed the toilet seat and plopped down, scrolling through my phone. I checked on Lucy, who was spending the evening at Oliver's and would be home by ten p.m., and texted Max, who was home for the evening, playing Xbox with Ryker. I had no reason to run home and was out of excuses. It was time to move things forward with Travis.

I exited the bathroom to find Travis leaning against his kitchen counter, phone in hand and a look of worry plastered across his face. "What's wrong?" I asked.

"Oh, it's nothing. Just a little work emergency."

"Work emergency?" I asked, wrapping my arms around his waist. "What kind of work emergency happens to pharmacists at eight p.m. Friday night?"

"You would be surprised."

"Okay." I shrugged.

"But it will be okay," he said, inhaling deeply.

"You sure you don't need to go in? I would hate to stand in the way of some innocent ninety-year-old lady getting her blood pressure medication on time."

"That's pretty specific." He laughed as he pulled me closer and kissed the top of my head.

"Authors don't really have emergencies."

"When do your book reviews come out?"

"Any day now," I said with a smile. "I'm freaking out."

"Don't freak out. You're fabulous, and your reviews will be too."

I stood on my tiptoes, gathered his face in my hands, and pressed his lips against mine. His mouth was warm as it pressed against me, and I melted into him as I had many times previously, rubbing my hands along his back and squeezing him to me. "Come on," he whispered as he lifted me up in one scoop, tossing me over his shoulder. "You're mine for the night."

"Travis!" I laughed, playfully hitting his back. "Put me down."

"Nope," he argued, his tone lighthearted and mischievous. "You're coming with me."

"I didn't agree to a sleepover."

"What? Do you have a curfew?"

"No, but my kids do."

"Well, you're mine for a couple hours, then. And I will take what I can get."

Travis carried me upstairs and down the hallway until we reached the master bedroom. He kicked the door closed, flopping me down on my back as he continued kissing my neck, his hands exploring under my shirt freely. "Lina," he whispered. "You are absolutely stunning."

I responded to this by pulling him down on top of me and wrapping my legs around his waist, feeling the heat of him against me for the first time as we kissed, waves of electricity streaming through me at lightning speed as I rolled him on his back and climbed on top of him, feeling vulnerable but safe in the grip of his large, strong hands.

We moved together like this for what felt like forever before he unbuckled my shorts and slid them off me, and I removed my shirt over my head. I hovered over him in my bra and underwear as he studied me intensely and lightly traced his fingers over my abdomen, stopping at the seam of my underwear and back up again until I couldn't take it anymore, and I tugged at his shorts and demanded he take them off.

Travis removed his clothing, and I removed what was left of mine. "Let me look at you," he pleaded, rolling me onto my back and kissing me all over. "Lina," he moaned. "I can't get enough of you."

My breath increased rapidly as his mouth traveled from my abdomen to my thighs and back up again until he pulled himself into a seated position, sweeping me up and onto him with my legs wrapped around his waist and as he pressed himself inside of me. My body was flooded with feelings that I hadn't experienced in so long, and my fears and anxieties drifted away instantly.

"Travis," I called to him repeatedly because I couldn't think of anything or anyone else but him. Travis knew how to move beneath me. He knew how to move our hips together like I had never experienced before, and I caught a peek of his smile in the stillness of the night, and for a split second as our shouts, gasps, and moans came together in what felt like perfect harmony, I decided that I just might be the luckiest woman alive, because for the first time in the longest time, I felt a glimmer of hope that maybe, just maybe, things were going to be okay.

***

Afterward, as I lay there on my side facing Travis Mullins with his nose inches from mine, I thanked my lucky stars that he was in my life. What were the odds that our paths would have crossed that day at the ice cream social? What if I hadn't called him? What if I had just walked out of the gym that day and never looked back? Who would have thought the chemistry between us would be so amazing? And the sex. Good God, that was the best sex I had ever had in my life. I didn't even know men knew how to move their bodies like that, and for a moment, I was hoping we could do it again. "That was amazing." I smiled, kissing his nose.

"You," he said, kissing me back. "You are the amazing one."

"We should do it again sometime," I cooed, raising my eyebrows.

"I would love that," he said. But something in his voice shifted, and his voice hardened.

"What?" I asked, concerned.

"Lina, I really like you. I know you've been through a lot, and you want to take it slow… But I really… I really want to be with you."

"You are with me," I teased.

"You know what I mean."

"You want to be my boyfriend?"

"I thought I was your boyfriend. What I'm saying is, I want to be more than your boyfriend."

"I'm confused."

"We aren't getting any younger, Lina. I want a family. You, me, Smith, and your kids… I want… I might even want more kids."

His voice trailed off as I pushed the blanket off me. "Is it hot in here?"

"Lina—"

"What are you saying, exactly?"

"I want you to meet Smith. And I want to meet your kids. I see this really working with you, with us. I want to be a family."

Panic climbed up my chest and into my throat, suffocating me instantly. "We just had our first night alone," I said, my breath catching, and I sat upright, gathering my hair over my shoulder. "Are you proposing?"

"I'm not proposing," he reassured me, rubbing my back with his palm. "Lie back down."

"I… I can't," I said, swinging my legs over the side of the bed and gathering my clothes.

"Where are you going?"

"Home. This is a lot, Travis." I stepped into my shorts and zipped them shut. I pulled my bra on and then my shirt before I made eye contact with him again.

"You still love him."

"Huh?"

"Your ex."

"That is *so* not true. I don't even talk to Jon anymore."

"That's not true, and you know it."

"Are you talking about the coffee thing? The Starbucks meetings?"

"Yeah, when *is* your next Starbucks meeting? It isn't normal to have biweekly coffee dates with an ex-husband."

"Soon. I need to talk to him about a couple things," I said, thinking of Max and Lucy and how I would brief Jon on Lucy's newest relationship and Max's overuse of Xbox.

"Can I come?"

"You want to come… to Starbucks? With Jon Cote?"

"Yeah. I want to do this. Like, really do this."

"You're out of your mind," I huffed, pulling my hair into a ponytail and tucking my phone in my back pocket.

"Come back to bed, please."

"I can't, Travis. Thank you… Thank you for a great night. Let's just… Let's pretend we never had this conversation. I need to take things slow… for me… for my kids. That's the only way this will work." I leaned down and kissed him before turning away and pausing in the doorway.

"Lina—"

"My ex-husband is my business. Please don't ever say his name. Never mention it."

"Just hear me out—"

"Never again," I repeated. "Just text me, okay?" And with that, I turned and exited Travis's bedroom, and I didn't look back.

Chapter Thirty-Three

Now

When I wake, I am in a tent, lying on top of a filthy, musty sleeping bag with limited airflow and that horrid rotten-egg smell consuming me. I immediately feel between my breasts for my necklace and phone and sigh in relief that the phone is still there, and the necklace is intact.

I prop myself up on my elbows, pushing through my headache and arm pain. I squint to see through the darkness. I can hear breathing nearby, but who could it be? Sure, it could be the missing girls, but it could also be Travis, Ace, Slinky, or any other idiots affiliated with them. "Hello?" I whisper. "Who's there?"

A small figure less than two feet from me releases a small groan. "Hello?" the voice cries out.

I crawl over to the voice, pain shooting through my shoulder and down my back. "Who's there?" I ask again.

"June," she says, her voice dry and cracking.

"June!" I shout through my whisper. "It's Gemma."

"Gemma?" she asks, reaching for me and patting my head, face, and shoulders as if to confirm it's me.

"Yes," I say. "Oh my God, are you okay?" I ask through tears, unable to believe Jon and I had done it. We found one of the missing girls.

"No," June cries. "I'm so scared. And I'm thirsty, Gemma," she whines.

"I know," I say, pulling her close and holding my breath as the stench of body odor and urine permeates my senses, and I can't tell if it's me or June or both of us who need to bathe like our lives depend on it.

"They took you too?" June whispers.

"Yes," I say. "But it's going to be okay."

"The others were here," June says. "They were here with me in this tent but left yesterday."

"All of them?"

"June shakes her head. Chloe and Teresa were here, but Alanna has been gone for a while. They shipped her away."

"Shipped her away?" I ask, confusion washing over me.

"They sold her."

"Oh," I say, my heart sinking further into the depths of my chest. "Are Chloe and Teresa okay?"

"They would just sleep," she says with a nod. "They didn't talk or eat. They just slept. I think they sold them too."

I nod, realizing more than ever that we need to get out of here. "Who else is in this tent?"

"Just us, but they guard it from out there."

"I have a phone," I whisper. "I'm going to take it out, and I need you to watch. Keep your eyes open and kick me if anyone is coming inside."

"Okay, Gemma."

But as I reach into my shirt to retrieve my phone, the tent unzips, and a gigantic figure crawls inside. *Travis.* As if she's done this a million times before, June curls up in a ball and pretends to sleep. "Come with me *now*," Travis demands, yanking my arm.

"Ouch," I say. "Stop. I think you broke my arm."

"There is no time," he says, his voice growing sharper.

I follow Travis out of the tent, and my jaw drops as I study my surroundings. We are still underground but in a large clearing the size of an empty parking garage. Hundreds of tents are scattered about and are lit up by flashlights and lanterns, and I realize there is a whole community of people living underground here, and my heart breaks for them. "Here." He points, unzipping a tent and pulling me inside.

Travis shoves me into the tent and zips it closed behind him. He lights a small lantern, and when I see his face in the light's glow, he pulls me against him, flooding my face with kisses. I crumble, and he does the same. The tears flow freely down my cheeks, and enormous sobs escape from within. I feel the tears on Travis's skin, and I am instantly confused. "What are you doing here?" I ask through my tears.

"Me? What are you doing here?" he asks, holding me tighter.

"You first," I demand, not giving him an ounce of truth until I know I can trust him.

"I'm being blackmailed," he explains, his chest heaving up and down through his sobs.

"Blackmailed? Who in the actual hell would blackmail a single father in his thirties? No offense Travis, but your life isn't all that exciting."

"Remember that colleague I told you about? The dean of the private school? Him. He's blackmailing me."

"What's his name? The dean?"

"Dean Orson Turner," Travis says, pressing his hands to his face and shaking his head from side to side.

"The dean of Emerson Academy?" I ask, eyes wide. "Molly's dad?"

"You know him?"

"*He's* behind this?"

"He's behind this."

"But why *you*? How do you even know him?"

"We met in college. We were in the same frat. His son, Emmett, needed drugs for his mental illness that the insurance wouldn't approve, and I was sneaking the dean his drugs. He's in over his head, Dean Turner. He's been blackmailed this whole time, Lina. He only threatened to go public with the drugs because he needed help to get out of this situation."

"This situation?" I ask, still confused that Dean Turner, Molly and June's *father,* is behind the kidnappings.

"It's a long story, Lina. We don't have much time."

"I need to know," I insist.

"Dean Turner's son, Emmett, got caught up in the wrong crowd a couple years ago at ASU. At first, it was just alcohol and then drugs, and before long, he started presenting with signs of mental illness. Slinky and Ace are leaders of a gang that run this community," he says, gesturing around him. "They found out that Dean Turner is loaded, so they took advantage of Emmett and extorted the dean for money."

"Did he pay?"

"Yeah, but Emmett was so messed up, and there was really no helping him. Emmett just kept coming back down here, and it happened repeatedly."

"So they kept making him pay?"

"Yeah, until he couldn't anymore. They threatened to go public with it and refused to let Emmett go. Turner cared about his own reputation and freaked out."

"What did he do?" I ask, knowing deep down that I have the answer.

"They found out he was the dean of Emerson. They demanded that he provide teenage girls in exchange for his son's freedom."

I nod, suddenly realizing that every missing girl has one thing in common—Molly. "He used Molly," I say.

"He used Molly's social circles to pinpoint girls and then used her Snapchat account to locate them online, and he lured them to Ace and Slinky through Snap... as you know," he said knowingly.

"Why did he need you?"

"Ace and Slinky are weak bastards." Travis laughs. "I'm the muscle."

"I can't believe… I can't believe you've helped kidnap children," I say, my hand covering my mouth as I ignore the pounding on the side of my head. "You kidnapped me."

"I can't lose my license. I can't lose my job."

"You could have gone to the police, Travis!"

"Once I got in, it got too hard to get out. You have to believe me. I never meant to hurt you."

"I'm not talking about me!" I wail. "Chloe, Teresa, June, and Alanna. Their families, Travis. They are so scared."

"You were my first, Lina. Emmett, Dean Turner's son, did the rest. I didn't kidnap those girls."

"Just me."

"Just you."

"Where are we?" I ask, gesturing around me. "What is this place?"

"This place is a series of underground tunnels. It was designed to transfer storm water from the city streets and into the river bottom. It's been taken over by hundreds of homeless people. And they have their own rules, Lina. And Ace and Slinky run it. They are dangerous, dangerous people."

"That's so… so sad."

"What are you doing here, Lina? How did you get involved in this?"

"Travis, are you sure I can trust you?"

"I swear on Smith, Lina. You can trust me."

He rubs my arm, and I cringe. "I think it's broken," I say through my tears. "It's a long story, Travis."

"Tell me what's going on."

"I'm undercover. I've been undercover at Emerson since September. I've been pretending to be Gemma Mendoza, a senior at Emerson."

"This has to do with Jon, doesn't it?"

"Yes, I'm working with Jon."

"Why were you undercover? Damn, Lina, this is so dangerous."

"To find the girls. Which I did," I say. "Except Alanna. Apparently, they sold her, whatever that means."

"It's human trafficking, Lina. This is no joke."

"It just doesn't make sense that it's Dean Turner," I say, ignoring Travis. "Why would he kidnap his own daughter?" I ask, thinking of June.

"He didn't. He told them he was done and that there would be no more kidnappings. Because he wouldn't cooperate, they took June. Dean Turner only assisted in your kidnapping to get his daughter back."

"Those assholes," I sigh. "Listen, Jon is tracking me, and I have a phone."

"You have a phone?"

I nod, reaching into my shirt and pulling out my phone. I power it on, and my stomach flips joyfully as it turns on but sinks when the screen flashes, *No service*. "I don't have service."

"Nobody does down here."

"Shit. That means he can't track me."

"Listen, Lina. I can get you out of here."

"No," I say, shaking my head. "Not until we find Chloe and Teresa."

"Lina, you need a doctor. You got whacked in the head with a baseball bat and have a concussion. Your arm, is probably broken."

"I'm doing this with or without you," I say, not taking my gaze off his.

"Do you love him?"

"Excuse me?"

"Your ex-husband, Jon. Do you love him? More than me?"

I laugh, a bit on the hysterical side. "*He* didn't kidnap me and knock me unconscious, Travis. So yeah, if this is a reality TV show and I'm the bachelorette, I think Jon gets the rose at this evening's ceremony, and *you* get sent home. Now shut the hell up and help me find the missing girls. We can talk relationship status another time."

Chapter Thirty-Four

Then (2024)

When I returned home from Travis's house, Ryker was perched on my sofa, eating popcorn and watching reruns of *Blue Bloods*, the clock on the cable box reading 10:30 p.m.

"Hey," I called from the kitchen. "I'm going to get comfy. I'll be right down."

Ryker gave me his best thumbs-up from the sofa, and I headed upstairs, changed into my favorite oversized T-shirt and leggings, washed my face, checked on the kids, and returned to the kitchen, opening a bottle of white wine and filling the glass to the rim.

"Need a beer, Ry?"

"I have one, thanks."

"What are you still doing here?" I asked, flopping on the couch beside him and resting my head on his shoulder.

"Nice to see you, too, Lina."

"You know what I mean." I sighed. "It's nice you hung with Max, but you know he doesn't need a sitter. You could have totally gone home. No need to worry."

"Maybe it isn't Max I was worried about," Ryker said, wrapping his arm around my waist.

"Lucy?" I asked, playing dumb and reaching for a handful of his popcorn.

"You, idiot," he declared between bites. "I was worried about *you*."

I nodded, sipping my wine and brushing a tear from my eye. "Do you still have a huge crush on Donnie Wahlberg?" I asked, nodding toward the TV to change the subject.

"Obviously. Stop changing the subject."

"Do you think it's weird that after all these years, my favorite New Kid on the Block has changed? I was obsessed with Joey for twenty years, but now I like Donnie. How does that even happen? It's like an identity crisis of some sort."

"How did it go with Travis?" Ryker asked, completely ignoring me.

"Best sex of my life," I said nonchalantly, chomping on an extra-buttery piece of popcorn. "Really. Hips don't lie," I said between laughs, cracking myself up and thinking about Travis and how he sensually swayed his hips beneath me Shakira style.

"Then why do you look like your cat died?"

"I don't have a cat."

"You know what I mean."

I watched Donnie Wahlberg as he and his partner chased down a suspect and tackled him to the ground. "Travis wants to be the effing Brady Bunch."

"What?"

"You heard me. The two of us, Max, Lucy, Smith, and oh… He wants to be my baby daddy."

"And… you don't want that, I'm assuming. You know, since you are sitting here on the couch with me, not in bed with Travis, going for round two."

"Round two, yes… absolutely. I could do *that* with Travis daily for the rest of my life. But… getting married again and having a future like that with Travis… another baby, no."

Ryker paused the TV and met my stare. "So, you are okay sleeping with him. But it's the commitment that scares you."

"Bingo."

"I'm really worried about you."

"Worried enough to pause Donnie?"

"Stop," he said firmly. "I want you to be happy. Since we've become friends, you've never been truly happy with a man."

"You make me happy. You're a man."

"Romantically happy."

"Well, I've been through a lot, Ryker."

"I'm not discrediting that you went through a lot. I hate your ex-husband with a passion, and you say you do, too, but you won't be able to move on until you let him go."

"Um, I don't know what planet you are on, Ryker. But I hate Jon Cote, too, and I have let him go. I only talk to him about our kids, nothing else."

"Lina... you're wearing his T-shirt right now."

"This isn't Jon's shirt," I lie.

"You're full of shit, and you know it. Honestly, Lina, what's wrong with giving this guy a shot? Is it so terrible that a man in your life who is hot, supportive, and great in bed wants to be part of your family? I would kill for a guy like that."

"He *is* really sweet... and he wouldn't hurt a fly, literally. I don't know, Ry. The second I get close to someone, it all comes crashing down, and I can't think of anything positive. I can only see the negative. My brain can only focus on the bad things that can happen, not the good," I said, sipping my wine and reaching for the popcorn.

"You need to cut ties with Jon."

"I can't." I chuckled. "We have teenagers together."

"People divorce *all* the time. People who have kids together divorce *all* the time. These Starbucks meetups are an excuse to stay connected with him, and you know it."

"Can we watch TV now?" I pouted. "You're really bumming me out."

"Fine," he said, kissing my forehead. "Promise me you will think about what I said."

"I promise."

Ryker turned the TV back on, and I snuggled up against his side. "Why can't *we* get married?" I griped. "You would make a great husband."

"We've been over this."

"I know."

"Now tell me about these hips," he demanded, his lips curling into a devilish smile.

"Excellent hip mobility." I winked. "Dude definitely does his stretches."

"Tell me more, sensei."

But I didn't. Instead, I placed my wine on the coffee table and curled up on Ryker's lap, but a loud thud from upstairs startled us both. "Did you hear that?" I asked.

"Nope."

"I swear I heard something upstairs."

"Probably the kids."

"Probably."

"Hey, Ryker?"

"Yeah?"

"What if you're my soulmate?"

Ryker leaned forward and brushed my hair from my eyes. "What do you mean?"

"What if I don't need a guy? Can't you and Daphne just be my soulmates?"

"Sure," he said, bending forward and kissing my forehead. "But you still need to face your feelings about Jon and Travis."

"Okay," I agreed, drifting softly to sleep and trying, with all my might, to push his accusations far away from my mind, a small part of me eager to meet up with my ex-husband for coffee in just a few short days and another part fearful that, although he was being obnoxious about it, Ryker just might be right.

The truth was there was a lot I didn't know. I didn't know that at that moment, Lucy was sneaking Oliver in through her bedroom window, that my book reviews would suck, and in two days, when I met with Jon at Starbucks, my world would be turned upside down because he would pitch Operation Superglue for the first time… and my life as I knew it would never be the same.

Chapter Thirty-Five

Now

June is helping me make a sling for my arm out of an old, hooded sweatshirt when Travis enters our tent. It has been the longest night of my life, and my arm pain continues to take my breath away. I'm starving and dirty, and I have gone to the bathroom in a bucket, which is my definition of rock bottom, and in the light of day, our tent is even filthier than I could have ever imagined.

"Hey," Travis says, entering the tent.

"Hey," I reply.

"You are scheduled to be transferred within the hour. I suggest you let me get the two of you out of here before that."

"What's going on?" June asks in confusion. "Aren't you... Aren't you the bad guy?"

"You didn't tell her?" Travis asks, his eyes wide.

"Didn't tell me what?"

I hadn't told June about Operation Superglue because I didn't want to blow my cover unless necessary, but now that Travis is helping us, it makes sense that she knows. "I'm here to help you," I say, choosing my words carefully. "And so is he," I explain.

"Um, didn't he break your arm?"

"Yes. But not on purpose. Listen, June. I need you to listen very carefully, and I need you to promise me that once I tell you this, you will stay calm and cooperate with us."

"Okay, Gemma."

"My name isn't Gemma. It's Lina. I'm a thirty-five-year-old mother of two from Scottsdale."

"You're joking, right?"

"No. I was undercover at Emerson, helping my ex-husband find the missing kids."

"Your ex-husband?"

"Mr. Jacobs."

"This is too much," she says, shaking her head from side to side. "I just want to go home."

"There's more," I say, rubbing my aching arm. "This is Travis. I'm dating him—or something like that."

"Something like that," Travis says with a roll of his eyes. "Lina, you're my girlfriend. Why is that so hard for you to say?"

I swat his words away with my good hand and continue. "And this last part, June. This will be hard for you to hear… like really hard. Your dad and your brother… They are the ones behind all of the kidnappings."

"No," she says, holding up her hand. "I don't believe you."

"Your dad is using Molly's connections, June. Think about it. Alanna volunteered at the soup kitchen, Chloe was on the volleyball team, and Teresa and Molly did the school play together. Every girl who went missing was connected to Molly."

"No!" June insists through her sobs.

"It's true," Travis affirms. "I know your dad. I've been to your house. Don't you remember me? Your brother was in trouble with these guys, and they dragged your dad into it. Your dad is a good man, June. He just got in over his head, and we will help."

June's expression changes at the mention of her brother. "Emmett is sick," she sniffs. "Not the kind of sick you can see. He's sick mentally. He's mentally ill, and we don't know how to help him."

"It's not his fault, June. And when all this is over, you can help people see that."

"Okay," she agrees.

"Do you trust me?" I ask.

"I trust you. What's your real name again?"

"Lina."

"I trust you, Lina."

I turn to Travis, who is trying frantically to get his cell phone to work. "If we go now, I can get you out of here before transport," he says eagerly.

"No," I argue. "I'm not going anywhere."

"What? Have you lost your mind? You need a doctor."

"I'm not giving up on the girls. Take June, get her out of here, and call Jon."

"I'm not leaving you, Lina," he says, narrowing his eyes.

"Me neither," June agrees.

"This is all very sweet, you two, but I need you to tell Jon where we are, and I want June out of here."

"If I leave and take June, they will kill you."

"Their names are Ace and Slinky. How bad can they be?"

"Bad, Lina. Really bad. If you aren't leaving, we all stay."

"Then it looks like we are staying." I shrug. "I'm not leaving here without Chloe and Teresa."

"Have it your way." He shrugs. "I'll see what I can find out about the transport."

"Try to get cell service," I beg. "We need to tell Jon what's going on."

"I'm so excited to talk to your ex, Lina. You have no idea," he barks with a roll of his eyes.

Travis exits the tent, leaving me to sit in awkward silence with June, who has hundreds of questions about me. I tell her about Max and Lucy and my career as an author. She wants to know what it was like to be undercover as a high school senior, and I find it refreshing to talk to her about my experiences, some good and some bad.

"Hey, Lina?" she asks, resting her head on my lap.

"Were you really friends with my sister, Molly? Or was that fake too?"

I smile at her question and think about it for a beat before answering. "I love your sister. That wasn't fake. Not one bit."

"Why is Mr. Jacobs your ex-husband? Why did you get divorced?"

"Oh," I say, sitting up a bit straighter and biting down on my swollen lip. "That's complicated."

"No, it isn't." She smiles. "You either love him or you don't."

"I wish it were that simple, June."

"Do you love him? Yes or no?"

A tear trickles down my cheek as I search my brain for an answer to the simplest but most complicated question I've ever been asked. I close my eyes and think of the first time I met Jon. How he looked as he stood in the Starbucks line, in uniform. I think of his smile as he ordered my margarita at the restaurant even though I wasn't old enough to drink it. I think of his body hovering over mine and the steadiness of his gaze as he made love to me in his apartment and the pride and joy on his face when they placed Max, our first-born twin, in his arms. I remember the way he proposed to me, down on one knee with the plastic Starbucks cup, and the look on his face as my father walked me down the aisle on our wedding day.

"Lina?" June asks. "Do you love him?"

The tears flow freely as I fondly remember Jon for the first time in years. I remember his words of encouragement when I was tired with the babies and when I was so frustrated with my first manuscript and how he reminded me that I could do anything I put my mind to. I think of the way he consoled Lucy after Oliver broke her heart, and then I think of the way he made love to me the night before. But it isn't until I think of him standing in front of art class in his white apron and khaki pants, winking at me from time to time from the front of the classroom, that I have my answer. "Yes," I say firmly. "I'm in love with my ex-husband."

"Good job," June says from my lap. "Now you just need to explain that to the big, scary guy."

"Travis?"

"Yeah, Travis. Cause he's *obviously* in love with you."

Chapter Thirty-Six

Now

I have turned my flip phone off and on at least twenty times when I notice one bar flashing on the tiny screen. "Oh my God, June. I have cell service."

"What? How?"

"I don't know! I turned it off and on like you said."

My fingers tremble as I press the call button, and Jon picks up, but his voice is muffled, and I can't hear him.

"He can't hear you!" June wails.

"No!" I insist. "No, no, no. Jon?"

"Hang up and try to text him," June suggests.

I do what she says. I hang up the phone and try to text, but my fingers shake, and I can't type correctly with only one working arm.

Ace barges into the tent, followed by Slinky and then Travis, and I am forced to drop the phone behind my back. I make eye contact with Travis, who sees the phone, but it doesn't appear that the other two have noticed.

"Cuff them," Ace instructs, tossing two pairs of plastic zip ties Travis's way.

"She's got a broken arm, man."

"Think I give a damn? Cuff them and meet us outside. This is for their mouths," he says, tossing him a roll of duct tape.

"I have cell service," I whisper to Travis once Slinky and Ace are out of sight. "But calling won't work. I need to text."

"Five minutes!" Ace calls from outside.

"I'm sorry," Travis says to June as he ties her hands behind her back and presses a piece of tape over her mouth.

"Take the phone, Travis. Text Jon, *please*. It's the only number saved in the phone."

Travis tucks the phone in this pocket and unties my sling. "I'm really sorry, Lina," he says as he pulls my arms behind my back. I feel like a knife is slicing through the side of my body as he clasps my hands together behind me, and I let out an animal-like yelp. "I'm sorry," he says again. "We should have gotten out of here when we had a chance."

"Let's go!" Ace hollers from outside the tent.

"Please, text him," I repeat as he rips off a piece of tape and prepares to press it to my lips. "Travis… I—"

"I love you, Lina. Trust me, we will get you out of this."

Travis kisses my lips before pressing the tape over them, and I catch June raising her eyebrows. Travis drags us out of the tent and presents us to Ace and Slinky, who are each carrying a gun—something I hadn't expected. My stomach flips and flops as we follow Ace out of the camp and back down the tunnels, my legs barely strong enough to support me and my arm so sore it has lost feeling.

We have been walking for what feels like hours before we exit the tunnels, and I'm hit in the face with daylight, and my head pounds harder than the worst hangover or migraine I've ever experienced.

"The van's that way," Ace tells Slinky. Slinky nods and follows behind Ace, who raises his hand to Travis.

"Thanks for your help, man," he says to Travis.

"I got you," Travis says, his voice catching.

Two men come up behind June and me, and without warning, we are dragged away from Travis toward a gigantic black van marked Super Scorpion Pest Removal. For real? I think, remembering the afternoon the pest control guy harassed me about my age. What are the odds? But Pest

Control Guy is not my worry right now. I am concerned that June and I are being dragged to the van without Travis and my phone.

A driver exits the van and tosses a large black bag to Slinky and Ace. "Pleasure doing business," the man says and gets back in the truck, and I'm left wondering just how much June and I are worth.

"Why don't I tag along?" Travis asks, trying to sound chill but failing miserably.

"Why don't you just get the hell out of my face?" Ace replies. "You're done here."

Text him, I plead to Travis with my eyes.

Travis nods, puts his hands in his jeans pockets, and strolls away from us, only turning back once, just in time for what I hope is to catch a glimpse of the van's license plate number and not my heart breaking into millions of tiny pieces as I climb into the creepy van, possibly leaving my life behind forever, as a blindfold is tugged around my eyes and everything around me turns to darkness.

Chapter Thirty-Seven

Now

It's funny, isn't it? How specific experiences change the way we feel about life? For example, being beaten, starved, handcuffed, blindfolded, and kidnapped can make you appreciate the little things. Like that first cup of coffee in the morning, texting your best friend, calling your mom... I would give anything now, at this moment, to call my mom.

I scooch closer to June, who tilts against my shoulder. My head rests against what I assume to be the van's window, and I silently pray that June and I get out of this alive. Part of me knows I should have allowed Travis to help us escape, but there is another piece of me determined to solve Operation Superglue and reunite the girls with their families that just won't give up.

I think about Jon and my recent confession to June. Would I feel the same way if circumstances had changed, and my life wasn't at stake? Did we sleep together because I was only minutes away from risking my life? Or is Ryker right? Have I always cared about Jon and fear getting hurt again? And because of this, I have chosen to hate him. But do I hate him? Or do I hate myself for not being able to forgive him?

If I am in love with my ex-husband, where does that leave Travis? Travis, who, before blanketing my mouth with duct tape, kissed me and informed me he loved me for the first time. One thing is for sure. If I do make it out of this alive, I will need to see Tanya, my therapist, STAT and drink lots of margaritas with Ryker and Daphne—*lots* of margaritas.

I also can't stop thinking about the pest control van. The man who came to my door months ago seemed normal enough. Could he have been surveying the area for young girls? Were there girls in his van that day? He mentioned my age more than once. If I allowed him in my home, would I have put my life at stake? Or Lucy's? Or was this simply a coincidence? Could the pest control van have been stolen? Or was this company directly connected to the kidnappings too?

The automobile suddenly stops, and I'm thrust forward, and I feel June do the same. The pain in my arm is causing me to feel nauseous, and I'm thankful I haven't eaten since the Cheez-Its in the motel room. I feel my necklace tickle the crease of my neck, and I relax a bit, hopeful that Jon and Travis are tracking us. That is, if Travis contacted Jon like I asked him to.

I push this thought far from my mind because Travis would contact Jon, right? But then again, he was so threatened by Dean Turner outing his pharmaceutical indiscretion, he could always put himself first and leave us here. Plus, Travis doesn't know about the tracker necklace. So, if he wants to, he can move on from all of this and pretend it never happened.

"Shipment leaves first thing in the morning," one man says to another.

"You know you can count on me, boss," the other man responds, his Spanish accent thick and prominent.

They speak back and forth for a bit in a language that sounds like Spanish, but I don't recognize what they are saying, and I took three years of Spanish in high school, clearly not enough. I listen closely and make out a few words here and there but nothing that will help us now.

I hear the van's door swing open, and June's muffled and ear-piercing scream pricks my soul. "June?" I try to say, but it sounds like a muffled moan beneath the duct tape.

"Let's go," a man's voice grunts as I am ripped from my seat and dragged from the van. Still blindfolded and utterly terrified, I am led up several flights of stairs and yanked in multiple directions by my bad arm before I hear the unlocking of a door, and I am thrust onto what feels like a bed. My head smashes against a metal object. A bedpost, maybe? Whatever it is sends immediate shock waves through me, creating a throbbing ache that syncs with the rapid beating of my heart and matches the pulsating pain in my arm.

I roll to my side and try desperately to pull myself to a seated position, but as I do, my body presses up against something, someone in the bed with me, and when I realize it's a person, I begin screaming into the duct tape, and I don't stop until the tape is ripped off my mouth and my eyes are uncovered.

"Calm the hell down," my kidnapper demands.

"Where... Where am I?" I demand as my eyes focus. I peer around the room through the pulsating of my throbbing head and gasp.

I am surrounded by at least a dozen teenage girls who look dirty, malnourished, weak, and terrified. It is hard to tell if any of them are Chloe and Teresa, as some are curled up on the floor, on the beds, and others lean forward with their faces in their hands. *June? Where is June?* "The girl who was with me. Where is she?" I ask the kidnapper, not removing my gaze from him.

He laughs an evil, Disney-villain sort of laugh, rips my necklace from my neck, turns from me, and exits the room.

"June?" I call out. "Did any of you see a young girl with brown hair?"

They all look at me like I'm crazy and seem to want to talk to me, but they can't, or they are too scared to. "Is Chloe here?" I shout, searching the room through my tired eyes. "Or Teresa?"

"We're here," a soft voice answers from the bunk above me. "Both of us. We are here."

A beautiful teenager with dark skin and black curly hair peers over the side of the bed and studies me. "Your head is bleeding."

"And Alanna?" I ask Chloe. My voice is weak but hopeful as I ignore the blood that is trickling down my cheek.

Chloe shakes her head. "Alanna wasn't here when we arrived. Nobody here has seen her."

"I'm going to get you out of here," I whisper to Chloe as the door is thrust open and June is shoved into the room. She lands with a thud beside me as her blindfold and mouth covering are removed.

I wait until the kidnapper exits the room before I allow the tears to fall freely, and I'm not sure if they are tears of sheer terror and fear or tears of relief and joy. Because I, Lina Rivera, a mother of two from Scottsdale, have done it. I have found three of the four missing girls plus multiple others I hadn't even known about. Now, all I need to do is figure out how to get us out of here in one piece. And our fate is in the hands of my current boyfriend and ex-husband, and instead of tracking me through my necklace, they are now tracking the evil kidnapper, and they have absolutely no idea.

Chapter Thirty-Eight

Now

It's impossible to know how long June and I have been here. It might be hours, or it could be days. There are no windows or way of telling time, and I am kicking myself for leaving my flip phone with Travis.

I am beginning to understand why the girls are so quiet and lifeless. It's only been a short time since I was kidnapped from the bus stop, and the lack of food and water and the emotional and physical trauma I have endured have started taking a toll on my body, and because of this, I have drifted in and out of sleep, not sure what is my current reality and how much I am dreaming.

When my eyes are open, I think of June. She is curled against me and sleeps most of the time. But when she wakes, she complains of pains in her stomach from dehydration and hunger, and sometimes, I reassure her that it won't be long until Jon finds us, and other times, I sing to her. I sing "Baby Mine," from *Dumbo*, my favorite Disney movie, a song I sang to Max and Lucy while staying awake with them throughout the night as infants.

I continuously drift off to sleep, sometimes mid-song, and I dream of Jon, Max, and Lucy when I do. We are together, all four of us. Sometimes, they are babies in my dream, and other times, they are their current ages. At one point, I dream that Jon and I are curled up together on that white couch in his apartment, each holding one of the babies, and we stare at each other with the biggest possible smiles, and I just know… I know how much he loves me and how much he loves our kids.

Then I wake up, and between comforting June, crying my own tears, and breathing through my pain, I drift back to sleep, and I dream of Jon and me. We lie atop soft white beach sand, holding hands as cool ocean water tickles our toes. Four eagles fly overhead. The same four eagles that are engraved on Jon's skin. We are silent as we lie under the warm sun, and Jon turns his head and says, "Tempe Police Department—"

Wait, what? Why would Jon say that? My eyes flash open, and I am immediately blinded by flashes of light and the sounds of my fellow kidnapping victims as they scream in response to the invasion.

Am I awake or asleep? Because I am too tired to try to figure it out, I shut my eyes again, determined to get back to that spot on the beach with Jon, and I ignore the sounds of voices around me, ignore June as she shouts for me to wake up until I'm back on the beach with Jon again, and we are together, under the Hawaiian sun, and this time, we have margaritas. Prickly pear margaritas, to be exact. "Lina," Jon says through his young, handsome smile. "Lina," he says as he sips his margarita. "Wake up."

I ignore his request and sip my drink, rolling beside him and kissing his nose. "It's you," I say through my smile. "I just can't let go because of you."

Jon kisses me on the forehead and lips, and it starts to rain. The kind of light, warm rain that falls when the sun is shining, and I love it. It flows over me, washing away everything that hurts, and I smile because I am happy. I am truly happy lying there with him by my side.

But then, he drops his margarita, and it permeates the sand beside us, staining the perfect white color a bright magenta, and Jon starts to shake me, and my arm hurts. My head begins to pound again as I'm ripped away from my beach paradise, and I'm back in the room with the girls and back in hell.

But this time, I'm not alone. Jon hovers over me, tears flowing freely, and I realize that I haven't been on the beach with Jon during a romantic sun shower. My ex-husband is straddling me and shaking me to wake up, and the rain is his tears. "Jon?" I ask, my voice cracking and weak. "You found us."

"Yes!" he says, relief flooding him as he collapses on top of me, kissing my forehead and my cheek and squeezing me tightly to his chest. "I told you I would."

I open my eyes and study him. Patches of my blood stamp his face as he works to get my plastic handcuffs off. I groan in pain and hear Travis remind him about my arm. *Travis.* Travis came back for us. Travis didn't leave me here.

"Jon?" I ask.

He places one hand behind my back and the other under my legs, the way he used to carry the kids when they were younger.

"Yeah?" he asks, squeezing me tightly against him, his face flooded with tears.

"I found the girls."

"Yes, you did," he says through his sobs.

"Everyone but Alanna. We need to find Alanna."

"We will," he says, kissing me, holding me against him.

"Jon?" I ask again. "Can we get that pizza now?"

At this, Jon smiles and stands up. He carries me out of the room, and I close my eyes and drift back to sleep in the arms of Jon Cote, my hero, with Travis Mullins, my boyfriend, following close behind.

Chapter Thirty-Nine

Now

It's been less than twenty-four hours since Jon and Travis rescued us from the abandoned warehouse in Tempe, where the kidnapped girls were being held between transports. At first, I found my hospital bed comforting. Just like after giving birth to Max and Lucy, I welcomed the rest and relaxation with round-the-clock assistance and free Jell-O and thought about it like a vacation—with hired help.

But I'm starting to get restless. Jon hasn't left my side even though I've begged him to go home and be with the kids. Jon reassures me that Lucy and Max are with Ryker and Daphne but promises I will see them soon. When I ask why I can't see them tonight, he hesitates and says nothing but guides me to the restroom, where I cautiously approach the mirror and gasp in horror upon seeing my reflection for the first time.

My left eye is swollen and closed, and the fresh stitches on my left temple are covered by white gauze. My bottom lip is swollen, and a large contusion covers the right side of my face, a deep purple swell forming from my temple to underneath my right eye. "Oh …" I can't get more words out before Jon wraps his arm around me and pulls me close, and I burst into tears. My broken arm has been set, rests comfortably in a sling, and will be cast once the swelling goes down. I consumed a decent number of painkillers, but I'm still sore and in pain. "It hurts to cry," I moan, laughing at how pathetic I look. "I look ridiculous, like I've been hit by a bus."

"Lina," Jon says, turning me around to face myself in the mirror again. "You look like a hero. Because you are... a hero. You actually look pretty badass."

Operation Superglue

I study my reflection and try to see past my bumps, bruises, and what will soon be scars. I want to see what he sees, truly I do, but as each wound stares back at me, I begin to remember how they got there in the first place, and I suddenly find it difficult to breathe. Panic consumes me. "I need to get out of here. Please?" I beg.

Jon shakes his head, leads me back to my bed, helps me up, and tucks me under the thin white bedsheets. "You have your CAT scan," he says, tucking a strand of hair behind my ear.

"Do we really need a picture to tell me I have a concussion?" I joke. "I have a concussion. Or two."

"They need to make sure you are okay. Plus, you don't want to go outside. Reporters are everywhere."

"I know," I say, turning the volume up on my TV. Jon and I have been watching the news for the last hour, and our story is on every news channel locally and nationwide. Dean Turner's face is plastered across the screen as reporters tell the story of Emerson Academy's missing teenagers and their link to the dean. Reporters have mentioned my name, along with Jon's, in the girls' recovery under the headline Operation Superglue, and Alanna's picture is featured as the only missing girl still unaccounted for.

"Imagine being Alanna's mother?" I ask, tilting my head and studying her photo. "Everyone but your kid turns up."

"Think about the girls you did save, Lina. You recovered twelve teenage girls in that warehouse."

I think about this for a beat, and I nod. "So, Operation Superglue is over." I sigh. "No more Gemma Mendoza."

"Nope, no more Gemma."

"It's a little sad," I admit. "I kind of liked her. And you made a damn good Mr. Jacobs," I declare, trying to crack a painful smile.

"I liked Gemma too," he agrees. "But I like Lina better."

I stare at him, the silence so awkward I could cut it with a knife. As if sensing my anxiety, Jon changes the channel to *Family Feud* and offers me more Jell-O. I turn it down and tell him I would love coffee. He kisses my forehead and rises to his feet just as Molly bursts through my hospital room door, her face tear streaked and her hair disheveled.

Jon and I stare at Molly, and I have no idea how to greet her. I reach for Jon's hand and squeeze it, holding my breath that she will be able to forgive me for the lies and hope that she doesn't hate me, especially because her father has been arrested and will probably go to jail for the foreseeable future.

"Thank you!" Molly bellows as she pushes past Jon and approaches my bedside. "Thank you for finding my sister."

Molly has been crying for so long and hard that she doesn't even try wiping her eyes. She allows the tears to fall like they have become a permanent part of her. "I'll be back with your coffee, Lina. Do you want anything, Molly?" Jon asks, looking from me to her and back to me.

"No, thank you, Mr. Jac—Sorry." She frowns. "I guess I don't know your name."

"Call me Jon," he says with a smile before turning and exiting the room.

"Bruh, you look awful," she says, looking me over.

"Have a seat," I say, tapping the side of my bed and scooching over a few inches.

Molly climbs in bed with me and lies on her side. She rests her head on my good shoulder, tucks her knees to her chest, and begins sobbing even harder.

"I'm sorry for lying to you," I say because I am.

"June told me everything."

"I never meant to hurt you."

"You didn't," she says, staring at me through tears. "I mean, it's totally wild that you're thirty-five. I hope I look like you when I'm *that* old."

"Old as shit?" I ask with a smile.

"Yeah." She chuckles. "You're old as shit."

"I have twins who turn sixteen in November," I confess. "Molly," I start but stop, choosing my words carefully. "My name is really Lina Rivera. I'm a single mom and full-time author. I went undercover at Emerson with my ex-husband to help find the missing girls."

"Wow, an author? June told me about the other stuff, but I didn't know you are an author. What do you write?"

"If I tell you, you can't tell anyone."

"Promise," she says, extending her pinky for a pinky swear.

"I write the Cat Rose books."

"Shut up, right now." She gasps. "You do not."

"I do. But you can't tell anyone about my pen name. Part of why I went undercover was to learn more about what it's like being a teenager. It's *so* different. My son was right." I sigh.

"You need to sign my books."

"I will."

"I can't believe Mr. Jacobs is your ex. I'm so embarrassed…the things I said about him…" Molly's voice trails off as she attempts to process everything.

"Don't be sorry," I reassure her. "It was kind of funny." I smile. "He is hot…and he is *old*."

"I really thought you were my age. I really thought we were friends."

"We are friends. All of that, Molly. All of that was so real. Part of why I went through what I went through out there was so I could bring June back to you."

"Thank you for that."

"How is she doing?"

"She's scared, but she's okay. She told me she would never have left there if it weren't for you. She told me how brave you were, how you got kidnapped on purpose. I'm so happy she's okay, but I can't…I can't believe my own father was behind this."

"I know," I say, running my fingers through her hair. "It's a lot to take in. But from what I know, Molly, your dad did what he did for you and your family. What he did was awful, but he was so worried about your brother and you."

"Do you know what this feels like?" she asks, her tone growing angrier. "Every girl kidnapped was taken because of their connection with me."

"I can't imagine what you are going through. But, Molly, I'm so glad you and June are safe. This could be so much worse."

"It's just so strange. My dad acted so upset after each kidnapping. He lied *so* much."

"He did what he had to do for your brother. Parents do crazy things for their kids. Maybe hear him out. You will feel better once you talk to him."

Molly is silent for a beat. "You love your kids, right?" she asks.

"Of course I love them."

"Would you put someone else's child in danger for them? Because that's what my dad did. He traded innocent girls from his school to pay off my brother's debt. It's not okay, Lina. It's just not okay."

"You're right," I say, pondering Molly's question. "I'm here for you and your family, though. Whatever you need."

"Really?"

"Really. I love you, Molly Turner. I hope that we can stay friends."

"Obvi." She smiles. "I couldn't do life without you. It's just going to really suck not having you in school. And it will be a while before I stop calling you Gemma."

"That's fine," I say. "I kind of like that name. And I will miss being in school with you too."

"Do you think my dad knows how to find Alanna?" she asks, staring at the ceiling.

"I hope so." I sigh. "I really hope so." Because deep down, I know that I won't back down from this, and I won't quit looking until we do find her.

"Hey, Lina?"

"Yeah?"

"Are you really that bad at art? Or was that just your excuse to see Jon."

"I'm not that bad at art." I smile. "But you know who is? Jon."

Molly and I erupt in a fit of laughter as Jon enters the room with a coffee for me and an ice cream for Molly.

"What's so funny?" Jon asks from the doorway.

"Nothing." I smile. "Just two friends sharing an inside joke. Right, Molly?"

Molly smiles and rests her head on my shoulder, and I breathe a sigh of relief that I was able to come out on the other side with Molly Turner by my side, friend for life.

Chapter Forty

Now

It's been two days since I returned home from the hospital, and I've had more visitors than I feel necessary. Ryker and Daphne have set up camp with me in the living room, and my parents have stopped by multiple times, along with Dean Elizabeth, Travis, and Jon. Although I am not always eager to talk and relive my heroic tale, they bring food, coffee, and snacks, and in the end, I am happy to be with others.

Jon's presence at the house initially confused Max and Lucy, but we have kept things platonic and casual, especially in front of them, and because of this, they have chalked it up to the fact that we have been working together, and since, the questions have ceased.

The news reporters, however, have yet to take a break. Even now, as Jon, Max, Lucy, Daphne, Ryker, and I gather in the living room, eating pizza with the words Operation Superglue flashing across our TV screen, a reporter waits across the street in her car, hoping for my statement.

At first, the Tempe Police Department took most of the credit for finding the missing girls, and Jon and I were okay with that. I was hoping to fly under the radar, but when June told the reporters everything, that all went out the window, and Operation Superglue became a nationwide phenomenon. I don't recall sharing the name of our operation with June, but I apparently had. Who knows what I rambled about that night in the abandoned warehouse.

As I bite into my second slice of pizza, the doorbell rings. "I'll get it," Lucy calls from the kitchen.

"If it's the reporter, tell her no comment," Jon reminds her.

Lucy opens the door and greets our guest. "Mom," she calls. "It's for you."

I turn toward the kitchen to see Molly standing next to Lucy. Seeing the two together is odd, but regardless, I am overjoyed to have her here. "Molly." I smile. "Come on in."

"Hi," Molly says, entering the living room and sitting beside me on the couch.

"Molly, this is everybody. Everybody, this is Molly," I say, trying to sound casual but failing miserably as my two worlds collide.

"I'm Lucy," my daughter says. "Want some pizza?"

"Yes," Molly says, reaching for a slice.

"How do you know my mom?" Max asks from his spot on the living room floor.

"She's my BAE." Molly smirks.

"She's your what?" Ryker asks, clearly confused.

"It means best friend," I laugh.

"Alrighty then," Ryker laughs. "I suppose there is room for another best friend. What do you say, Daph?"

"Any friend of Lina's is a friend of mine." She smiles.

"There is room over here," Max says, patting the ground beside him.

"Thanks," she says.

"I like your sneakers," he says, gesturing toward her Vans. "Those are fire."

Molly blushes and turns toward me, and I nod in silent approval. Lucy joins them on the floor, and the three begin talking like they have known each other for years. And my heart flutters with happiness, and I am overwhelmed with joy.

"Need anything?" Jon asks as he takes my paper plate from my lap.

I think about this for a beat. "I'd love to walk, but that reporter won't budge. I haven't left this spot in days."

"Want to go out back?"

I smile at this, thinking about the first year Jon and I bought the house, when we used to sit outside on the back porch after tucking the twins in. "I'd like that. Glass of wine, for old time's sake?"

"Doctor said no drinking," he says, lightly tapping my head.

"Oh, come on," I whine. "It's one glass of wine. I'm fine, and you know it."

***

A few minutes later, Jon and I sit on our old porch swing, my feet dangling beneath me as I hold my wineglass with my good arm, my other hanging supported in my sling. "You get your cast on tomorrow, huh?" Jon asks as if reading my mind.

"Yup. I'm thinking hot pink. Thoughts?"

"Sounds perfect." He smiles.

"You're gonna sign it, right?"

"Of course."

I sip my wine and stare up at the stars, and no matter how hard I try, I can't stop thinking about Alanna. I think about her being kidnapped, just as I was, and I think about how scared she must be. I was rescued from that warehouse, but we were too late for Alanna. She must have been shipped out, far away, and who knows where she is now.

"So, nothing from Arizona PD?" I ask Jon.

"No, nothing," he sighs. "But Lina, you need to let this go. You need to rest. You've been through so much."

"I can't let it go," I say firmly. "We were supposed to save all of them. Not *most* of them."

"Let the police handle it. They have Turner, and they are questioning him. Just let them do their jobs."

"Like they did their jobs the first time?"

"It's on their radar now. They are way more equipped to handle this than we are."

"Did they look into the pest control van? I told them about that."

"I'm not sure." He shrugs. "If you told them about it, they are looking into it."

I sip my wine and lean back, frustration flowing through me. "Why don't you care?" I whisper.

"Lina, I care. I just… I care more about you. And you need to know… it's over. Operation Superglue… It's done. You did a great job, and now you need to heal. You need to rest."

"I can't," I say, a tear trickling down my cheek.

"One day at a time," he says, his tone soft. "Okay?"

"Okay," I agree.

Jon rubs his thumb under my chin and gently kisses my swollen lips. "I'm so glad you're okay, Lina."

"I'm okay, thanks to you," I remind him.

"I have a confession to make," he says, his words catching in his throat.

"What else could there possibly be to confess?" I laugh, sipping my wine.

"I love you, Lina Rivera."

My wine trickles down the wrong pipe, and I cough. "Sorry," I say between breaths. "That went down the wrong pipe."

"I love you," he repeats again, his tone serious and grave. "I've never stopped loving you."

I stare at him under the moon's light, and I have no idea what to say. I know the right thing to say is that I love him, too, but my head is spinning, and I've been taken off guard, so all I can say is a soft, "Thank you."

"You don't have to say anything back," he says, his eyes smiling. "I just need you to know that."

"Okay."

"And there's more."

"How on earth can there be more?"

"When I asked you aboard Operation Superglue, it was to find the missing girls and to help you with your books, but… it was also an excuse to be around you. To be with you."

"Shut up right now," I say in my Gemma voice.

Jon laughs at this, and I am thankful for the break in silence. "Seriously," he says. "*You* are the glue, Lina. You've always been the reason we keep it together like we do. Even though we aren't married, you've always been the glue."

I think about this for a moment and study his teary eyes. "Operation Superglue," I whisper slowly. "I'm the glue."

"You're the glue."

"It wasn't just about the girls?" I ask again.

"It wasn't just about the girls."

"You're something else, Jon Cote," I say, resting my head on his shoulder. And for the first time in years, as I study the stars in the sky, I know, without a doubt, that everything will be okay, and maybe, just maybe I've found a way to forgive Jon, and even more importantly, I'm ready to start being honest with myself, and although that realization is terrifying, I'm ready. Because let's face it, I've been through much, much worse.

Chapter Forty-One

Now

November in Arizona is my favorite time of year. The heat dissipates, and my favorite holidays are around the corner—the twins' birthdays and Thanksgiving. My reasons for loving the kids' birthdays are apparent, but Thanksgiving is my favorite because my mother makes everything and all things prickly pear, from prickly pear salsa to her unique turkey glaze and prickly pear stuffing. But my absolute favorite is her homemade prickly pear pie. I, of course, make the drinks with my dad, which has become a tradition I hold dear to my heart. And this year, Jon will be invited back for the first time, and this fills my heart with such happiness that I can't actually find words to explain it.

It's only been two weeks since Operation Superglue came to a close. I have been working hard on my newest project, a young-adult crime suspense novel about a seventeen-year-old protagonist with a knack for solving crimes. The information I gained about teenagers in 2024 has provided me the knowledge I was lacking, and I'm sure I will impress my agent and editor with the sample chapters. I've done this with the help of dictation software that I installed, seeing as though my arm is cast from my wrist to my shoulder, and I will be living this way for at least the next eight weeks. Writing this way has been an adjustment, but not impossible, and with the help of Daphne, Ryker, Jon, and Molly, I've begun to recover physically and emotionally from my kidnapping experience.

Jon and I have been texting and talking on the phone, with an occasional dinner at the house with the kids, but we have kept things low-key. As far as Max and Lucy are concerned, we have become friends since working together, which is a perfect place to be right now... at least until I can talk things through with Travis and sort out my feelings for Jon.

So now, as I open the door to Starbucks with my good hand, I inhale deeply and encourage myself to relax, which is easier said than done. It's *Travis*. I've known the man for quite some time. He's seen me naked, for heaven's sake. It's just a coffee date. But I'm not nervous about seeing Travis. I'm worried about my conversation with him because now, more than ever, I'm ready to be honest with myself, which leaves me in an uncomfortable place with Travis.

I glance around the room, and my eyes shoot to Jon's usual table, occupied by a woman and her laptop, and continue scanning until I find him seated across the room in a booth against the wall.

"Hi." I smile, approaching his table.

"Hey," he says, taking a sip of his coffee, and I realize at this moment that I have no idea how Travis takes his coffee at Starbucks, and this actualization sort of takes the wind out of the part of me that sees things for what they are and not what I want them to be.

"Sorry I'm a few minutes late."

"No worries," he says, standing and wrapping his arms around me in a caring embrace. I find his strong arms comforting and the familiar smell of his aftershave soothing. He pecks my lips, and we smile uncomfortably, like we aren't sure we did the right thing. "I... I didn't know what you like to drink."

I start to say Frappuccino, but I stop and think for a beat. "You know," I say with a smile, "it's been a while since I looked at their menu. I'll be right back."

I walk to the register, where Jon and I first met, and my smile grows wider as I remember the moment fondly. I scan the menu and land on a pumpkin cream cold brew, and for the first time in over fifteen years, I try something new.

"That looks good," Travis says as I sit across from him and breathe a sigh of relief, as this is my first time seeing him since he and Jon rescued us from the warehouse. I was worried that seeing him might trigger a panic attack, which had happened frequently at the weirdest times. "Didn't take you for a pumpkin spice kind of girl."

"I guess I'm full of surprises." I wink.

"Yeah," he says, shifting uncomfortably. "I guess you are."

I sip my drink and study his expression, trying to figure out what he might be thinking. I adjust my arm in my sling and lean forward, locking eyes with him. "I couldn't tell you about Operation Superglue. You know that, right?"

"Yeah. I get it. It sure explains a lot, though."

"I feel the same," I say boldly. "Your involvement with the dean... I knew something was up. Did the cops question you?" I ask, surprising myself with my ability to be so direct.

"No," he sighs. "Thankfully, Dean Turner has kept quiet. Although I feel that it's only a matter of time before my name gets dragged through the mud."

I nod. "I haven't said anything," I reassure him, but I am dumbfounded about why Dean Turner wouldn't rat out Travis. And if he isn't outing Travis, what else is he keeping from the cops?

"I appreciate that."

"I appreciate you... coming back for us. You didn't have to do that."

Travis takes his hand and wraps it around mine. "I would never leave you there, Lina. I meant what I said. I... I love you."

A lump fills my throat as tears form involuntarily, and I blink them back. "I... I care about you, Travis. A lot."

"But you don't love me?" he asks, letting go of my hand and sitting back in his seat.

"It's… It's so complicated."

"No, no, it isn't, Lina. You are in love with your ex."

"It's not that simple, Travis. Like I said, it's complicated."

"I've got time." He shrugs. "Were you ever really into me? Our last night together, you bolted out of there like you were breaking out of jail when I told you how much I cared for you and wanted to start a family with you."

Heat rises to my cheeks, and I nod. "You're right." I sigh. "I wasn't emotionally available, and I'm sorry I acted like I was."

"Thank you."

"I don't want any more babies," I say, a soft laugh escaping from within. "I have two kids and could never start over. Not now."

"But it would be *our* baby."

"It's a hard no," I say softly. "And I'm not ready for anything serious. Not right now."

"Even with Jon?"

"Even with Jon," I agree, although I'm just not sure about how I feel anymore.

Travis nods. "I care about you, Lina… but I'm not getting any younger. I want to give you space, but I can't guarantee that I will be available if and when you change your mind."

"I—" I start and stop, choosing my words carefully. "Travis… I'm not going to change my mind. I care about you too… but with everything we have been through," I say, gesturing to my cast, "I just don't see this going anywhere, and I'm sorry." I bite my lip and hold my breath. It takes a minute before I make eye contact with him again.

"I'm sorry about your arm, Lina," he says, his tone soft.

"It's not my arm. It's everything. I get why you did what you did. You couldn't blow your cover. But if you knew what I went through in the past"—I wipe a fallen tear with my finger—"if you knew what I went through with Jon, back when I found him cheating on me and he couldn't blow his cover… if you knew what that was like and how that felt, you would understand why this is such a complicated mess."

"Can you tell me? What happened?"

I frown and start to shake my head but then decide that maybe, just maybe, Travis deserves to hear the truth. "Jon was undercover at a college, living in a frat house. I found out he was cheating, so I stormed into his room and caught him. He was so far under that he fell for the girl… and I couldn't handle it. I outed him. And if Jon hadn't kept his cool, this guy would have killed Daphne, Jon, and me… but instead, Jon pretended he didn't know me. And when he did, the guy, Owen, threw me to the ground and kicked me." I winced. "He broke my ribs. And Jon let it happen. He had no choice… but by doing so, he saved our lives."

"Oh my God, Lina—"

"Please don't. It's taken me a while to understand why Jon did what he did. But when I was undercover with Operation Superglue, I realized how hard it can be to live two lives simultaneously, and I guess… I blame him less, and for the first time in years, I've started to forgive him, and I've started to stop hiding behind everything. I want to forgive. I want to love, like really love. I want to put my heart out there and trust again."

"Just not with me."

"Just not with you, Travis. I'm sorry."

"Wow, I was hoping this would work out differently." He chuckles.

"You are an amazing man. And I loved our time together," I say, blushing.

"The sex was great because *we* are great together," he says, leaning forward and taking my hand in his. "We are great together," he repeats.

"It *was* pretty great." I smile. "But as great as it was physically, I need some space to figure myself out emotionally. And I'm sorry that leaves you in a crappy spot."

Travis nods and sips his coffee. "I understand."

"Really?"

"Really."

"Can we be friends?" I ask, my tone hopeful.

"I'm not really sure how to answer that."

"I get it."

"But with time? Maybe."

"I'll take maybe."

"You really are a fantastic woman, Lina Rivera. Jon Cote is one lucky man."

"I'm not—"

"One lucky man," he repeats, kissing my hand gently. "You have a beautiful family, Lina. Nobody would blame you if you tried to put the pieces back together."

Or glue them back together, I think, smiling about Jon and his super-glue reference. *I'm the glue. I've always been the glue.* "Thank you," I say through my tears. "And like I said, I would love to stay friends."

"I'll have to get back to you on that." He winks.

"I understand," I say, standing from my seat and kissing his forehead gently. "Take all the time you need."

With that, I turn and exit Starbucks with my new favorite beverage and head out into the fall Arizona air with positive thoughts about my new life, my new dreams, and a new *me*.

Chapter Forty-Two

Now

It's been a week since I sat with Travis at Starbucks, and within that short amount of time and the conversations I've had with Jon, I decided to take Jon up on his offer for an official date. So now, as I sit across the table from Jon at the same Italian restaurant where we started our first date, I couldn't be happier.

I smile at him as I sip my prickly pear margarita, and we laugh about how much has changed since the night I wasn't old enough to order my own drink. I remember that night fondly, and the fact that I can do this is worth a million dollars.

"This would have come in handy when the kids were younger," he says, gesturing to the paper-tablecloth covering and the Crayola box the waitress left for us after writing her name in the center of the table.

"Right," I agree with a smile. "Max probably would have thrown the crayons across the restaurant, and Lucy would have eaten them."

"Yup," he says, removing the red crayon from the box and drawing me a heart.

"You didn't break the crayon!" I say in my mom voice. "Great job."

"You're a comedian," he says, his smile proud. "But you must admit, that's a good effing heart."

"It is a good effing heart," I agree, removing the yellow crayon and drawing him a sun. I reach back into the box for the orange and then grab the red and sketch him a sunset.

"See." He smiles. "You aren't so bad at art after all."

I nod in agreement, reach for the green crayon, and smile proudly as I draw a cactus. "It's a desert sunset," I proclaim. "I totally get an A."

"You can't get an A." He sighs. "That would mean no more office hours."

"Stop," I say, rolling my eyes. "Those days are gone."

"They are, aren't they?" He sighs, and for a split second, I see a flicker of sadness in his baby blues.

"Are you... Does that make you—"

"Sad?"

"Yeah," I say, thanking the waitress as she places our appetizers between us.

"A little," he admits, reaching for a slice of garlic bread.

"Which part?"

"Come on, Lina," he says, lips curling into a soft smile. "You know what part."

"You miss Gemma?" I ask between bites.

"I don't miss Gemma. I miss *you*, Lina. Seeing you every day, spending time with you in my office, collaborating with you, your theories, and your ideas. I'm lonely now without you."

"Aw, shucks, Mr. Jacobs," I sing.

"I'm serious, Lina. I miss you."

"I miss you too," I say, sipping my margarita, "And I miss Operation Superglue. I love my writing, but now that I've been a part of something big, I feel... I don't know... like what I'm doing lacks some sort of significance."

"I can see that. But what you do is so important, Lina. You are an amazing mom. Your writing career means much to you."

I dip my bread in the sauce and sigh. "Can I be honest with you?"

"Always."

"Sometimes, especially when I can't sleep, I think about Alanna, and I try to piece together her kidnapping and figure out where she might be.

I know I'm supposed to put it behind me… but there is this ache in my gut, and it won't go away, and I… I need to find her, Jon. I just *need* to."

Jon wipes his mouth with his napkin and clears his throat. "What are your theories?"

"Really? We can talk about it?"

"We can *talk* about it, yes."

"Okay," I say, reaching for the crayon. I slide into the booth beside Jon and start drawing pictures and listing bullet points. This continues through the main course and into dessert as Jon and I collectively list possible leads, from the pest control van to the driver's Spanish accent, and by the time we are through, we have two to three potential working leads.

"Not too shabby," Jon says, snapping pictures of our table covering with his phone.

"Right? We sure do make a good team," I say, resting my head on his shoulder.

Jon bites into his dessert and smiles. "I love this," he says, his tone even and serious.

"The chocolate cake?"

"Well, yeah, the chocolate cake… but *this*, Lina. I love working through cases with you. You're good at it," he says, kissing my head.

I take his fork and eat a bite of cake. "Delicious. And yeah, I like doing this stuff with you too. I just want to find Alanna, and I feel like if we could find the other girls, we could find her too."

"Well, it isn't that simple, but I think you know that."

"I do."

Jon rests his head against the booth and rubs his fingers over his scruff. And then he gets that look on his face, the same look he got when he had the idea for Operation Superglue. "Hear me out," he says boldly.

"Oh no." I chuckle, reaching for my drink. "I've seen that face before."

"Yes," he agrees. "You have."

"What's your bright idea, Jon Cote?"

"Come to work with me," he says, turning in my direction and tucking a strand of hair behind my ear.

"Huh?" I ask, confused. "Do you have another case that involves going undercover as a teenager or something?"

"No. Not like that. Come to work for me at Cote Investigations."

I laugh at this, although I'm not sure why. "What would I do? I'm not a PI."

"So become one," he insists, not backing down. "In the meantime, you can work as my apprentice, but get your PI license and come to work with me. We are a great team, Lina."

"Could we try to find Alanna?"

"I can look into it," he says, his eyes not leaving mine. "Consider it. You can still write, but you can also work alongside me. Think of the material you would get for your stories."

"You're not wrong about that," I agree, biting into another piece of cake. What would this mean for me, my kids, and my relationship with Jon? What if I ventured into this with him and things got messy again? What if—and then I stop myself because I'm doing it again. This downward spiral of pessimistic predictions that stem from past experiences annoys me in ways I can't even begin to describe, and at this moment, I am determined to break this pattern.

"What are you thinking?" he asks, his tone hopeful.

"I'm thinking that this could work," I say, wrapping his hand in mine.

"Really?"

"Really."

"Lina, this is going to be so great," he says, his smile wide.

"On one condition."

"Anything."

"Anything?"

"If we are partners, we need a better name than Cote Investigations."

"Well, I've purchased the trade name, and it's an LLC."

"Okay then, no deal," I say, pouting my lips.

"What do you have in mind?" he asks with a slight roll of his eyes.

"Prickly Pen Investigations," I say with a smile. "That's what I'm naming the PI service in my novels."

"It's always prickly pear with you, isn't it?"

I lean forward and press my forehead to his, so his eyes are centimeters from mine. "There are worse things."

"There are. But what does prickly pear have to do with anything?"

"Well, the dessert, duh," I say in my best Gemma voice. "And pen, because I'm a writer, and it sounds pretty badass."

"Fine," he agrees. "Prickly Pen Investigations it is. I do need to change things up now that we were all over the news. Sort of hard to fly under the radar when everyone knows your name."

"Exactly. And I get my own desk," I say, rubbing my nose against his.

"Done," he agrees, his voice increasing at least an octave.

"And I pick my hours," I add.

"Copy that."

"And I get to choose what we order for late-night takeout," I insist, brushing my lips against his.

"Whatever you say."

I gently place my hand on his jeans and glide it along his thigh. "Thank you," I whisper through my smile, excitement gushing through my veins. "You're right. We will make a great team."

"I have my conditions, too, you know."

"Oh yeah?" I ask. "Nothing too demanding, I hope."

"Kiss me," he says, his breath tickling my nose. "And come back to my place after we get the check."

"Deal," I say, pulling his face to mine and bringing our lips together in one of the most passionate kisses we have shared thus far.

Jon wraps my face in his hands, kisses me back, and takes my breath away, pulling back only to ask for the check.

It's funny, isn't it? How sometimes things find a way of working themselves out? Because in this moment, back where we started, Jon and I have found our way back to each other, which I never would have thought possible—not in a million years. But yet here we are, back at square one, with endless possibilities ahead of us. Possibilities that would never have been made realities if I hadn't taken that leap with Jon. Operation Superglue has put us back together, and in this moment, in the booth with Jon, I make a silent promise to both him and myself to keep looking forward and stop looking back, because we do have a beautiful family and we do make the best team, and those two reasons alone are enough for me to keep trusting, to keep reaching, and to keep dreaming.

"You ready to go?" Jon asks, pulling away from me to sign the check and then pulling me close for another kiss.

"Yes," I say through my smile. "I'm ready," I say because I mean it. I'm ready for whatever comes next. The good, the bad, the unknown, and everything in between. "But, Jon," I say, my tone serious.

"What is it?"

"No tattoos tonight."

Jon throws his head back in laughter before pulling me close to him. "No tattoos, Lina. I promise. Come on, let's get out of here," he says with raised eyebrows, looking me up and down like I'm dessert.

"Yes," I agree. "We have a lot of work to do. Prickly Pen Investigations isn't going to start itself."

"Yeah." He hesitates. "But first, I thought—"

"I agreed to go back to your place." I shrug. "I didn't agree to actually doing anything once we get there."

"O-oh," he stutters, cheeks flushing.

"I'm joking," I laugh and reach for my purse. "Take me back to your place, Jon Cote. This is *not* a business meeting. And if you still have your Mr. Jacobs apron, that would come in handy."

"Copy that, Lina," he says, reaching for my hand and pulling me toward the exit. "The night is young, and so are we."

"Well, I'm young," I correct. "You're old as shit."

"You're trouble, you know that?" he asks as we slide into our Uber and close the doors, kissing again before the driver even puts the car in drive.

"I'm trouble," I say between kisses. "But you love me."

"Yeah," he says, pulling back for a brief second. "I do love you."

"I love you, too, Jon. I always have… and I always will."

Epilogue

Six Months Later

My fingers type briskly on my laptop's keys as I put the finishing touches on my manuscript from my desk at Prickly Pen Investigations. It has been six months since Jon and I solidified our business partnership with a kiss at our favorite Italian restaurant, and things couldn't be better.

The business has been relatively quiet, and for the most part, Jon heads up the investigations while I stay and write at our office, stopping only when he wants to brainstorm on cases late at night with yummy takeout. We have not been technically rehired on Alanna's case due to a lack of evidence regarding our theories, so our cases have been much less exciting. Aside from hiring a new employee who is also desperate to locate Alanna, things have been on the quiet side.

On the other hand, our dating lives have been anything but boring. Jon and I have been spending lots of time together at his place, and our physical and emotional connection has been more intense than ever. Daphne has been incredibly supportive of this development, while Ryker remains hesitant to fully accept that Jon has changed and worries that I might be getting a bit ahead of myself.

"How's it going?" Jon asks from across the office at his desk.

"I should be done within the hour." I smile.

My cell phone rings from my desk, and I swipe it open, taking a call from my agent. "Catalina," she says, extending my name into what feels like five syllables through her thick Russian accent.

"Ana," I say, placing her on speaker phone and gesturing for Jon to come listen. I cross my fingers and squint my eyes closed as I ask,

"What did you think of the proposal? What did the editor think of the sample chapters?"

"It's wonderful, Catalina," she exclaims. "Everyone loves your idea. The Prickly Pen series is sure to be a hit. We have a deal."

"Really?" I scream, pumping my fists into the air.

"Really, Catalina. You have really outdone yourself this time. The knowledge you have gained about teenagers today is truly remarkable."

"Thank you," I squeal. "Thank you so much."

"No, thank you, Catalina. For your hard work. I knew you could do it."

I hang up with Ana just as Jon picks me up and spins me around, hooting and hollering. "Told you you could do it!" he roars.

"Thank you," I say, wiping a tear of joy from my eyes. "I can't believe it. I'm back!"

"Yes, you are. Back and better than ever." Jon places me on my desk and wraps my legs around his waist, pulling me close and flooding my face with kisses. "I'm so proud of you, Catalina," he says in his best Russian accent.

"I can't even believe it," I say, squeezing him tightly. "I could never have done this without you," I say because the truth is I couldn't have—not without Operation Superglue, not without Jon.

"You would have figured it out," he argues.

"No," I say, shaking my head. "This was a team effort. It's your win too."

"Okay then." He shrugs. "We need to celebrate. What should we do?"

"No," I say again. "I don't want to go anywhere or do anything big. I just want to be here with you."

"You don't have to twist my arm," he says with a smile. "I'll do that any day."

"Let me just finish this chapter," I say. "Then I'm all yours—"

But Jon has other intentions because he has left me on my desk and is digging through his backpack.

"What are you doing?" I laugh.

"Hold on a sec," he says before returning with a Starbucks cup and holding it out to me. Taped on top of the plastic cup is a ring with the word *promise* written on the cup in Sharpie.

"Jon... I—"

"It's a promise ring," he interrupts with a smile.

I breathe a sigh of relief and attempt to slow my beating heart. "A promise ring?"

Jon peels the tape off the top of the cup and slides the most beautiful silver band with a magenta-colored stone onto my left ring finger. "It's pink tourmaline," he says proudly. "It's the closest color to prickly pear I could find."

"Jon, it's beautiful," I say through my tears.

"Lina Rivera," he says, pressing the ring to his lips. "I promise to always be honest with you and to be up front with you. I promise to never lie to you again. When things get hard, I will run to you, not away. I promise to always love you and to put you and our family first."

"It's beautiful," I say again, my face flooded with tears. "Those are great promises, Jon," I say, pressing my lips to his and kissing him deeply and passionately.

"It's not an engagement ring," he says, clearing his throat. "I know that would be moving way too fast, and I would never put that sort of pressure on you... but you need to know, Lina. I'm not going anywhere anytime soon."

"Good," I say, my voice catching. "I don't want you to go anywhere."

Jon wraps my legs around his torso and pulls me closer, and I do the same. He presses his lips against mine, and I open my mouth as he dips me back against my desk. I cling to him as his tongue does the talking, and my heart rate increases as I kiss him back, and I feel like the luckiest girl alive. I pull back and whisper, "I love you."

"I love you, too, Lina," he says, wrapping his hands under my shirt and gripping my waist, but then the sound of the door opening startles us both.

"Oh—I'm sorry, guys," a voice says from the door.

Jon and I pull away from each other and begin to fix our clothes and hair. "Sorry about that, Travis," Jon says through a goofy, caught-in-the-act smile.

"Sorry, Travis," I say, hopping off my desk and plopping back in my chair.

Travis drops his backpack on the white couch and looks from Jon to me. "Now that I'm working here, you two think you can get a room?" He smiles like a dad catching two teenagers, something I know way too much about.

"Sorry, man," Jon says again, his cheeks flushed.

"Not a problem," Travis says.

"How was your date?" I ask Travis, eager to hear how his most recent dating-app experience has turned out.

"Not great." He shrugs. "Turns out she is married and just wanted to know what online dating is like, just in case she leaves her husband."

"I'm sorry," I say.

"Don't be. I got the bartender's number, and we have a date tomorrow night. Legs for days. Anyway, what's going on here?" Travis asks. "Looks like you guys were celebrating."

"Lina got some good news on her book proposal," Jon explains, and I am thankful that he left out the presentation of the promise ring for Travis's sake.

"That's awesome. Great work, Lina," Travis says.

But I'm not paying attention to Travis and Jon anymore. Instead, my attention is turned to the van parked across the street, so I stand and walk toward the window to get a better look. Sure enough, it is a black van with the Super Scorpion Pest Removal logo printed in bright-green letters. "Jon," I say, my jaw dropping and eyes wide. "Look."

Jon follows my gaze and lands his eyes on the pest control van. "Hey, Travis," Jon says, voice steady. "I need you to get that plate number for me. And don't take your eyes off it. The second it moves, call me and let me know your location. If that plate matches the one from the tunnels, we might have something."

"Copy that, boss," Travis says, hopping to his feet.

We watch Travis as he snaps a picture of the plate and then jogs toward his car, signaling us to join him. The van's engine turns on as Jon and I bolt out the door and into Travis's car.

"Follow the van," Jon directs.

"Copy that," Travis says as he turns his ignition and puts his car in drive. "I'm pretty sure the plates match."

I buckle my seat belt and grab Jon's wrist, hoping for the first time that we might have a lead of some sort.

"We've got this," Jon says as he slides beside me and holds me close.

"I know we do." I smile. Jon kisses my cheek and rubs his fingers over my new promise ring.

"I promise," he whispers in the darkness.

Operation Superglue

"I promise too," I say because I do. I promise to keep looking forward and hope for the best and to see the positives in my life as the blessings that they are.

We follow the pest control van, into the darkness and into the unknown, hoping to bring Alanna home, put bad guys behind bars, and move forward together as business partners, parents, friends, and simply Jon and Lina... *us*.

And that is the best possible ending I can hope for. Right? Because let's face it. Sometimes, when life gets tricky and everything falls to pieces, someone needs to be the glue. And those bad times, the times that seem the most impossible to forgive? Those are the times we need to be the stickiest.

Lina Rivera, mother of two from Scottsdale, private eye, signing out. Until next time... Operation Superglue 4 Life.

About the Author

Stacy Lee, the acclaimed author of the best-selling *Nubble Light* series on Amazon, is eagerly diving into her new venture—the captivating *Prickly Pen Investigations* series with Speaking Volumes Publishing.

A proud New Englander through and through, Stacy calls New Hampshire her home, where she resides with her endlessly supportive husband, two exceptional teenagers, and two cherished rescue pups.

Stacy's creative pursuits extend beyond the written page. Alongside her compelling fiction, she's currently engrossed in crafting a thrilling TV series based on the Prickly Pen Investigations, diving into the dynamic world of television production. Stacy's enthusiasm for storytelling spans her written works and her dedication to scriptwriting, where she eagerly collaborates within the vibrant and ever-evolving landscape of the entertainment industry.

Upcoming New Release!

STACY LEE'S

OPERATION CACTUS BLOSSOM
Prickly Pen Investigations Series
Book Two

Get ready for another thrilling ride with the Prickly Pen Investigations team! After the success of Operation Superglue, they're back and more determined than ever in *Operation Cactus Blossom*. Follow along as Jon and Lina continue their daring undercover missions and race against time to bring home the indomitable Alanna Foster, affectionately known as "Cactus Blossom" for her tenacity and courage. But amidst the action, a bombshell revelation threatens to cast a shadow over Jon and Lina's bright future together. With secrets unraveling and tensions rising, can they navigate through the twists and turns to emerge victorious once again? Join the adventure in this electrifying sequel!

**For more information
visit:** www.SpeakingVolumes.us

Now Available!

JORDAN S. KELLER'S

Ashes Over Avalon Trilogy
Books 1 – 3

**For more information
visit: www.SpeakingVolumes.us**

Now Available!

CYNTHIA AUSTIN'S

The Pendent Series
Books 1 – 3

**For more information
visit:** www.SpeakingVolumes.us

Now Available!

TONI GLICKMAN'S

Bitches of Fifth Avenue
Books 1 – 2

**For more information
visit:** www.SpeakingVolumes.us

Now Available!

MARK E. SCOTT'S

A Day in the Life Series
Books 1 – 3

**For more information
visit: www.SpeakingVolumes.us**

www.ingramcontent.com/pod-product-compliance
Lightning Source LLC
LaVergne TN
LVHW091623070526
838199LV00044B/912